The Unpassing

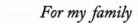

For my family

The Unpassing

1

DURING AN UNEVENTFUL PART OF MY CHILDHOOD, MY mother walked into the room with a plate of loose washed grapes. She collapsed. Grapes thudded dully on the carpet. One rolled under the couch. The plate lay overturned, and my mother's body was beside it, limbs splayed.

My sister Pei-Pei and I remained very still. "Don't cry," she whispered to me. But she was the one who was starting to cry. Her bottom lip hung open, and her halting breath slid out.

Sunlight glossed the spread of my mother's hair. I saw veins of red in all that black. I felt a compression of everything I knew to one hard nut. Things ended. You couldn't stop things from ending.

My mother's back twitched. Her limbs reordered themselves; she sat up. "I was testing you," she said. She was angry. She clawed at the grapes on the carpet, collecting them to be washed again. "Why were you just sitting there? Why didn't you call for the ambulance?"

Neither Pei-Pei nor I could say a word.

"You didn't do anything." As my mother rose from the floor on a swell of indignation, the plate she held tipped forward and back, and grapes rolled right up to the precipice. "What kind of children have I raised? Tell me, do you want to be orphans?"

I wish I'd never felt it, that relief—that total unburdening. My mother had wanted to teach us a lesson; what I'd learned was reversal. Things that had been splintered could be intact again.

Not long after, when we faced events that caused us sorrow, I yearned for that same erasure. *Undo this.* But although we tried, each in our own way, no one was able to go back even one step.

———

MY FATHER liked to declare that he had moved us to Alaska so we could be closer to the stars.

"And now you're digging down instead of up," my mother said.

By day, he drilled water wells. In winter, when the ground froze and cinched tight, he took the odd plumbing job. ("Plumbing," my mother said, "is reaching your hands into other people's toilets.")

In late summer or early fall, when the strung-out sun began to set again, we lay out at night and offered ourselves to the hungry sky. If my father had not mown the wild grasses, I would scratch my neck and ears and wrists and, in the dark, think of the smallness of ants.

"What did I tell you?" my father said. "The stars are so close, you can feel their heat."

Sometimes I thought I could feel it, too, a rope of warmth in the cold air. Other times it seemed nothing at all was close to us, not those pinpricks, not a breath of sentient life. But when we shifted, there was a faint crackling, the grass stirring where we had flattened it, trying to rise back up. Then I felt a surge of hot animal blood and the expansion of my senses. Was this what he meant? I was his son, and for a flaring second I understood him. Something diabolical was about to swoop down from the monochrome sky.

"Did you see that?" he asked.

I squinted straight up at the scattered grains of light.

"A meteor," he said. "With a tiger's tail."

"Another one?"

"I'm certain."

Either my eyes were not fast enough, or he willed those fragments of space debris into being. They flamed with the intensity of his wanting.

"You could not do this in Taiwan," he said. If you believed him, the stars there hid themselves out of spite. That junk island. Where you couldn't find pizza or even a good, thick napkin to wipe your mouth. You couldn't talk about history. You couldn't mention certain dates. For a brief time his family had owned land, given by the Japanese and taken away by the Chinese. There was nothing left there for my father now, no family and no land.

Some nights, when the moon outshone the stars and we couldn't search for meteors, my father said it was the Trans-Alaska Pipeline that had called to him. That black steel artery

zigzagging across eight hundred miles of shifting permafrost—
hot oil over ice. Made by man, like the pyramids. When a
single valve popped off, forty-two thousand gallons leaked out.
At Woolworths we met a rig hand who had worked the North
Slope. He told us the winds were so muscular, you could unzip
your coat, open your arms, and fly.

We had lived briefly in Michigan, but my father had lost
his job as a wastewater engineer. He mistimed our move to
Southcentral Alaska; we could prove only five months of resi-
dency instead of six, and so we missed the first and largest
payout from the Permanent Fund. Before Ruby was born, we
were a family of five, which would have meant five thousand
dollars—one thousand each, even for baby Natty. We could've
bought an aluminum boat, my mother said. Never mind that
the closest water was a spittle creek, and after that, Turnagain
Arm and its barricade of mudflats.

Thirty miles outside of Anchorage, our small house sat by
itself at the end of a short gravel road. It faced several acres of
half-cleared land. To the back and sides were spruce woods that
had lived through world wars, the gold rush, homesteading. But
in a country where we had no ancestors, in a state only twenty-
some years old, the past felt irrelevant to us. Only later would
I realize that even our house harbored its own history. There
were figure-eight gouges on the kitchen floor where furniture
had rolled like marbles during the big quake. Mushrooms
sprouted in our bathroom with the seasons, tracking time. They
grew from the seam between the floor and wall, and the caps
were perfect and unblemished, curving over their stems like
modest skirts. The house had been built on the tail end of the
World War II boom, part of a subdivision that had never materi-

alized. Wanting nothing to do with it all, the chimney detached itself and crumbled. The wall was patched using cement instead of plaster, so that even after it was painted over, there appeared a permanent, textured shadow, the ghost of the old fireplace. In the woodstove, there was a thick layer of ancient soot.

My father told us that other houses would be built around us, that a small neighborhood street would spring up; we imagined deciduous trees and curbs and tricycles. "When the others move in," my father used to say, followed by his own vague wishes: the road might be paved, the mailbox might be relocated, the wind might not blow so hard on us. At some point the future ossified, our ghost neighbors vacated, and he talked in should-haves—we should have double-paned the windows, we never should have bought that used dresser, which was how the carpenter ants got in—and my mother was quick to jump on this train, from which she never disembarked. Even three decades later, she suddenly said to me, "Back then we should have planted chokecherry trees to poison the moose." I couldn't help but remember how in the summer and fall, the four of us children would press our flat faces to the same window glass that my mother was smacking with her palms, trying to scare the moose away. Once a bull moose spent hours rubbing its mossy antlers against a cluster of young spruces near our house, thrashing the trees silly, and my mother had stood behind the front door with a piece of steel pipe in her hand.

———

BY JANUARY OF 1986 we had been following the goings-on of Christa McAuliffe for many months, fighting to claim first discovery of the briefest snippets, sharing bits of information as though she had confided in us herself. Her children were six and nine. She felt safer on a space shuttle than driving around New York streets. As a psychological test, she had sat inside a zippered ball in complete darkness; when she got scared, she bit down on her tongue.

The *Challenger* launch would be broadcast in class. But the day before it happened, I started feeling sick. On the bus ride home, every jostle of the bus twinged my spine. The trees ticked by, scraggly and bare where snow had dropped off in chunks. The asphalt blurred and liquefied, and even the potholes smeared away. I nodded off, and when I woke, I felt worse. The bus dumped me at the Qwik Stop. Usually I walked in a trench of snow along the road until I got to our gravel turnoff, but on that day I walked right on the asphalt, and the rare vehicle went around me.

Pei-Pei's boots were toppled at the bottom of the stairs, a sign she had gone straight to our bedroom, pulled on her headphones, and made herself deaf to us. I wanted to join her, but the stairs seemed mountainous. Instead I sat in the den with my coat on and leaned against a crate, causing books to slip to the floor. We bought our books at library sales—one crate for one dollar, and we piled those crates high.

The little ones were beside me, drawing on the backs of torn envelopes. "He's home," Ruby whispered to Natty, waggling a finger in my direction. In the mornings, she pressed her hand down on the sandwiches Pei-Pei and I made for school. She squashed them flat as punishment for leaving her.

"You," Natty said.

"No, you," Ruby said. "You do it."

They giggled into their fists. Ruby didn't have much in the way of hair, just some patchy tufts, and she was dressed in Natty's outgrown overalls. Once in a while my mother slid a barrette in her hair to mark her as a girl, but it never stayed on for long; her hair was too wispy. Side by side, they looked like brothers, four and five years old, small and dark and cagey.

Ruby lunged at me. "I'm going to draw on you," she hollered.

I put my hands up to block her. "Don't," I said. "I don't feel good." But she head-butted me and slashed at my face with a crayon.

There was pressure at the center of my skull, deepening. I grabbed hold of her waistband and turned her sideways so she flailed at air instead of me. She was only four, but a few months ago she had broken Natty's tooth with a stray kick.

"Let her go! You let her go!" Natty slapped at me and hung on to my coat.

I flipped Ruby onto her back and worked a crayon between her lips. "Eat it," I said. She sputtered, and I used my fingers to shove the crayon in farther. I tried to notch her teeth with wax.

While Ruby squirmed, Natty wrapped his arms around my neck, choking me. Then he was clawing. I had trouble ducking my head away.

"Okay, okay, stop," I said, holding my hands up and dropping the nub of crayon.

Ruby let her head fall back and became so limp she nearly slid off my lap. It was a sign she was tired, and I liked her best in this state, all droopy and sweet, leaning heavily on me and asking for nothing. Natty slumped on top of us, and we stayed in this pile, heaving in sync, our six legs and six arms twisted together like a boneless creature at the bottom of a sea.

With great effort, I extracted an arm to shield my eyes. The sun was boring through the den window. How could this be? These were the darkest days of the year. It was late afternoon; the sun had retreated. I knew the snow out there was gray. It was melting; craters of dead, matted grass were expanding in the side yard. Where was the brightness coming from? I fell asleep.

When I woke again, I was lying on the sofa by myself, while Pei-Pei sang with the radio. She was doing something with her voice that made it sound like a washing machine.

"Turn off the light!" I yelled.

Pei-Pei's singing stopped. "What'd Gavin say?"

My mother: "He didn't say anything."

I swallowed, and the spit raked my throat. My eyelids trembled. Light was trying to force its way through. If I opened my eyes, they'd be torched. I tried to sit up, but no part of me moved.

Later someone carried me up the steps, jostling me at the hinges. I didn't know if it was night or day; my eyelids had fused together. I heard my parents fighting. It was a familiar, comforting sound.

For a while, there was a different bed. Too cool and too quiet. Then I was in my own worn sheets. A crust of sea salt coated my throat, like rocks at the edge of the ocean, pleading for a sip, a cold wash. "It's over," Pei-Pei said. I dozed off, but the thirst stayed with me.

—

PEI-PEI WAS the only one home when I woke.

"How are you feeling?" she asked. It was a real question, without sarcasm.

The door was open, but no sounds drifted in from the other parts of the house. From my bed I could see Pei-Pei lying on her stomach, kicking her legs. My pillow obstructed part of my view. Her bare feet swung in and out of my sight.

"What time is it?" I asked.

"One or two."

She was still in her sleeping clothes, a set of faded blue long johns with sleeves that were too short. The elastic at the wrists was loose. Her long black hair was tied back, and the shorter front pieces were matted to her temples. When I swung my legs out from the covers, I was wearing pants I had never seen before.

"It's Tuesday," she added. "You went to the hospital."

"You're not in school?"

She didn't respond. Her legs pedaled the gummy air.

"We have to go," I said. "They're showing the launch. Did we miss it already?"

She nodded. "Yeah, it was last week."

"Last *week*?"

"It exploded."

"What?"

"Everyone died." She sat up and stared at me, evaluating something in my face.

"What are you talking about?"

"There was a huge cloud of smoke, and then nothing came out of it—no shuttle."

"What?" I looked around to see if someone, my father or Natty, was laughing at me from the closet. But the door was open, and there were no legs or feet beneath the hanging clothes.

"Believe me. I saw it happen."

I shook my head, trying to find room for what she was saying.

"There's something else," she said. She pushed at a spot on the bridge of her nose. Her face was completely bare and her hair was clawed back. Behind her thick glasses her lashes were sparse, and her eyes were very small and black.

Suddenly I was afraid to look at her face. I tried to smooth the folds in the fitted sheet. It was not my usual one, and the fabric was all twisted and bunched. Later I would discover it was too big for my bed. When I helped my mother change it, we had to shove handfuls of it under the mattress, hiding its excess.

"Ruby's dead."

I laughed. I pressed on a wrinkle in the sheet with the heel of my palm, trying to spread it flat.

Pei-Pei took off her glasses and shook them as though they were filled with dust. "You heard me," she said, "and I don't want to say it again."

"Stop joking," I said.

"I'm not joking," she said. "It happened two days ago."

"How?" I asked. As I said it, I pressed a hand to my throat to stop a noise. There was an expanse between what I was saying and what I understood myself to be saying, and the giggle in my chest was trying to morph into something else.

"She got sick. There was an outbreak at school."

"But she doesn't even go to school yet."

"No," Pei-Pei said. "She doesn't."

We stared at each other. Without her glasses on, Pei-Pei's eyes had expanded. They were not quite black, but the color of winter soil after the snow was scraped away.

Pei-Pei came to my bed. "It's no one's fault."

"Get away," I said.

She slipped her glasses back on and stood up. She walked to Ruby's bed, leaned over it, and pulled the blinds up. Light washed over the room; the carpet turned from tan to blond, and the walls glowed. "We're having a warm spell," she said. The faded floral blooms on Ruby's sheets were almost translucent as they bore the brunt of all that sun.

I gazed at Ruby's bed. It was neat; she almost never slept in it. Her pillow was missing, though, and that one small absence made me uneasy.

After Pei-Pei left, I made my way to the window. I sat there trying to adjust my eyes to the light. Outside, at the end of our dirt driveway, were four trash bags, each opaque black and straining with contents I couldn't fathom. The bags were knotted, dimpling on top, leaning on one another. One had fallen on its side. Soon I would find myself searching for things around the house: my backpack, my coat, my shoes. My mug, which I had chipped against Natty's mug in a test to see whose was stronger. It began to seem that everything I had ever touched was missing. Or at least the things most familiar to me were gone.

AS THE SUN SET, the windows in the house turned into sapphire glass, then into mirrors, and then we had the sense of being downright trapped. The nineteen-hour night had begun. My father had locked himself in my parents' bedroom. When he left to use the bathroom, I walked right in and sat on the depression in the bed. Spread across the covers were newspaper and magazine clippings and an empty manila folder. They were all photographs of Christa McAuliffe: a great force of hair and what my father called a champion's smile, though it looked a little nervous to me.

There wasn't a scrap of text. Just pictures: black-and-white, color, thumbnails, spreads, Christa in her blue NASA jumpsuit, Christa floating sideways in microgravity. She looked like what she claimed to be, just a normal person headed to space.

"Don't touch anything," my father said when he came back. He used a fingernail to nudge the thin edge of a clipped portrait back in place. "And definitely don't touch her on the face."

In the kids' room, my mother took my hands. She swung them, as though to begin dancing, but it was not a dancing expression she wore. My arms began to hurt. I was afraid she would pull them off.

"How are you feeling?" she asked.

"Fine."

"Is there some part of you that is hurting?"

"Not really," I said.

"What part? Is it your head? Do you need medicine?"

Pei-Pei was already asleep, or pretending to sleep, though it was only eight or nine. I went to lie down, too.

"Are you cold? I pulled these from the basement for you."

My mother patted the stack of extra blankets at the foot of my bed.

"Did you get these from the basement, too?" I gestured at the strange sheets I was lying on and the comforter she was trying to pull up to my eyes. They smelled earthy, a kind of settled damp. That afternoon they had given me dreams about old furniture and broken clocks whose hands spun and spun without anything happening to time. I kicked the whole stack of blankets to the floor.

"What hurts?" she asked. "Please tell me what hurts."

"There's something heavy," I said.

"What do you mean? Where?"

But the weight on me made it hard to speak.

From his bed, Natty said, "When is Ruby coming home?"

My mother's eyes stretched to fill her sockets. "Ruby is still lost," she said. "She can't find her way home."

"Still?" Natty asked.

"We don't know where she is. So we can't get her back, you see. Because we don't know where to look." My mother drifted to Natty's bed and squatted down to his height. "You're the smallest one now. Sometimes it's nice to be the smallest."

"Where can we find her?"

"I don't know. I don't know where. That's what lost means."

"But where is she lost?"

"I said I don't know."

"Where?"

My mother stood up. "I told you. I can't do anything. You don't think I'd find her if I could?"

"Why are you doing her laundry?" Natty asked.

I scanned the bedroom. Ruby's bed was now missing its sheets as well as its pillow. On the other side of the dresser, where my mother couldn't see, was a small heap where the laundry basket used to be; Pei-Pei had been piling up our dirty socks, underwear, and chocolate bar wrappers, and it stank like it was harboring something more.

After my mother left, Natty came to the edge of my bed and said, "Do you know where Ruby's lost?"

"I don't know anything," I said, and it was utterly true. I scratched at the wall.

"Where is she lost?"

Each time he asked, it was like the fireweed turned to seed in autumn, sending so much fluff into the air we were choking on it. I squeezed my eyes shut as he said, "Please tell me. Where? Please." He sent his cottony seeds up, and they drifted around, trapped in the room with us.

We lay in the dark, shifting between fretful wakefulness and rickety sleep. They were hard to tell apart. Whenever I was awake, someone else was, too, rustling or flipping over or coughing—the kind of cough with intention behind it, placed out there just to puncture the silence. In the early morning I opened my eyes. From the window there came a deep blue luminescence. By feel I knew it was around five or six on this winter morning. Dark and joyless but with a scrap of a promise: more than this, there would be more than this. Someone was sleeping in Ruby's bed. My whole chest seized. But almost instantly I saw, even in the minimal light, that the figure was much too big. It was not Ruby but my father. He slept on the bare mattress without a single sheet or blanket, wearing his heavy work clothes. His belt buckle was off to one side. I couldn't tell if his eyes were closed, and watched to see if he was awake or asleep. He did not so much as twitch—it meant he was awake. Studying him, I drifted. When I woke again, it was eight, and Ruby's bed, in its entirety, was gone.

I went to the window. The mattress had joined the pile at the end of our short driveway. One long edge rested in the remnants of snow. Soon my father would load it in the truck and haul it away.

The legs of Ruby's bed frame had left four divots in the bedroom carpet, and when I sat inside those corners, I could pause the emptiness cracking open in me. But if I was on the other side of the room, sitting in my own solid bed, then I could plainly see that the room had changed, and I could feel it, too, not just a shifting or rearrangement but a gutting. When Natty woke, he sat up and stared at the void. He might have been caught in the head fog of any ordinary morning, except he continued to sit there, without speaking, for a period of time that grew and grew. The longer he sat there, the more unfamiliar he looked, both smaller and older than I had ever known him to be.

"Natty," I said. I placed myself in his direct line of sight.

His eyes finally focused on mine.

"We're late for breakfast," I said, feeling that I had taken a great leap. I didn't know whether there was any breakfast. I didn't know what was down there waiting for us.

He started to cry. His voice was shredded. I realized he was forming words. "She needs her bed," he said. "She needs to have her bed."

I sensed I should touch him. He was only an arm's length away. But the way he was crying scared me. It felt risky even to glimpse it. I thought of a place we had once seen while picking blueberries. Above Turnagain Arm, along a dirt path that followed the bluffs, where sour blueberries grew low to the ground, there was a spot of earth that had fallen away. You could inch up close and look way down the scoured face of the cliff and see a small, dark, rocky cove, which had surely never been touched by a human being. It was refilled and refilled and refilled by the unknowable ocean.

2

WE USED TO DRIVE FORTY MINUTES INTO ANCHORAGE TO shop at a Korean grocery. The one vaguely Chinese store was associated with a Chinese mainlander, and mainlanders lacked values. That owner, my mother said, stirred rat meat into the ground pork; when you unwrapped the butcher paper, you might catch a faint scent of urine. Pork, in turn, was passed off as beef with a squirt of red dye. So she shopped at a Korean store no bigger than our garage, blocking pinched aisles to ponder the mystery of Korean packaging, while I snuck promising foods into the cart: purple rice, tofu that came in a squeezable tube, a can of what looked like shiny pretzels but turned out to be candied lotus root.

At the end of winter, my mother and I made our first visit to the store since Ruby had died. Six weeks had passed. Halley's Comet had been visible as a smudge. It was to return bigger and brighter in 2061, but which of us would be alive to see it? Our aliveness was precarious. Divers had found the crew compartment of the *Challenger* with all of the bodies inside. Soon the wreckage would reveal that four emergency air packs had been activated; not all of them had died instantaneously.

At the grocery store my mother stood in an aisle and stared at the bottled vinegar. She walked the length of the display, following the spectrum from clear to black, and then stood staring at the blackest vinegar. We left the store without buying a thing. She pulled off the road and parked. In a series of actions that startled me, she hopped a guardrail, scampered across the forbidden railroad tracks, and led me down to a huge rock at the beginning of the mudflats. The rock was shaped like a fist, knuckles down. Standing on the rock, towering over the low beach, she said she was trying to listen to it speak, the water, but she couldn't hear it from there. The tide was low; the mud-flats were vast.

Across the rippled terrain was the same ocean she'd grown up beside; here was Turnagain Arm, which was part of Cook Inlet, which was part of the Pacific Ocean. If you cut a slanted path through the water, she said, you could end up on the eastern shores of Taiwan. Her village, even. You could stagger to land as the first light broke, coming in with the fishermen who'd just climbed down from their anchored boats. They dragged swollen nets of fish behind them on Styrofoam flats. As they came to shore in their rubber waders and boots, long squeaks marked the rhythm of their walking. On the sand, in early light, my mother waited for her father with a bamboo pole. They'd string the net over the pole and carry the fish between them. The short beach was sloped upward, so she walked at the front, and the load was easier on her.

My mother climbed off the rock and tested the hardness of

the silt. These days, the sun was setting during dinner; we watched each other chewing and gulping in coppery light. In a couple of months the sun would be glowing in electric perimeters around our blinds into evening. Giving us all a charge. The previous summer, Ruby had insisted she was a fish, and my mother had fed her huge sheets of dried seaweed, folding and crumpling them into her mouth. Pei-Pei had asked to go camping with her friends. Camping! my mother exclaimed. Here, where black bears lumbered down from the Chugach Mountains, gorged on salmon at Campbell Creek, and then stuck around to swipe at your garbage cans.

Beyond a scrawny, twisted tree was a huge white boulder at the edge of the water. A person was squatting beside it. "My heavens," my mother said, and started running. I tried to grab the bottom edge of her coat, but caught nothing, which made my hands feel empty. We ran past the tumbling of rocks and stray driftwood and made our way toward the boulder. For a while we followed the arcing tracks of a bird, stamped into the silt, a trail of half asterisks.

It was a whale, and my first impression of it was its whiteness, unsullied. It was nearly as long as my father's pickup truck, lying in a puddle. The slump of its body came up to the chest of the squatting man, who stood up. "It's still alive," he called to us. "Bleached," I thought he said, but of course he must have said, "Beached."

"What is it?" my mother asked, though she knew about the belugas in Cook Inlet. On certain stretches of Seward Highway she told us to watch the water for their writhing bodies, whiter than the crests of the waves. Just once I'd seen a short, misty spray. But she didn't know how to make conversation in English.

She was always asking, What time is it?—with her watch curled in her coat pocket.

"Beluga," he nearly sang, and each strange syllable was liquid and warm.

The man was short, with a wide, deep chest and arms so muscular they hung away from his sides. He was wearing a neon-orange cap with earflaps, from which a few gray curls escaped. I'd never seen such a funny hat, or such a happy color. My mother approached the whale and stopped two yards from its face. I hurried to her. The whale was situated in a crevice of mud and was wriggling its head side to side. I froze in the steady gaze of its small, oily black eye, not so much bigger than a human eye, embedded in a thick ring of skin. The protruding forehead and long mouth gave it a strange expression—a pained smile—as though we'd asked, Shouldn't you be in the water?

"Go back," the man said. "It's dangerous, this glacial silt."

"Is okay," my mother said, and tapped the toe of her loafer against the ground. When nothing happened, she dug her toe in harder.

The whale lifted its head and slapped it back down. There was a cool, silty splatter on my arm.

"Oh," my mother said, delighted. Her sweatpants were streaked.

Its flippers pressed against the silt and its flukes fanned the air twice. The heft of its midsection was too great for it to do more than flex. Here is a whale, I told myself, and then I wondered if it would die. It looked too big to die, too big to vanish during a sudden, silent creak of the world.

And what, I thought, had they done with Ruby's body?

The man scratched his bristly neck and flicked the brim of

his cap up. "Best she can do is stay still and wait for the tide to come back in."

My mother sprang forward, and with a shock I saw her put her hands on the body of the whale. She ducked her head and shoved, arms locked straight, her loafers gouging tracks into the packed silt. Her feet slid out of her shoes. Her socks darkened where they soaked up water.

The man belted out a laugh. "That's, like, two tons you're trying to roll."

My mother's face hovered beside the blowhole, from which a milky foam was leaking. She slipped her shoes back on and walked around to stand before the whale's face. She touched its forehead bump, the same gesture as when she pressed a palm to our sternums to put us to sleep at night. Pei-Pei, me, Natty. "Sleep," she would say. And, so quietly we could barely hear, "Wake up again tomorrow." The heavy weight of her hand, like sleep itself bearing down on us, paralyzing us where we lay. "Come here," she said to me now. She lifted my hand to the whale's forehead.

It was not especially cold or warm. The skin had a rough, porous texture, and behind the skin its flesh was soft, like a ripe peach; I could have left dents with my fingers.

I don't know what kind of expression I made, but the man, a yard away, started laughing again. "This kid," he said. I liked the way he laughed, upward, without self-consciousness.

He swept an arm back the way we had come. "Nothing to be done. We should get out of here."

My mother did not move. She was staring hard at the whale, which began exerting more effort, its head and extremities whapping against the ground.

"Do you understand what I'm saying?" His voice sounded far behind me, and when I felt his hand on my shoulder, I started and flung it off. "Easy. Does your ma speak English?"

The wind lifted my mother's permed hair into a mane, making her taller and more savage.

"Do you? English? Hey, kid. English?"

I looked up. A neat mustache hid half his mouth, and his eyes were translucent.

"What's your name?" he asked.

"Gavin," I said.

"How would you spell that in English?"

My mother kicked off her shoes. She peeled off her wet socks, rolling them into a single ball that she stuffed into her coat pocket. She picked up her loafers, one in each hand.

Immediately I wanted to be barefoot, too. The man offered an arm to me as I balanced shakily on each leg and removed my sneakers and socks. When I ran to my mother, my feet stuck to the cold silt, which turned softer, muddier, where it met the water. It sucked on my heel.

"It's thirsty," my mother said. "The poor thing. It's dry and it's thirsty. The air hurts its skin." She dipped a loafer into the puddle and dribbled water onto the whale's back, spreading the liquid with her hands.

I became aware of my own thirst, big and insatiable; I looked past the flats at the glinting water, out of reach, and the wind felt sharp and dry.

The man said, "Tide's starting to come in." There was an icy splash at our legs. The puddle around the whale overfilled. I raised one clean foot to my hand; the foot was cold and foreign.

"Let's go," the man said.

My mother nudged me away from the water. The man began to walk, turning around to check that we were following. He held the laces of my sneakers in one hand, and below it my sneakers danced. In front of me, my mother swung her shoes in arcs to dry them, and there was an easiness to her walk. I watched our bare feet keeping pace with his boots. His khaki pants were folded once at the hems, showing the inside threads and exposing strips of wool sock at every step. My mother's pants were darkened up to midcalf, and mine to my knees. Though my legs were wet and cold, I felt a slow loosening in my chest as the three of us walked, as though my windpipe were untwisting and clear, unobstructed air coming in.

At the fist-shaped rock, my mother took a seat at the far end. Her legs fit perfectly into two scallops on the rock's front edge. She pulled me up beside her. The man stood for a while, then leaned against the rock, then scooted in until he was sitting beside me.

The water had come in; it was maybe a foot high around the whale. Even from this distance we could see the whale pulsing. I rubbed the tops of my cold feet. They were nearly dry and a little ashy. Beside me, the man was working his thumb through a hole in his windbreaker sleeve.

Then he bent over and grabbed my left foot, setting it on his lap and sandwiching it between his hands. He began to rub my foot. His hands were rough, and I could feel a snag of dried skin scratching the center of my sole. He moved his hands faster, making a rasping sound, and the resulting friction was very warm. I raised my other foot in the air, and the man chuckled and warmed it, too.

He and my mother conversed haltingly about the recent spell

of rain and the plummeting oil prices. It was the kind of conversation I might have overheard any afternoon at Carrs or the Qwik Stop, and I was proud that my mother was part of it. The man absently alternated between my feet, and I sat rapt at his hands.

They fell silent, then the man said, "Where are you from?" and after my mother had answered, he asked, "And what's that like?"

My mother tilted her head. "There, not so many signs," she said. "Danger. Stay away from tracks. Don't fall off cliff. Do not drown. There are no signs like this."

The man laughed, and his eyes struggled to expand below his heavy brows as he looked at my mother in a way that made me turn to her, too. The curls of her hair had been loosened by wind, and they moved restlessly about her narrow shoulders. In her wool coat, gray sweatpants, and bare feet, she belonged nowhere but this forsaken beach. She paddled her callused feet on the rock, and the man looked down at her toes. There were threads of dirt beneath her toenails.

"And children there," she said, nudging me, "are more useful." In her childhood, she had tied nets and cleaned fish and scraped tiny oysters from rocks.

The man was still rubbing my feet, but more slowly. I could feel the warmth slide from my heels to my toes and back, following his large and heated hands. The skin pooled, darker, around his knuckles.

"And do you have a dad?" he asked me.

"Yes," I said.

"And do you live with him?"

My mother moved her hand very slightly and dug her fingernail into my arm. She said to me in a low voice, in Taiwanese, "Say no."

I looked at the notch her fingernail had left on me. "Yes," I said.

Silence followed, and then my mother said in the same tone, "Couldn't you just have pretended?"

"Pretend what?"

"That you don't have one."

The man stopped rubbing my foot, and I was very sorry for it. The wind that bore down on us seemed to have traveled from afar; it carried a cold, unfamiliar scent. My damp pant legs turned icy.

My mother lurched forward and said, "Whale."

I had to squint, for the sun had sunk lower. The whale was gone, and all that was left was water. I felt we had done this by waiting and watching over it.

"It went home," my mother said. Her voice sounded strange to me, soft and full of too much air.

"It won't die?" I said.

"Not today," the man said. He flung his head back and let out a long whoop.

My mother jumped from the rock, hooked my elbow, and pulled me down, half catching me but allowing me to fall to my knees. It hurt but I didn't show it. She picked me up by the armpits and started to run, staggering. I thought we were headed back to where the whale had been, but then she veered away. She was only running. I could not stop laughing at how she carried me, careening yet strong, each bare foot anchoring us as it drove into the ground. My legs swung like a doll's and my toes dragged. The mudflats were clean and gleaming, raw batter shaken inside a pan, and we zigzagged across them, too nimble to sink.

When she stopped to catch her breath, I stared into her wind-raked face and said, in a voice that came out scratchy, "I love you."

She narrowed her eyes to consider me. "Where did you learn that?" she asked.

The sound of clanging and the freight train's whistle made my mother whirl around. The boxcars kept coming. I couldn't have said if it was an eighty-car train or whether the cars numbered in the thousands, only that they kept barreling by, bringing their own wind, metal scrubbing metal, the couplings rattling. In winter, moose preferred the easy walking on the tracks when the snow was deep, and just two months earlier, a single train had killed twenty-four moose in one round trip. The cowcatcher mounted at the front had plowed right through them, fourteen on the northbound, ten on the southbound. My father, reading the newspaper, had rested his forehead on the dining table with a sadness that astonished us.

The freight train left behind a spoiled space and silence. My ears could still create the tone of the last whistle burst. Beneath it, a wheezing sound came from my mother.

"Let's run again," I said, but she didn't respond. She was gazing at the rock. When I looked, the man was no longer there. I searched in vain for the bright blip of his orange hat.

"Let's run," I said.

"I don't feel like it."

I picked at my pants below the knee, trying to keep them from clinging to my skin.

"When can we go home?" I asked.

When she didn't reply, I said, "I want to go now."

She scratched hard at her jaw, where there was a trace of mud. She tossed her head back so her hair settled behind her shoulders. "Why do you want to go home?"

I was stumped. A single gull cried far above us. "Natty," I said. "Natty and Pei-Pei are home."

"Don't you want to go somewhere else?" she asked. "Anywhere else?"

I scraped hard at my upper lip with my lower teeth. I tried to imagine another home. Neither my mother nor father had taken to Michigan. We had lived in another home in Taiwan but had left when I was three. I could not picture it, though I had a feeling of dim, oily rooms, soggy air, sticky skin. Home was a place you could see every detail of. Not-home was a void, the outside that crept upon you when you were about to fall asleep—the thing you tried to keep at bay as you jolted yourself awake.

"Is there anything at home for us?" she asked.

I gnawed at my lip and tasted salt or blood, and when I pressed the side of my hand to my mouth for confirmation, it came away with a tiny red print.

"It's possible to be someone else," she said. "I used to be."

I pretended to think about this, but the wind was constant now, as though it no longer needed to gather breaths, and I was trying not to shiver. The gull laughed. Where the sun met the water, it pulled wide into a tomato-orange strip and sent a corresponding line over the surface of the water straight at us, hot-forged steel.

My mother pinched my earlobe hard. "I'm just kidding. Of course we're going home."

"Yeah," I said, "we're going home."

She grabbed my chin and pushed it up. "Don't talk in English," she said.

"We're going home," I said in Chinese.

My mother made an ugly face. "You never speak Taiwanese anymore," she said. "It's all your grandfather knows. When we visit, will you be able to say anything to him at all?"

I took a few steps toward the train tracks.

"You never speak it anymore," she said. "Can you, even? Can you still speak it? Say something."

"Khah kín-leh," I said rudely, the phrase crooked and angular in my mouth.

But she didn't hurry up. "Yes, speak like that when we visit." Extending her arm over my shoulder, she pointed at the water, as though my grandfather were swimming out there, a speck but visible, waiting for us. I knew that in fact he was bedridden; once a month, my aunt pulled him on a wagon to the village school, where there was a phone, and they waited for my mother to call.

"Let's go," I said.

"You tell him you've missed him, that you remember him. It wasn't so long ago. You remember him, don't you?"

The tracks were still many yards away, up a little stretch of scree. Beyond that was another small slope, then the road where we had parked. We would have to cross the tracks and climb back over the bent guardrail. It wasn't far, but I had a hard time lifting my feet. A couple of weeks after Ruby had died, my mother had woken us in the dark, running from bed to bed, her large fearful face so close we could smell the decay of her teeth. I could still hear her cracking voice, saying again and again to us: Never cross the train tracks. It's dangerous to cross the tracks. Promise me you will never cross the tracks. Promise. Promise me.

———

DECADES LATER, a woman ambling along the coastal trail told me this with the grave authority of a tourist: The mudflats here, they were not to be trifled with. A man had died on these flats, two legs rooted in the silt as the tide came in. Drowning or hypothermia, she didn't know. They attached a rope to his body and the other end to a helicopter, but only managed to tear him in half. For the mudflats could turn watery on you, like quicksand, then cement you up to your thighs. Maybe she thought I was a tourist, too: an Asian man in Anchorage, carrying a backpack. Or maybe it was the way I stood at the edge of the flats, seduced, toeing the start of the sodden beach.

3

THERE WAS SNOW INTO LATE MARCH, AS WELL AS MOMENTS
so clear and bright, I could turn my face up to the sun and oblit-
erate my mind. The weather changed from morning to afternoon, and back again, and it was hard to dress comfortably. To
and from school, I wore Pei-Pei's old parka, which reached
down to my knees, and often found myself sweating in it, too
hot to muster the energy to shed it. One afternoon, a scant
snow gave way to a flaring sun, and I came home to find the snow
had melted and refrozen into crispy sheets of glass all over the
yard. I crunched around in my sneakers and lobbed shards of
ice at the door. The ice tinkled cheerfully when it shattered.

My mother opened the door and said, "Hurry in, we've got
to go." I held on to a disc of lacy ice as I followed her into the
dark entryway. In the kitchen, the glowing windows refined
Natty's bent silhouette. He was sitting exactly where we had
left him that morning, as though someone had screwed his

elbows into the table. I held the ice to one side like a Frisbee, threatening to fling it at him, but he never looked up, so I laid it on the floor.

"We're going shopping," my mother said. "We need to buy you a coat and some clothes and shoes."

"I hate shopping," I said, just to say it, though the only thought I'd had upon stepping in was that I had to get out again. There was an odor like the insides of our suitcases, which smelled like herbs turning to dust. A potted ficus tree wedged against the stairs was dying. When I brushed against it, dry leaves crackled and fell off.

"I had to throw so many things away," my mother said, kneeling in front of the closet. "Those boots of yours," she wailed. "Such nice boots. But they might have gotten infected."

"I need underwear," I said. "You threw almost all of it away, you know."

Pei-Pei sat on the floor and shoved her feet into her tied sneakers. It seemed to require some violence. She said, "There are things I need to get, too."

"You?" my mother asked. "I didn't touch your things."

"I need a skirt," Pei-Pei said.

I laughed because I had never seen her in a skirt.

"Need?" my mother asked.

"Yes, I do," Pei-Pei said. "If I don't have it, I will die."

My mother swung the shoe, hard, and hit Pei-Pei across the face. "Speak nonsense again."

Pei-Pei did not react, except to suck her lips in, so her mouth made a perfectly straight line. Perhaps it had not hurt. My mother's shoe was bendable, with a thin, flat rubber sole.

"Let's go," my mother said. She left the door open behind her.

I went back to the kitchen for Natty. "Come on," I said. I pulled on his arm until he slid off his chair. I found his shoes in the closet and carried them to the door.

He stopped. "My socks are wet," he said.

I looked down. He had stepped in the puddle of my melted ice.

He jammed his wet feet into each shoe, stepping on the backs of them. As he walked into the sunlit day, he looked like a sandpiper, jabbing himself forward with each finicky step.

As we drove through the soft, thick slush, Pei-Pei drummed on the window glass in time with the radio. I didn't recognize the song. A woman was crooning about being sorry.

In the store, Natty drifted around the perimeter, and I followed a few steps behind. While Pei-Pei and I went to school every day, Natty had nowhere to go. He hadn't left the house in two months. Now he stayed on the edges of the store, his shoulders hunched, but it was impossible to hide from the rows of fluorescent lights; they ran the length of every aisle. When an elderly woman stopped him and warbled, "Aren't you pretty," rubbing his hair between her fingers as though testing fabric, Natty cowered in place.

Every item in the store had two price tags. One tag was the price you paid at the register, and the other was what you would have paid at a more expensive store. Sometimes I tore these fake tags off and hid them. I raked my hand across a long-haired coat, a velvety table runner, a few ceramic ornaments separated from their box. Half the things in our house were from this store, from spiral notebooks to stale crackers to the ice cleats my father strapped to his boots.

"What's wrong with your foot?" I asked Natty as he hobbled along in front of me.

"I'm trying not to touch my sock."

I ran my hand back and forth along a rack of belts, making the slatted leather curtain undulate. Somewhere in the thick of the store, my mother and Pei-Pei were working the racks; they slid each hanger to the left, as though whipping a page in a book, and did not stop until they had reached the end.

"What did you do today?" I asked.

Natty rolled his head from side to side.

"I said, what did you do today?"

"Nothing."

"What did Mom do?"

"Nothing."

"Was Dad home?"

"He brought lunch."

"What did he bring?"

"McDonald's."

"McDonald's!" I hit the belts with the side of my fist, and they danced.

"We threw it away."

"Why?"

"It didn't taste good."

Pei-Pei had left for school first that morning, and then my father had gone to a job site. The sun was slow in coming out, and no one had turned on the kitchen light, so it was still dark when I left. It felt strange to abandon my mother and Natty in that cave with its gray frosted windows. As I'd crept along the little gravel road that turned onto the asphalt road to the

Qwik Stop, leaving them behind, the sky had lightened rapidly. Gladness and guilt fought over every last space in me.

In the single aisle of toys, there was an enormous stuffed bear. It was too large to fit on a shelf, and too ugly to be bought. For as long as I could remember it had lived on the floor, patrolling the toy section with a moody expression. Both price tags were missing, though a plastic loop still pierced one ear. Its matted coat had a lifelike look to it, a texture that might have been acquired by slogging through the wet understory of a forest.

Natty laid the bear on its side so its legs reached out stiffly.

"What are you doing to him?"

"Go away," Natty said.

Normally I would have shoved him, or kicked the bear so it spun to the end of the aisle, but I couldn't gather that surge of energy. Or at least I couldn't direct it at him. Without Ruby, Natty was soft and listless, like a mollusk without its shell. I left him in the aisle.

In the boys' section, a rack of jeans caught my eye. That morning, a girl in my class had asked me, "Why do you always wear the same sweatpants? Don't you have any other pants?" People had begun to study me. They looked at my hands, my face, any exposed skin. Only two other students—neither of them fifth-graders—had contracted meningitis, and both had died. I, who had never done anything noteworthy in my ten years of life, had lived. I wanted to tell them they would find no explanation on me. I had already searched for it.

I swiped a pair of jeans at random and brought them to my mother. She flipped the orange tag and frowned. "These are too big," she said.

Pei-Pei peered over from her rack and cackled. She grabbed the jeans and held them up to me. The legs bent against my sneakers and the hems lay flat on the floor. She danced the legs like a puppeteer. "You thought you'd fit these? Just how tall do you think you are?"

I snatched the jeans and hooked them onto a rack of skirts. One skirt was so long it dusted my toes. I kicked it.

"I hate shopping," I said.

"Try these on," my mother said, pointing at the pile in the cart.

"You try them on," I said, and ran. I darted between racks and hid inside a broken tent whose side was caving in. Someone had placed a bin of loose fake flowers in there, and their wire stems jutted every which way. I organized them into a bouquet and laid it on the floor. Was this how a funeral went? We had not had one.

When I returned to the toy aisle, Natty was still there, sitting on his pliant ankles, gazing dumbly at neon sports equipment—plastic paddles, foam footballs, something green that claimed to be a basketball. This was the kind of garbage we used to beg our parents for, all of us except Ruby. She favored things that were not toys at all; sometimes she walked around wielding a carrot from the fridge.

"I'm back," I said.

He shifted on his ankles and did not turn.

I dropped to sit beside him. "Look at me," I demanded.

When he did, I couldn't breathe. There was a clot in my throat, but I couldn't push it down. I swallowed twice, but it only grew. I saw the blur of neon in front of him, and the shelf of dolls above that. One doll had fallen on her face, and her hair spilled over the edge.

Natty kept peering at me with that sideways squint. Every opening on his face was a thin, dark breach. His eyelids drooped low, and only his black irises showed. His mouth hung open just far enough to see the darkness inside, without any glimpse of teeth.

"Stop looking at me," I said. "I didn't do it. I didn't—It's not my—" I couldn't speak. The heaviness on me was like dread. But what came after dread? What was on the other side of it, once a thing was done, done, and done, and dread had thickened into something solid? I leaned forward until the top of my head rested on the cold floor. I gazed at my shins, the tight knit of my sweatpants. In this small cavern I could hide from his gaze. His awareness of what I had done.

"What are you doing?" Natty asked.

"Nothing," I said.

For a time, Natty had constantly asked for help. "Can you put on my socks?" "Can you turn on the light?" "Can you pull up my sheet?" One night, after his bath, he had sat shivering on the edge of the tub while Pei-Pei refused to help him into his clothes. I shook his underpants at him.

"Help me put them on," he said.

"Don't help him," Pei-Pei said. "He can do it himself."

Natty tugged on the sides of the towel, closing it tightly in front of him, and sat there for nearly an hour. His only movement was to maneuver his knee into a threadbare section of the towel.

Finally Pei-Pei said, "Okay, okay," and gave him light, quick pats. She rubbed his head with a hand towel even though his hair was already dry. "Let's get you dressed, then," she said, and pulled him into her arms. "You're freezing!"

In the rare, puny circle of Pei-Pei's tenderness, Natty had cried. Whispery wails that ended in openmouthed silence, his face contorted with the need for air. It made me gulp and gulp, trying to compensate. Even after Pei-Pei had managed to pull his pajamas over his limp body, he was still crying. We ushered him to the bedroom. Something kept rasping out of him. It shook his whole body.

That had been nearly a month ago. Natty hadn't asked me for help since.

My mother stepped into the aisle. "Where have you been?" she demanded. "We're not here to play." She gripped my arm. Instead of resisting, I let her yank me up and away, to the new, dismal clothes that awaited, always just a notch away from normal.

While we were in the store it had started to storm, but under the perpetual glare of the fluorescent lights we hadn't noticed the weather. By the time we returned to the parking lot, the sky was the milky gray of old paintbrush water, and filled with churning lint. Only three cars remained. Perfect squares of snow rested on their hoods and roofs.

As we drove back out of Anchorage, the road narrowed and the rhythm of the streetlamps slowed. Stripes of asphalt tapered off into white-blue drifts. We saw only one car on the road, and it was just a haze of light. My mother switched off the radio and gripped the steering wheel, and when the back of the station wagon slid a little, she muttered something like, "Go ahead."

As the snow accumulated, the tires made a crunching sound over the thicker spots. Everything was padded—by snow, by silence, by graveness. I wished Pei-Pei were not angry, so that she would chatter about the clothes she had seen or ask Natty if he could guess the number of trees in the world, or the color of fish urine, and then say, "Wrong, wrong, wrong." But in the store she had wanted a skirt that was too expensive, and she and my mother had fought. Pei-Pei had come away with nothing. She sat beside me with her hand on the door handle, as though she might spring out and roll into the soft streets if we so much as glanced at her. The windshield wipers made the sound of a nervous heart beating.

When we turned up our driveway with a creak, we saw the yard was fluffed. The damage I had done had vanished, refreshed by the snowfall, and a feathery joy filled my chest.

"I want to play outside," I said.

"It's time for dinner," my mother said.

"But you haven't made anything yet."

"It's too dark."

"Please," I said.

"It's too cold."

"Please."

My mother turned off the car and the headlights and whirled around. "I can't do this anymore."

Natty, Pei-Pei, and I sat still in the backseat. Snow silently struck the windows.

"You don't know," she said. "None of you know." My mother breathed through her teeth. I wondered if there was enough air in the car for all of us. With the engine off, I could feel the heat dissipating.

We trudged through the garage and basement and up the stairs, and everything looked exactly as we had left it—junk, so much junk, like the store. Stacks of old blankets and twenty-pound bags of rice and dusty boxes of things we had bought on sale and never used. In the kitchen, there were pans covered with scratches and grease, and disposable cups that had been reused instead of disposed of, and all of it continued to give me that funny feeling. That we had replaced something important with this junk. That we had traded something for it.

As I kicked off my shoes, my mother said, "Well, go out and play in the dark. Isn't that what you wanted? Do as you want."

Outside the kitchen window, behind the reflections of our indoor lights, was the steady descent of snow, that constant downward drift. The falling clumps were like the sheddings of an immense white bird beating its wings above our house, distraught by something headed this way.

"I don't feel like it anymore," I said.

"Go play," she said.

"It's too cold."

"I'm not stopping you."

"I changed my mind," I said.

"Don't change your mind because of me."

My mother kept standing there, spinning the plastic shopping bag so the top twisted tighter and tighter. I put my shoes back on and reached for the zipper on Pei-Pei's jacket. I ran it from my knees all the way up to my throat and headed for the front door with a feeling of doom. A scattering of dry leaves fell off the ficus tree as I pushed by, and when I opened the door, the leaves swirled low along the linoleum tiles. Outside, the snow careened. I nudged the door closed behind me, sealing off the light and warmth, butting into the night. The sky was chock-full of snow, yet the night felt empty. I walked to the bottom of our drive. Across the gravel strip was the abandoned development project. Strange shapes had formed in it; snow had softened the tree stumps and filled the gaps between piled branches. White mounds, like the backs of huge sleeping animals, filled the clearing, and seemed almost to breathe.

I headed for the pond. It was a deep man-made crater, maybe the early stages of an old foundation. In winter and spring it was filled with ice and water, and all around it, leafless trees pricked at the sky. A single spruce leaned over the water at a forty-five-degree angle, testing gravity. When I got to the edge of the pond, I saw how smooth and black it was. There was no reflection of stars or moon; the snow had shaded them out.

I turned around and saw our little house with its honeyed windows, and the quiet abyss of snow and woods around it. This was what our home looked like when I was not inside. Dinner was on the stove, and my sister was sulking upstairs, filling the whole empty floor with her foul, reassuring presence. I felt hunger like a tiny seed of pain.

Suddenly the cold came, slamming me like a rogue wave. How long did my mother want me to stand here? Was it the beginning or end of my punishment?

4

WHEN THE SUN TUNNELED THROUGH IN TIME FOR SPRING
break, we played rapturously in the clearing, and each day was
less muddy than the last. The pond settled, the water cleared,
and the paste at its edges turned ashier by the hour. Out of the
mess of stumps rose a few trees, preparing to leaf lushly over
their fallen kin. A handful of abandoned logs not worth pulp-
ing had turned mealy, forming a massive, soft heap of slash.
We buried our hands in this mush or jumped from stump to
stump, or took turns standing still while the other two pelted the
frozen one with chunks of gravel from the road. Natty was too
small to aim well, but I was afraid of Pei-Pei's arm; she threw
with precision and without mercy.

Natty found an empty liquor bottle sitting with two beer
cans on a stump. He filled the bottle with water from the pond
and shoved a fistful of cotton grass in. The tips looked like
scrubby old brushes, but in summertime they would turn white
and silken and smear the clearing with a layer of gauze.

When he brought the vase home, my mother screamed, "Don't touch that!"

The bottle hit the floor. Water pooled on the linoleum.

"Get away from it!"

Natty backed up to Pei-Pei.

"Where did you find that dirty bottle?" my mother asked him.

Pei-Pei said, "It doesn't look dirty."

"You can see germs with your eyes?" My mother's gaze jumped between Pei-Pei and Natty without a glance at me, but at the mention of germs, I stiffened.

"It's just a vase of grass," Pei-Pei said.

None of us pointed out that both the bottle and the cans were the same brands my father drank. My father, who had come to the doorway of the den, retreated, so that all I saw was a flash of his tumbled hair and fearful eyes.

"That is a bad spot," my mother said. "A spot where strangers drink by themselves is a very bad spot." With that, we were forbidden from playing in the clearing.

Half of spring break remained, and we took to the deeper, more bewildering woods. Behind our house, we followed the faint path farther than we ever had, and found it went on and on through the endless white spruces that released a scent like damp cleaning rags. And making our way along the lumpy path was not unlike stamping through a giant spread of rags, for the ground was thickly cushioned with needles, soft branches, and crumbling trunks. The path faded out in a few stretches, but several days of bolder and bolder exploration brought a discovery: it ended in the yard of the Dolan house. It was a shortcut between our homes, which by car were nine or ten miles apart. The Dolans—that was something.

Ada Dolan was in my class at school. I sat right in front of her. She was partial to overalls and spent the day hooking and unhooking her shoulder straps, which made a secret snapping sound behind me. Once she reached out and tugged on my sweatpants until the waistband slid down my stomach and sat on my hips. "That's how you wear it," she said.

Her brother, Collin, was seventeen, but he talked to us anyway. The first thing he showed us was his garden of stolen street signs, a few still on their posts, planted into the dirt and leaning every which way like the drunken trees that grew in permafrost. HANDICAPPED PARKING, WOMEN, BEWARE OF DOG, GIVE MOOSE A BRAKE. When Pei-Pei complimented a highway sign lying on the grass, Collin beamed and lifted one side of it up to show her his real prize underneath: PLEASE DON'T CLIMB ON THE PIPELINE.

They lived with a monstrous dog named Baby and their father, a similarly large, slow-moving man whom we occasionally glimpsed ducking into the doorway of the shed or moving split logs around to adjust his enormous stockpile of firewood. Behind their shed was a trailer propped up on cinder blocks with rust streaks running down its broad face, so it looked to be grieving its loss of the open road.

Spring break came and went. After school, we continued to romp around until we forgot about nights, about walls, about homes. Along the trail, we broke off discs of fungus that grew along the live trunks or stirred at the spongy orange innards of a dead trunk with a good stick, trying to flick the ants at one another. Though he was three years older, Collin knew Pei-Pei from the high school and called her Paige. The first time, Pei-Pei had cocked an eyebrow at me, daring me to say anything. It vaguely reminded me of some trouble a couple of years back, when she had tried to pass herself off as an Athabascan native. I found myself mumbling, "What time do we have to be home, Paige?" and "Paige, I'm thirsty," and she thought I was making fun of her, but I'd been trying to play along.

One weekend, while we were arguing about whether Ada had in fact seen a black widow spider in a hollowed stump before it had skittered into shadow, there was an earth-rending crack and the arcing movement of a brittle crown high above us. A massive tree came to a slanted standstill against the trunk of another spruce. Its roots had wrested up a great clod of earth.

Ada broke the long silence that followed. "Did you see that?" She fell to her knees and squashed Natty's face between her hands.

"I did," Natty said.

"Tell me," Ada said. She put her face right in front of his, practically touching noses. Her freckles ran together into whole dollops, and only very close-up could you make out the individual dots. "What did you see?" she asked.

Natty's hair was pressed funny from the way Pei-Pei had held him against her stomach, and it rose up and gave him a defiant look as he said, "The tree. It fell."

His pronouncement released us from our dumb fright.

"Motherfucker," Collin said.

I kicked a damp mound of rotting needles, spraying them into the air.

Collin planted himself on the trail in front of Pei-Pei. "That tree almost fell on top of you." It was true she had been standing most directly in the path of the tree. I studied the second tree, the one that had stopped it. It was squat. All its branches pointed downward, so it gave the impression of being burdened.

Pei-Pei said, "Didn't you see I jumped away?"

"Not in time," Collin said. He shook his head several times, and the bill of his cap sliced and resliced a line in the air. "If it wasn't for that other tree, it would've been the end for you."

"Maybe, maybe not."

"It would've fallen on you for sure."

"I'm faster than you think."

"You wouldn't have been fast enough. You would've been pancaked." Collin smacked his palms together.

Had Pei-Pei almost died? No, it was impossible. She was laughing so hard she had to press a fist to her stomach to make herself stop.

"And we wouldn't be able to get it off of you," Collin added. "It's too big to move."

Pei-Pei quieted down and bent over to reroll a pant cuff. She nudged her glasses up with her wrist. "You could've tried to help me."

"Help you?"

"You're quick, anyway."

Collin was a hockey player. Pei-Pei said he hovered over ice like a dragonfly over a pond. He shrugged—awfully slowly, I thought.

"No one's quick enough for that. Anyway, what kind of idiot would I be if I jumped in front of a falling tree?" He lobbed

49

a chunk of dead branch straight up. It rustled through several boughs as it came back down. The end of it just missed Pei-Pei's shoulder. Collin giggled.

"Fuckwad." Pei-Pei whipped a stray twig at him and took off down the path toward home.

"Come back," I said. I couldn't keep the whine out of my voice. I tried to decide whether to follow. It was an unspoken pact that we stay out until the last possible second. At home, my mother was bent over a spiral notebook at the kitchen table, a row of blue pens lined up beside her. Her knuckles dug into the paper. Beneath the nib of her pen bloomed precise Chinese characters with severe hooks and wild, unleashed strokes. Her list of good ideas, she called it. Ideas of jobs she might start, with no correlation to her skills or actual openings. "I could repair washing machines," she would say. "Those guys, they charge whatever they want to charge."

Collin ran and grabbed Pei-Pei by the elbow.

"Get off me," she said.

"I didn't mean to throw it at you."

"I have to go home." She shoved the whole mass of her hair to one side.

"I said I was sorry."

"I have to make a phone call."

"Who you running to call? When you got us?" Collin looked at Natty and me, then at Ada, who was sitting on the path, picking bits of forest floor from the knees of her pants.

"Let's get out of here," Collin said. "Let the kids play by themselves."

"Pei," I said.

She spun around, and I realized I'd used the wrong name. "Go home," she said.

"It's not time yet."

"Then stay here. I don't care."

I tried to catch her gaze, but she was busy shaking the coins in her coat pockets.

"Come on," Collin said.

"Where are we going?"

"Where we went last time."

She zipped and unzipped her jacket just an inch at the throat. When he gave her hair a flick, one side of her mouth twitched up. Collin began to walk, and Pei-Pei shuffled behind him.

"Runts," he said, showing us his pink palm, "catch you later."

I shook an alder shrub and made the leaves slap one another. The catkins wobbled. When I looked up, Collin and Pei-Pei were past a large patch of cow parsnip thirty yards away, about to take a curve in the path.

I hurried over to Ada. "Should we follow them?" I asked.

"Nah," she said.

"We could stay back so they don't know we're following."

"Nah."

I considered pointing out that if we kept playing here, she would have to walk home alone. But she seemed to think nothing of walking the entire length of the path on her own. Maybe, at ten years old, I should have been as brave. But it seemed to me the woods wanted something of us. And the farther you went into the woods, the bigger that thing was, and the more intensely it was wanted.

I gazed up for signs of beetles on the trees directly over us. They left their mark in the form of rust-colored boughs that scarred the blue-green woods. The boughs drooped and shed needles until they were nothing more than prickly netting. Then the netting disintegrated, and entire trees stood stripped and spindly, like the old tube brushes in my father's plumbing box. Any gust of wind might topple these husks, and even from the house we could occasionally hear the splitting of bark, sounds of surrender.

Ada played with Natty's hair, standing it up, wiggling it at the roots. She slapped her thigh. "I almost forgot! I saved this for you." She worked something out of her pocket. A Tootsie Roll. When Natty opened the wrapper, we saw it was half eaten. Before I could say anything, he popped it into his mouth. I stared at him. He stared back, chewing. It was too late. The germs were in his body.

He squatted beside Ada on the path. His hair had gotten long. If he didn't push it out of his face, it would cover his eyes and brush the tops of his cheeks. I scratched at my forehead, suddenly aware that my own hair was also the longest it had ever been. Ada and Natty bent their heads together. Ada had yanked a horsetail stem from the ground and broken it in half, and they were trying to piece it back together.

I rotated my watch; it was too big for my wrist and the heavy face always hung on the wrong side. Just past four o'clock. My mother was at the kitchen table making her list, talking out loud as she wrote. My father didn't have a job today; we had left him in the den, digging in the crates for a book none of us remembered. "The one with the photographs of the poisonous frogs," he kept saying.

"It doesn't exist," Pei-Pei had said. "I'm the one who reads all those books, and I'm telling you it doesn't exist."

"You know," he said, "with the shiny green frogs that have got tiger stripes on their legs. Or the blue frogs that look like they've been dipped in paint."

"Did you dream this?" Pei-Pei said. "Is this from your sad childhood?"

"The book was in the house," he said. "Who took it?"

"What do you want with it anyway?"

"I want to show Natty the frogs. Don't you want to see the frogs?" my father asked.

"Yes," Natty said. "But first I want to play outside."

That was hours ago. It was possible my father was still looking for the book.

The days were longer now, but the woods would still dim. I wished I could stop the day from darkening, or the trees from leaning into the path, making you wonder what, in the thick of the forest, they were trying to escape.

"Let's do tattoos," Ada said. She plucked a few leaves from an alder shrub and worked on Natty's arm. When she finished, she pointed a hooked finger at me. I knelt and held my arm out to her, ready to receive her gifts.

She turned my forearm up and pressed the underside of a jagged alder leaf to it. She rested my arm on her thigh, stacked her hands over the leaf, and leaned all of her weight on top. When she flipped my arm over, the leaf was pasted on. "This one will be good," she said. She breathed out of her mouth. After she peeled the leaf off, she rubbed a handful of dirt into my arm, then brushed off the excess. Leaning low, she blew the last of the dust off. Her blond hair fell onto my arm, and her breath was cool yet not chilling like wind. "There," she said, and wiped her hands on the front of her pants.

"It's better than mine," Natty said.

I examined my tattoo: the leaf and its branching veins, imprinted on my flesh. That night I would take care not to wash it off, so I could study it in the near-dark. What I had brought back from the woods.

At school, I had tried to climb a rope tied to the limb of a tall, smooth tree. A piece of yellow tape marked the height we had to climb to pass the unit for gym. I wiggled but couldn't move upward. Eventually I just hung on the very end of the rope like the bob on a pendulum, and a boy named Dean said, "Don't laugh. He can't help his brains got scrambled."

It was the sickness. Now people were noticing me. But it was possible to get away from them. Recently Ada and I had snuck into an empty classroom, where she pushed me into a cabinet. We discovered the whole length of cabinets along the wall was connected. Or perhaps Ada had always known it. We huddled in the dark while the second-graders shuffled in, and stayed there for an entire language arts class. When it got quiet, we knew Mr. Hammel was walking up and down the aisles to straighten or expand or shrink students' hand-formed letters by writing over them with a red felt-tipped pen. He mutilated the letters; they bled into their forced shapes. In the cabinets we lay our heads down on boxes of manila folders and card stock, and Ada held on to the shell of my ear. She smelled like peanuts. It was dark, but I forgot to be scared.

5

THE DAYS WERE RAPIDLY LENGTHENING; I COULD BARELY remember the spun-out dawns and twilights of winter. But although the nights were short, they felt long and wild. We had rearranged the beds again, each one against a different wall, and Pei-Pei and I were sleeping with our heads pointed to the same corner. Sometimes, when I breathed too loudly, Pei-Pei scrambled out of bed in a huff. She grabbed hold of my feet and rotated me like the hand of a clock. She tossed her pillow to the other side of her own bed, and suddenly she felt far away.

"I can't sleep," I whined.

She forced out a long, voiced sigh. "Why not?"

"Thoughts," I said. "Dreams." I described one. A dot of mold was on my forearm, an ash-gray spot like the ones we excised from bread. I couldn't wash it off. It's spreading, Pei-Pei had informed me as she handed me a knife.

There was silence. Had she gone back to sleep? But she

appeared over me. She whispered, "It's okay. Ruby didn't die that way."

It was a while before I could whisper back, "What are you saying?"

"She didn't rot. They burned her."

I jammed my fingers under the mattress until I found the cool metal mesh of the bed frame. I could hear Natty's sharp little sleep breaths from his adjacent bed.

"They burned her body."

The night-light by the foot of Natty's bed seemed jittery. It flickered, but when I stared at it, it stilled.

"She's in their closet. On the high shelf. I've seen it." Pei-Pei's hair trembled as she bent further forward. I could perceive the outline of her figure as it hovered over me, a blanket draped over her shoulders so she was the shape of a leaf pile. And her short, breathy utterances were like small, unknown animals darting out of that pile; they kept coming, from the darkness, rustling at me.

"The urn is really small," she said. "The size of a large soup can."

I swatted at her face.

"What was that for?"

"Get away from me."

"I'm just saying, go to sleep. It's okay. You can go to sleep." She turned and retreated to her own bed.

Soon I could hear her clear breaths, sipping air and letting it go. Would Ruby fit in a soup can? All of her? Wouldn't some part of her have to be left behind? I grunted. The night-light strobed. My whole body contracted, trying to rid itself of a foreign object. A knuckle in my throat.

———

SOMETIMES WHEN I COULDN'T SLEEP, I crept down the stairs to the kitchen or den, where I flipped on the lights to push the darkness back. Things had a sheen of unfamiliarity in those hours, or non-hours, as they felt: the strange pattern of Natty's crayons scattered over the den carpet; the wrinkled surface of the couch cushions, which my mother had sewn into unbleached canvas casing to preserve the maroon velour; the closet in the cramped entryway of the house, with its door left ajar. The closet was very narrow, perhaps two and a half feet across, and our coats were crammed in so tightly, a sleeve sometimes reached out and kept the door from latching. Every item in the house seemed slightly askew, as though a stranger had been handling it.

One night, in those viscous hours meant for sleep, I found my father sitting on the couch in the near-dark. Feet planted wide, elbows on his knees. The small lamp that Pei-Pei had made in school from a soda can had been moved from a folding chair down to the carpet, where its crooked shade leaned against the base of the couch. Its bulb was the size of a cork, and it gave off the only weak light in the room. My father was leaning between his legs and staring at the carpet, where Natty had left one of his drawings.

Unsure if he'd seen me, I thought about retreating to the kitchen, but as I took a step, I stumbled on an encyclopedia volume and then knocked into a folding chair. Without looking up, my father pointed to Natty's drawing. "Look at that," he said. Resting on the cushion beside my father was a mug, and as he moved, liquid swelled to the lip of it. I watched to see if it would spill over.

"Really look at it," he said.

I stepped to the other side of the drawing, which lay in the orb of lamplight, and became distracted by the little bulb. I had a straight view of it from the top, right through the opening in the shade, and its sudden brightness in our dark den was searing.

"What do you think?"

I blinked spots away, then considered the drawing. Natty pressed hard on his crayons, and the strokes were thick and waxy. He'd unearthed a book of old space photographs from the bottom of a crate and had been copying them in crayon. I recognized this one as Mars, seen from the *Viking 2* orbiter. In the photo, it was dawn, and most of the planet was subsumed in darkness, save an arc of red land. Natty hadn't outlined the red arc, drawing a banana shape and coloring it in the way Pei-Pei or I might have, but instead had layered stroke after stroke after stroke so that even though the strokes weren't precise, exactly, in sum the planet looked red and swirling and the polar cap like a blotted, bluish patch of ice that palmed the curve of land and faded at the edges into vapors. The land was pitted and scarred.

I knew the drawing was good because, like the photos, it made me dizzy. The idea of space gave me a spinning feeling; it was too big and unbounded, and the more I tried to believe in it, the more I believed in nothing.

My father shook his head. "Just what do you do with something like this?" There was a sudden movement on the wall, and I turned around to see his massive shadow, stretching up the wall and folding onto the ceiling, where it waggled its vague, enormous head.

"What was that for?" he asked.

It's possible I had shrunk away from him, or raised an arm to shield myself, or maybe I had cringed.

"What has your mother told you about me?"

"Nothing."

"She said something, didn't she?" My father grabbed the sleeve of my long johns, pinching my skin near my elbow. "What did she say about me?" His leg jerked, kicking the lamp over, and he let go of me to right it. When I glanced at where it had fallen, I noticed a large envelope on the floor, beneath a small, neat stack of paper. All of the text was in English. Sometimes, reading the newspaper, my father would point to a word and ask Pei-Pei if she knew what it meant, pretending to test her.

"It's not true," he said. "Or not the way she tells it. I didn't do anything wrong."

Like all of his children, my father had a very round face, but that night the cheek farthest away from the lamp was hollowed out by shadows. The right side of his face was lit, and his right eye seemed to stare at me harder than his left; there was a strange gleam in it.

"It's not my fault," he said.

I glanced at him through my bangs. It was hard for me to meet his uneven gaze. I unrolled the cuffed sleeves of my shirt so they hid my hands completely. I looked down and up and around. The room seemed off-kilter, with all its shadows thrown upward, at a slant.

When I tilted my head, I could see the top half of the first page on the stack. In the left corner was the incomplete border of a rectangle and several words printed in capital letters. My father's name, TSUNG-CHIEH HSU. The word DEFEN-DANT. To the right of the box was the word SUMMONS.

"There are things that happen," he said, and he seemed to be talking to someone suspended in the air above me. "The very things you fear. For a while you don't believe it, because you've spent so much energy fearing it, keeping it away, how could it have happened?" He curled his knuckly toes as he took a large gulp from his mug and balanced it back on the cushion. His hulking shadow moved again, too large for the low-ceilinged room as it tried to straighten itself.

My father gathered the wool military blanket bunched at the back of the couch and folded it in half. He draped it over my shoulders and held it closed below my chin. It pooled around my feet.

"I've turned off the heat completely," he said. "You'll have to wear more at night. And you'll have to eat more. Listen, you've really got to eat."

I couldn't think of a way to explain that something was stuck in my throat—that was why I couldn't eat. As I reached for the corners of the blanket, my father let go, and it fell off my shoulders. There was a draft in the room.

"You've got to put on some weight for next winter." He waved a hand at the length of my body as though he almost couldn't bear to consider it. He grunted. "At least we've got four walls and a roof." He reached over to the wall and slapped it, just beside the window that looked onto our dark yard. My heart pounded at the dim, shadow-etched face staring at us from outside, in the instant it took to realize the face was my father's reflection. As he brought his arm back, he tipped the mug beside him, and a portion of his drink splashed out. He swooped to rescue Natty's drawing. He shook the page, a sheet of green-and-white-bar paper with the perforated edges still attached, but it was dry.

He took hold of both edges and studied the drawing again, lowering it for light. "Do you think he's a genius? Do you think he'll be famous?"

My father had told us that he used to be a genius, that he had an advanced degree from Taiwan. My mother had never denied it, so I knew it was true.

"Yes," I said.

"You think so?"

"Yes."

"Painter, you think? Or something else?"

"Cartoons?" I said.

"No." He dropped his hand. "Do you see this?" He shook the paper again. "It has an essence." He closed his eyes nearly all the way, and half-moon shadows clung to his eyelids. "They might put his paintings up in a museum, all in a nice, straight row."

I stayed quiet.

"With a special light for each painting."

I pressed the damp blotch on the couch cushion where his drink had spilled.

"Does Natty do anything strange?"

I lifted my hand. "What?"

"Anything out of the ordinary." My father held the paper by the lamp again. "Michelangelo wouldn't take off his boots. Not even to sleep. When the boots finally came off, they peeled his skin away."

I stared at my father's bare feet. They were softer than my

mother's, whiter. The toenails had a yellow cast. He had not grown up beside an ocean, scrambling over rocks. During the day, his feet were swaddled in thick socks and boots made of rubber.

I thought of Natty sitting naked on the edge of the tub, lacking the will to seek something so basic as warmth. "Natty isn't strange," I said.

"Maybe that will come later," he said.

"It won't," I said.

He rose and pinned the drawing to the bare wall with his open hand, leaning over two rows of crates. "Go get the tape."

I ran into the unlit kitchen and rummaged in the drawer. Something gouged my hand, and I closed my fingers around the plastic case.

When I returned, my father was in the same position, his index finger tapping a dark spot on the red arc of Mars—the volcano Ascraeus Mons, which I knew from the caption in the book stood fourteen miles tall. A tallness that stretched beyond our comprehension on earth.

I tore a strip of Scotch tape. My father centered it over the top edge of the drawing and jammed his thumb against the tape. "Right there," he muttered. He ran his thumb back and forth, hard, so that it would be impossible to remove the tape without an accompanying strip of wall.

When I wandered down the next morning, the drawing stuck there gave me a start; hadn't it been a dream? Within days the paper had curled forward, as though trying to hide itself.

——

ON THE WAY to the buses, I saw two boys trying to set fire to piles of dead grass on the concrete step of the school.

"Give me that," I said, holding my palm out until one of them placed the plastic lighter there. But then I didn't know what to do with it. Throw it? Give it back? I turned a full circle. Just inside the front doors was a stack of newsletters.

"I don't know if . . ." one of them said as I knelt over the stack. I lit a bottom corner. To make sure it caught, I held down the wheel and fork until they left ruts in my thumb.

A handful of kids gathered several yards away, watching me as I watched back through the streaks of my long hair. No one stepped any closer. There was this between us: I had been tested, and I had survived.

It wasn't really a fire at all, just a hint of orange flame and a blackening that seeped across the paper. After the others had wandered away, I sat there, disintegrating the charred paper with mere touch.

I missed the bus that afternoon, and my mother refused to pick me up. I hid around the schoolyard and waited for my father, who came after dark. The truck idled, my father waiting for an acknowledgment of his presence. I sat with my window open and stuck both hands out and tried to tell if the stars were moving. They seemed to want to move.

"Does it even count?" I said. "First teacher in space? Was she? Were they high enough up? To count as being in space at all?" I made a smacking sound with my mouth. "It doesn't matter if she was first anything. In a year no one will remember her."

"What kind of person says things like this?" my father said. With one hand on the wheel, he craned his neck to peer up at the night sky, as though to ask the universe whether it could comprehend my wickedness.

The stars. What was so great about puffs of dust and gas? Even Natty, with his planetary masterpieces, was only interested in the colors and patterns. Not our world and its edges. Not the delusions that celestial objects had meaning to us, or that they—or we—were anything more than garbage floating around in a rubble-strewn world.

As we pulled onto the gravel road, my father whispered, "Me. I will remember."

6

RUBY OFTEN LEFT OUR BEDROOM TO SLEEP WITH OUR parents. They kept their door open for her. The hallway was so short I could hear the creak of the old mattress as she crawled between my parents, and my father's mumbled Taiwanese: "I was waiting for you, little muē."

Even though I knew she was gone, I couldn't help but listen for it. Sometimes Natty kicked his covers aside, and I wondered if he was listening, too, and whether the silence made his whole body prickle the same way, like a swarm of insects sweeping around inside, trapped and buzzing and wanting.

One night, we did hear something. Not Ruby's ghost footsteps, but a skittering across the ceiling. A clatter. The sound of marbles being rolled. But there was no access to our attic—it was completely sealed off. My father talked about cutting a hole and stuffing more insulation up there, but it was only talk. By spring he would forget how cold it had been.

Pei-Pei said children dwelled above us—paler, thinner versions of us who played in constant darkness. A flash of their wet teeth or the foggy whites of their eyes—this was all they could see of one another, and only on nights when the moon poked through the clouds and slid through a splitting seam in the roof. Once the sky turned its darkest cast, the children began to play marbles with—what? Dried wads of bubble gum, I said, but Pei-Pei asked where they would've gotten their spiny hands on a pack of gum. "It's bones," she said. She grinned at us, and her big plastic glasses slid down to the tip of her nose. "Because they live and die up there. And their own bones is all they've got. A shinbone for a bat and a knee bone for a ball, and the small bits for their marbles. Like toes," she said, dragging a fingernail across the tops of my feet.

"Upstairs?" Natty whispered.

"Right on top of our heads," Pei-Pei said. "Don't you hear them now?"

We strained our ears and were rewarded with a thump.

Natty's dark figure shot up in bed. The night-light made one of his cheeks glow. "Someone's upstairs," he said. His voice was clear and full, almost happy.

The ceiling percussion continued. Finally I turned on the light to find Natty lying with an ankle propped on his knee, hands laced behind his head, listening to the noises as though to fragments of an aria. As I sank away from consciousness, the overhead glare kept me swaying in the shallowest layer of sleep, a net of two-second dreams. A transparent tree. A train towing a house. A wet road and a troubled feeling.

I woke long before dawn. There was a chill. The light was off again. Natty was facing the window beside his bed, and it was open. He pressed the flimsy screen, which bent outward against his hand like a sail.

Our beds were in a U-shape arrangement, and my head was within arm's reach of Natty's bare feet. His soles were stained, as though he'd been padding around in soil, or maybe it was a trick of the night-light and the shadows.

"What are you doing?" I asked. "Close the window."

"I saw them," he said, leaning further into the screen. His eyes were swollen, and he had rubbed an extra fold into one of his eyelids. "The people from upstairs."

The window was too far and too dark to make out anything but blots of lucent clouds. "Don't fall out," I said.

"They were singing. Like this." He cupped his hands to the sides of his mouth and said, "Down. Down. Down."

"Down what? Down where?"

"Down. Down. Down." His low, raspy voice scraped my ears.

"You were dreaming."

"I heard it." Natty pressed both hands to the screen and peered at the driveway below. He craned his head. "Here. Next to the window. They were climbing down the wall. They grabbed the ledge—I saw their fingers—and they jumped all the way to the ground. I think maybe they flew." His face was warped by some kind of joy, an expression so unfamiliar I couldn't stop staring.

I leaped from my bed to his, dragging the covers with me. I closed and latched the window.

"They went that way, into the woods," he said.

I lay down next to him and tried to stop the images. A band of children popping the screen on the gable vent. Their feet scrabbling over the bones lining the attic floor, making them clatter. They weaseled down the vinyl siding. On the driveway, they shielded their eyes from the harsh light of the moon.

There was a slight crack across our plaster ceiling, and I watched the length of it, waiting for it to expand, for soft hands to reach through.

"They'll be back," Natty said.

"Just lie down."

"I'm waiting for them—"

I pulled him toward the bed, and he landed hard on his side, facing me with his mouth open.

"I'm waiting for them to come home," he said. He struggled to get up. Soon he was sitting on his heels, keeping watch at the window again.

As I slept I was half aware of the cold. Clean-smelling and ruthless. It seeped through the covers, making me huddle tight as I tried to hold on to the string of warmth that was slipping away. When I opened my eyes again, there was a dash of acid-pink in the black square of sky, a crack in the night, morning showing through. The window was open again, and Natty had fallen asleep on top of the covers. I touched his cheek: cold as the bed's steel frame. His skin was soft, his whole face tranquil. How could he sleep like this? Completely unharassed.

Through the window screen came a deep, sad voice. It stopped. It started, it stopped. I sat up and leaned over Natty's sleeping body, pressing my hands to the windowsill. There was just enough light to see the wetness of the driveway. Something massive and white-throated swooped toward the house, its wings like a blanket being shaken out, and just as swiftly it was out of view.

Then I heard the faint murmurings of a radio. My father was sitting in his truck with the windows down, refrigerating himself in the crisp air. His arm moved up and down in a small arc as he drank from a cup or can. It was all Chernobyl these days. We caught only snippets: a great plume of radioactive smoke, poisoning, abortions.

"You saw them," Natty said. How long had he been watching me at the window? He was still lying down. His mouth did not close all the way. His broken front tooth looked more jagged than usual, and the small bit of whiteness shone.

"What?" I said. "No."

"You did. Did you see Ruby?"

I didn't reply.

"Did she come back? Is she in the attic?"

A feeling seized me. A single shiver, slowed down and drawn out—it wouldn't release me.

"Is she upstairs?"

Something about Natty's expression made me scared to answer either way. But as I sat there gripping the cold windowsill, I started to imagine her small silhouette marching up the driveway. I wanted badly to have seen her. I wanted badly to be Natty, who believed I had seen her, and who had done nothing to her in the first place. Wasn't it just as fantastic to have seen an owl the size of a sofa?

"Yes," I said. "She's upstairs."

———

THE NEXT NIGHT, I felt my mother crawl into bed. She scratched me lightly on my forearm.

"What is it?" I whispered.

She settled herself on the mattress, completely off my pillow. Her elbow grazed my shoulder as she wedged her hands behind her neck. We fit well; the twin bed felt neither cramped nor empty.

Across the room, Pei-Pei moved an arm or leg, rustling her sheet. A minute later, Natty made a small puffing sound. After that was silence. And my mother's whisper in the dark, dispersing like vapors.

"I'd like to be a fish," my mother said. "Deep in the water. Never getting cold. No home but the ocean. Barely aware of yourself."

"I'd like to be a fish, too," I said.

"Maybe I would rather be the ocean," she said. "Just a drop of ocean water."

I didn't care to think about that. "Do you want some pillow?" I scooted my head to the side.

"I heard something." She pressed herself up on her elbows.

"Get under the blanket," I said. She was on top of the covers, which pinned me down. I yanked on it. "Get in."

She lifted the covers and crawled under. Her cold toes prodded at my leg. Under the blanket with me, her whisper had a different quality, more intimate but also sharper, honing in on me. "Your grandfather is sick," she said.

"Will he get better?" I asked. "Or will he die?"

"What a question!"

"Is he going to die?"

"Stop saying that." My mother pulled hard on my ear, and I slid my head toward her so it would hurt less.

"He's just sick." She flicked me on the temple. "When I

talked to him last week, he asked when we were coming home. I think you should say something to him on the phone next month."

I hadn't talked to him in a long time, not just months but years. It was hard to understand his pinched voice on the phone, and anytime I spoke, he would shout in a wheezing panic, "What's that you're saying? I missed it. I missed what you said!"

"How about I write him a letter?" I said.

"You know he's illiterate."

"Someone can read it to him."

"How many words can you write in Chinese?"

"Maybe twenty," I said.

"Just say hi on the phone. It's so easy, to make him happy." Her voice grew low again. "Leave, he told me. Start your life somewhere else. Now he says, Come back. He says, You never should've left. He doesn't remember that he wanted us to go."

There was a boy in her village, she said. They had swum together in the ocean. When the water ran down his arms, he was as brown and shiny as a lychee seed. Her father hated this boy.

"When is he going to die?"

"Shush."

There was a thump from the attic. My mother flipped onto her back. "There it is again. What is that?"

"Nothing."

"It's coming from the ceiling." She turned to face me and held my chin so I couldn't turn away. "What's up there?"

"Nothing."

"Bats?"

"No."

"It could be mice."

"No."

"Animals don't belong in a house."

I inched my legs toward her, trying to feel her warmth now that it was trapped under the blanket. Strangely, she gave off none. When I finally touched her cold legs, they sucked my own precious heat away.

"A house is clean," my mother said. "Dirty things belong outside."

I thought of how trees were washed by rain and the ground preserved under snow and cleansed by thaw, and how we closed up the house and shed our hair and skin and wiped our greasy fingers on the underside of the kitchen table. I liked to wedge little pieces of trash into places they would never be found: the inch of space behind the couch, the gap between cabinet and wall, the cracks in the basement floor.

"Tomorrow," my mother said, "we are going to fix this." She touched my nose, my mouth, my hair. "We are going to do things properly. For once, we are going to begin and end things the right way."

———

IN THE MORNING, my father pushed my bed aside and took a saw to the ceiling. He cut a square right over where my bed had been. As he finished the fourth side of the square, white dust poured out like sand.

"Maybe you should stop," said Pei-Pei. "Maybe stop right about now."

"Too late," my father said. "I've finished cutting it." He towered over us on the ladder, looking more awake than he had for weeks. He handed the saw to Pei-Pei and tucked his shirt into his pants. He brandished a screwdriver from his tool belt.

"We can tape back over it," Pei-Pei said.

I stood with Natty in the doorway. Behind us, in the hall, my mother slapped our backs. "Cover your noses and mouths," she said. Neither of us moved.

When the dust stopped trickling, my father pried the entire panel off. Then he was yelping, but we could barely hear it. Spruce cones were tumbling down, mixed with pulpy handfuls of insulation and what had to be gallons of dust. Cones kept coming. For a moment I thought we'd opened a portal into some other world. The cones bumped over the carpet and a few rolled to the wall.

When it was over, my father straightened from his crouch. He teetered off the ladder, hair frosted with dust. Near his stumbling feet I saw a tiny intact skull, no more than an inch in height. It had two long, curved teeth at the front and a great hollowness where the eyes had been.

"My God," my mother said. "Move away. Everyone get away." When I glanced behind me, she was backing down the hall all the way to the bathroom. She knelt in front of the cabinet and pulled out rags and sprays and bleach. "It's in the carpet," she said, and her voice was hoarse and frightened.

Beside the ladder, my father folded at the waist and ran his hands over his hair. Particles rained from his head.

While my father was bent over, Natty rushed the ladder, his bare feet raising dust where they stamped the carpet. He began to climb. The rungs were spaced so far apart for him that he had to spring from one to the next. He froze near the top, his head swiveling from side to side, scanning the dark attic. In the column of sunlight from the window, a million dust particles shimmered below him, freewheeling. A juicy river of light. For a moment Natty appeared to be floating. Suspended in the air, he twisted and gazed down at us. "There's no one up here," he said.

My father laughed. "Who did you expect to find?"

"Come down," I said.

My father was still laughing. "There's no one up here," he repeated, as though he had never heard something so clever.

"It's empty," Natty said. He let go of the ladder completely.

"It's not empty," my father said. "Can't you see it's full of trash?"

"It's okay," I said. "Come down." I stepped into the fog. I was aware of my mother behind me, coming in and out of the doorway, busy with her mission. In the corner of my eye, Pei-Pei waved my father's saw in the air. I approached Natty. His small, empty hands fluttered. "Hold on to the ladder," I said. I stood behind him in case he fell.

"A big step down," I said.

He wobbled down a rung.

"Two more," I said.

My mother tossed a sponge at my father. "Take care of this." She gestured to the arsenal of cleaning products she had lined up against the wall.

"Where are you going?"

"I'm going to buy poison. To make sure nothing comes back."

"Poison," echoed Natty.

My mother glanced at us. "I'll take the boys with me." She nudged us toward the door.

The dust around my father was so thick he seemed to be standing on a rug. He balanced a sponge on one flat hand, as though weighing it. Even I knew he needed to start with a vacuum.

———

AT THE HARDWARE STORE, the clerk said, "You hearing them by night or by day?"

"Night," my mother said.

"It's the flying ones," said a squat man who had stopped to join the conversation. Instead of a belt, he wore a piece of rope around his waist. "You got the flying ones."

"Agreed," the clerk said. "Flying squirrels, they forage at night. You're hearing their comings and goings."

The other man said, "Got yourself a den."

"A family," said the clerk.

"And poison?" my mother asked.

The short man grinned. He hitched his pants. "Antifreeze. You already got it at home. They'll lick it right up. They'll get the shakes and then they'll die."

"Yes," my mother breathed. "The antifreeze."

"No, no," the clerk said. "You don't want that. They'll drag themselves into some crevice to die. Be near impossible to find them before they start to rot. Let me show you something else." He led my mother out of the aisle.

Natty sat down on the concrete floor and rubbed his thumbs together. I studied the fragile tops of his ears, exposed and bare-skinned like the backs of newborn mice.

"The attic was empty," he said. He kept working his thumbs, scrubbing.

"Yeah," I said. Something filled my stomach and weighed me down, as if I'd drunk a glass of wet concrete.

"They weren't there. They left the house."

I nodded and tugged on a shoelace until it came undone. Its ends lay soft on the floor.

My mother returned, swinging a jug of ammonia in one hand and antifreeze in the other. She knocked the jugs together, and her smile was full of long teeth. As she ushered us to the checkout line, I watched my laces lash the floor.

Back at the house, my mother busied herself with her chemicals. I ran into the bedroom. Pei-Pei had fallen asleep, her arm hanging off the side of her bed in a way that looked precarious; I slept with everything tucked in. My father was in the attic, filling a garbage bag. His socked feet peeked over the edge of the ragged hole in the ceiling. He cleared his throat over and over.

"We're back," I hollered.

My father's legs searched for the ladder and took a few steps down. He wiped his nose on his sleeve and hacked out a few dry coughs. "There's too much of it," he said. "You wouldn't believe how much of it there is. I'll have to get more bags. I'll have to go to the store."

"There are trash bags in the kitchen," I said.

He pressed his nose with the side of his finger. "This dust. There's just so much. Every bit of movement makes more. It's not a job for one man." He unclipped his tool belt and let it thunk on the carpet. Without it, he looked thin and insubstantial. He sat on a low rung. "I think I'll take a rest."

I glanced into the empty hallway.

"I'll take a shower and then a rest." My father eased himself up and wandered to the bathroom. A few minutes later, my mother came in. She was holding a small armful of unmated socks. She scanned the fallen tool belt and the chalky carpet, then peered up into the attic and said, "Where'd your father go?"

At the spitting sound of the shower spray, she dropped the socks. "You better not be done," she yelled, barreling toward the bathroom door. She tried the knob, but it only rattled and would not turn. "I'm ready to do my part, but you haven't done yours." She kicked the door hard enough to make us flinch in the bedroom. Pei-Pei's eyes were closed, but from the jut of her jaw I knew she was only pretending to sleep now.

In the hall, my mother hollered, "Come out now. Finish this! You're holding me back."

It was impossible that he didn't hear her, but the only sound from the bathroom was the water splattering on the floor of the tub.

"Come out!" my mother screamed. "Finish this one thing in your life!"

———

AT DINNER, I stirred my rice porridge around the bowl, making ridges rise in the wake of my spoon.

Pei-Pei knuckled the corner of her crooked glasses. "Gavin hasn't taken one bite yet," she said. Natty slid off his chair and headed for the den. Flashing her teeth at me, Pei-Pei followed. I watched their backs. Over the table was a thick, gluey mood; they had forsaken me.

"Eat," my father said. His hair, still wet from his shower, had a metallic sheen.

"You think you can tell people to do things?" my mother said to the table. "You, the one who does nothing?" She snagged a few fixings and dropped them into my bowl. She clinked her chopsticks against the rim, pointing to my favorite, the shriveled coins of sweet seitan.

"It's not a difficult thing, to eat." My father dropped his newspaper, and it billowed up from the table, riding a draft of air from the vent behind him.

My mother laughed. "What do you know about difficult?"

I picked up my spoon and dipped it into the porridge. A few bloated grains clung to the tip.

"Is that called eating?" he asked me.

"You shut up," she said. "You should be ashamed to eat. What you've done." She looked at me. "I can't even talk about it. The children. If only they knew what their father's done."

"I haven't done anything."

"I can't even say."

My parents spoke Taiwanese to each other and a mix of Taiwanese and Chinese to us. Pei-Pei, Natty, and I spoke English to each other and a mix of Chinese and English to our parents. I thought of all the notions that got trapped. The expressions that caught and went stale before we could get them out.

"Oil prices can't fall any lower," my mother said. We can't

even afford a plane ticket to see my father. And you go and do this."

My father whipped the newspaper so it cracked. In one swoop, he was leaning across the table. He'd picked up the dish of bamboo shoots and was clearing it into my bowl. They were unsalted and reluctant to slide down the plate and I hated them. On top of this he dumped the remainder of the tomato and eggs. Lastly, the seitan. "I'm your father," he said. "And I'm telling you to eat."

I shoveled a piece of egg into my mouth, then two slices of bamboo shoot that smelled like pond water. I gagged. It didn't feel right, all that food in my mouth. It didn't belong there, and it wouldn't go down.

He began to mutter. "Small as a fingernail, this one. I give him food, and he acts like I'm trying to kill him."

Saliva rushed into my mouth and I had to blink wetness from my eyes.

"Keep going," he said.

"Leave him alone," my mother said.

I looked down at my bowl, piled high. I blinked several times, then everything fell out of my mouth. Clumps, thinned with saliva, hit the table, my bowl, my lap.

"You can stop now." My mother dragged her index finger across my forehead, sweeping my bangs out of my eyes. I shook them back in place where I liked them.

My father came around the table and grabbed my jaw. "Open." I felt the pressure and strength of his hand. He stuffed a piece of egg into my mouth with his fingers.

"Get away from him," she said.

"I have to teach him to eat. He doesn't know how."

She started clearing the table. She was sloppy with the stacking of bowls and dishes, clamping them together instead of nesting them. "Stop yelling."

"Who's yelling? Who's yelling so loud she can't hear herself?"

"One of us is yelling, and it's not me."

I spit the unchewed egg into my hand and eyed my escape route; I just had to make it to the kitchen counter, then follow it to the wide doorway of the den, through which I could see Pei-Pei on the couch and part of Natty's legs where he lay on the floor.

When my mother clattered everything into the sink, I made a run for it.

"You're not done," my father said. He threw his newspaper section at me, but it only flapped onto my empty chair. He picked up the remaining stack and whipped it hard in my direction. It fluttered and multiplied as inserts and coupon pages fanned from it.

When I was safely at the doorway of the den, I turned and watched my mother bend down. She gathered the pages on her hands and knees.

Against the back wall of the den, Pei-Pei sat motionless on the couch, reading, her legs folded to the side. On the floor, Natty had pushed back the mess around him; he lay on his belly on a small clearing of carpet. Around him, like the ruins of a fortress, were stacks of books of varying heights; one stack had toppled, so that the books lay at a slant.

I settled myself on the far side of the couch.

From the kitchen, we heard my father say, "Leave it."

I grabbed Pei-Pei's elbow. "What are you reading?"

She shook her head. "You made them fight again."

I opened my fist and dropped the clump of egg on her book. It was still wet with my spit. Pei-Pei brushed it to the floor and wiped her hand on her shirt, but there was a mark on the page where it had been.

"Tell me what you're reading."

"Read it yourself." Pei-Pei tossed the book at me and got up.

I ran my fingers over the embossed, glossy cover, but I didn't feel like reading. I felt like listening to her talk. I peeled the hardening rice off my sweatpants.

Pei-Pei headed up the stairs. Her footfalls were so light I heard only the first two or three, and then it was as though she had vanished. I stared at the top of Natty's head. He flipped a page in a photo book.

"What are you looking at?" I asked, though I could see the whole thing from where I sat. Photos of solar flares—great splashes of fire leaping from the surface of the sun.

He didn't reply. There were three of us, but it wasn't enough. More and more, I had this sense—that we were insufficient. After Ruby died, I'd heard my father and his partner in the driveway. Hoyt said, "Good thing you had so many children." The words kept coming back to me. Because we weren't so many, we were so few.

———

MY MOTHER filled trash bag after trash bag in the attic. Pine cones, insulation that had hardened into crumbles, scraps of old tar paper, wood chips, nails, fragments of rib cages, bones as thin as the shafts of feathers. I also glimpsed a broken cup and a ceramic thimble. When Natty tried to dig through the bags, my mother shoved him away. It might have been the look on his face, the determination to find something in that trash.

After the attic was empty, she gathered old socks and torn shirts and doused them with ammonia. She stood on the ladder, and Pei-Pei and I passed the cloths to her. Using the end of a broom, she pushed each wad farther into the recesses of the attic. The ammonia seared the membranes of our noses and traveled upward to pickle our brains. Pei-Pei and I dared each other to take sniffs when my mother wasn't looking. By the time she had shoved the whole lot in, we were stifling coughs and our eyes were leaking hot tears.

"Your radio," my mother said, reaching out her hand. Her approach was twofold: change the environment with smell and noise, so that the squirrels would be frightened away—and antifreeze, for the ones who stayed.

"Don't break it," Pei-Pei said. She held her boom box by the handle, low by her side, away from my mother. She'd won it at a school raffle and listened to it only one or two hours a day, so as not to wear it out. Although Natty and I were forbidden to touch it, we opened and closed the tape deck in secret.

"Just give it here," my mother said. She swooped an arm down to grab the boom box. When she turned it on, a nasally man's voice said, "If it's not one thing, it's another." She wrenched the volume all the way up. Just as a song came on, she pushed it deep into the cavity.

We gazed up at the two exposed rafters and the square of dark attic space they framed. We couldn't see the boom box, but it buzzed against the wood with each beat of the song. My mother snaked an extension cord up there, and from then on, music and the affected voices of advertisers came from the ceiling all day and night. As I drifted toward sleep, it became a kind of weather, like the pounding of rain, or a storm that whipped up static and swirled voices around like leaves, hurling branches that fell like drumbeats.

Then the smell came. Something like vomit and rot. Pei-Pei produced a peach-scented spray and proceeded to dispense the entire bottle in the room. She spritzed it at the carpet, the walls, our beds, then straight up so that when it fell, it misted our faces like light rain. Her glasses were speckled. When she wiped the lenses, they smeared. For a few hours, it was blissful, like living among piles of unwrapped candy. But soon our room smelled even worse, an unholy pairing of rancid flesh and artificial fruit.

When it was finally done, my mother stuffed batts of insulation between the rafters and later between the studs. Above our beds, the silence was cavernous. I knew there was only empty space up there, and a new swamp-yellow stuffing that smelled like pee.

"Doesn't it feel strange?" I asked Pei-Pei.

"What's strange?"

"There's no sound from upstairs."

"That's called peace."

Was it? A few weeks after the attic was silenced, Natty woke me with his urgent whispers. I crept to his bed. When I leaned in close, he was saying, "We have to make the chicken porridge. Ruby will come to dinner if we make the chicken porridge."

"Don't say things like that," I said. But he was not in a responsive state. When I shook his arm, his body stayed still, as though his arm were not attached to him. I pinched him hard, and finally his eyes opened. As the night-light flickered by his feet, I saw his pupils were the darkest thing in the room, two machine-punched holes.

"Don't say that," I said.

"Don't say what?"

"Don't say anything."

"Anything," he said, and giggled. "Anything, anything."

We were quiet, and soon I heard the little sleep whistle of his nose. I said, "Ruby can't come to dinner because she's not lost. She's not anything anymore except nothing, she's nothing."

I knew he was asleep. I was talking to ease the pang that had hit me—that pang of someone inhabiting the dark with you, then leaving you for sleep. In one lurch a person could be gone, just as if she had never been there, and the only thing that remained was your mind in the dark.

Ruby never stayed in her own bed; there was movement in these deep night hours. She drifted between our beds like a vagrant, favoring my parents' and Natty's. But once in a while she crawled under the covers with me. In the dark, she rooted in the folds of fabric; her fingers wriggled upward. We held hands under my pillow, and within seconds we were out.

7

IN THE LAST WEEK OF SCHOOL, I GRABBED THE KNOTTED end of the rope I had failed to climb all year and ran with it up the steep hill behind the tree. The rope grew heavier and heavier, resistant to straying. By the top I felt nauseous from the full-blown exertion. I gazed at the back of our school, where a few heated trailers had been towed in and dumped to accommodate the growing student population. It looked a mess.

I had asked to use the bathroom while everyone was in class. No one was outside, no one was watching. I wiped my hands and re-gripped the rope. Now was the time. I started running down the hill, just a jog, but the momentum took over. Soon I was pumping my legs as fast as they would go, giving it my all just to stay upright, on the cusp of scraping the whole hill with my face. When I lost every last thread of control, I jumped. I tucked my legs in and pinched my feet together above the knot. I was hurtling toward the school.

I couldn't climb the rope, but now I could fly, weightless and the owner of glory. At the end of the long arc, I jumped and soared. Finally I landed on my side, my whole body skidding across the grass. Things went dark for a second, and then they were too bright. I tried to breathe in, but I was trapped in an exhale.

"That," said a voice, "nearly killed you."

I rolled a few degrees to the right and saw Ada's pale jeans. They were exactly the right length for her and hit the tops of her sneakers.

"I looked for you in the boys' bathroom," she said. "I opened all the stalls." She offered her hands to pull me up to sitting.

I grinned at her even as her tugging motion caused a stabbing pain in my side. She had seen me sailing through the air. It was undeniable; it had happened. "How long was I up there?" I asked.

"Maybe five seconds?"

I tried to process this.

"I almost saw you die," she said.

The Rogers Commission Report on the *Challenger* had come out that week. Long excerpts of it were reprinted in the paper. For days Pei-Pei had sat with my father at the kitchen table, and they went sentence by sentence, pausing so my father could underline certain phrases. "I don't know what the aft field joint is," she would say, "but I think it's a piece that connects the segments of the booster rocket." Slowly they pieced together the demise of the shuttle: two rubber seals had become brittle during the cold-weather launch. Hot gases leaked through the seals onto a tank full of liquid hydrogen and oxygen. Boom. Between liftoff and the explosion were seventy-three seconds. After the shuttle was torn apart, the crew compartment continued to ascend more than three miles into the sky before it began its long free fall into the Atlantic.

Ada sat down beside me. She pointed at the rope, which was still swinging.

I laughed but the pain in my lower ribs cut it short.

"Did you break something?" Ada asked.

"Nah," I said.

"Good," she said, and that single word with its fullness of meaning—I'm glad you're not hurt—knocked me back down. The weight of happiness was too much. On my back, curled a little over my bruised ribs, I gazed into shredded clouds and thought of the summer about to unfold, all the long days ahead and the retreat of nights into their five-hour pens. It was finally here, summer, and the feeling that was the opposite of dread.

———

ON THOSE NIGHTS in early summer, I'd become accustomed to my father and Pei-Pei muttering over the *Challenger* report. But at some point, the aerospace terminology gave way to legal words. I didn't notice the moment it shifted, only that their voices grew lower and quieter, until they seemed to be communicating like horses, with infinitesimal flicks of the head. If I snuck up to them, I could catch a mysterious fragment.

"Every time you see the word 'aforesaid,'" she said, "just cross it out. Same with the words 'direct and proximate.'"

"But what do they mean?" My father held the dictionary in his lap. "They must mean something."

"They mean the writer's a jerk."

I remembered the day Pei-Pei had slapped an open thesaurus

in the den, cackling that she'd found eight synonyms for the word "inexpressible." Now she was hunched over the table, and the only thing that was moving was her eyes, ticking back and forth across the papers.

When I asked her about it in our bedroom, Pei-Pei started whispering in full force, like a faucet sputtering trapped air. "Something broke in one of the wells he built," she said. "Stuff got into the water. Stuff that poisoned it—the family's drinking water."

The way she said "poison," with a puff and a hiss, frightened me. I reared back and hit the frame of Pei-Pei's bed.

"Did anyone die?"

"A boy got sick. They're asking for money."

"How sick?"

"Sick enough to ask for money."

"How much?"

"Everything. All of it."

When I didn't continue my inquiry, Pei-Pei spread her fingers wide apart, a gesture of anguish or excitement. Gray triangles of diffuse light glowed between her fingers. "It's bad," she said. "But don't worry." She reached out and laid a cold hand on the side of my neck, and I tried not to flinch. "I'll take care of us." The thin light made her cheeks velvety, and she looked younger than her age.

———

IN THE WOODS, Ada and I chewed on spruce tips plucked from nearby trees. Early in the summer the young needles had been lime-green and soft, newly emerged from their papery buds, but even as the needles became tougher to chew and more astringent, we kept on. I liked the way Ada looked, yanking on a small, prickly branch as she bit the end of it.

The tree that had fallen last spring left a hole in the canopy, and a beam of syrupy light streamed through. Summer afternoons, Ada and I liked to haunt this spot. The toppled tree leaned against the trunk of a stouter spruce, and Ada was fond of walking up and down the incline, which would have made for a long, fast slide. She thrust out her arms like a tightrope walker. When she was about ten feet off the ground, she lowered herself into a crouch, her skinny thighs trembling, and sat all the way down so her arms and legs dangled on either side. From that position she spit wads of spruce needles at my feet.

One day she leaned forward, resting her chin right on the bark, and said, "Did you know that my mother is dead?"

I tried to make out her expression, but the trunk blocked most of her face. "Yeah," I said.

"She died seventeen days before my birthday."

"Oh."

"She's in heaven."

"Heaven?"

"She is," Ada said.

When I didn't reply, Ada said again, more loudly, "She is."

It was misty out, the air heavy with recent rain that still lurked. Where we sat, it was brighter than the rest of the forest, but a frosted kind of bright. The old man's beards that hung from the branches were heavy with dew, resembling nets that had been pulled up from the ocean.

"My mom had an accident. She didn't mean it. Now she's in heaven."

"But where is her body?" I asked.

"In our yard."

I gnawed on a single spruce needle, gently crushing it with my teeth so it released a small burst of flavor. There was a trace of citrus in it.

Ada lifted her head from the trunk and leaned to the side to get a good look at me. "Accidents don't happen in the same place twice, so now our house is safe." She kicked one foot. Even from the ground I could see the blue veins in her white legs, like trickles of watercolor paint.

"She's in your yard?"

"The backyard."

"She's buried? Her whole body is buried?"

"Of course."

I looked in the direction of her house. The fog had thickened or sunk, sealing off the view down the path.

Ada peeled off a strip of bark and dropped it. We watched its long, twisted fall. "I have to go soon," she said. "I'm eating meatballs tonight."

"And spaghetti?"

"Just the meatballs. My dad says it's okay." She shimmied a few inches down the tree. "What are you having?"

Nothing I could think of was uninteresting enough. "Maybe some kind of soup," I said. My mother spoke aloud now when she cooked. "Beef bones," she might say, unlidding a pot that had been simmering all day. "The soft marrow. We'll cook them until they crumble, until they release their animal souls." When she went on like this, talking to someone we didn't know, the air felt thinner in the room.

I began to crawl up the dead trunk. Ada was so high up,

the fog was licking her head. The bark scratched my palms and knees, and bits of it flaked off as I climbed. The closer I got to her, the more slender and brittle the trunk became. But she scooted down to meet me. When I eased myself up to sitting, she leaned back on me. It was a good height, eight feet or so off the ground.

We kicked our feet in unison and watched the scrolling fog. Where there were clear patches, we could see the understory. We gazed over the tops of the same ferns and shrubs we had fought along the path. They seemed inconsequential from our height.

"Put your hand on my head," she said.

I touched the side of her hair and took a furtive whiff. Candy and forest mushrooms.

"Not there," she said, and rearranged my hand so I was palming the ridge where the back of her neck met her skull. She pulled up her legs, crouched, and with some effort maneuvered her whole body around to face me. "Push my head," she said.

When I didn't do anything, she pressed on my hand, driving her own head forward until her lips were smashed into mine. Her lower lip rolled open, and the inside of it was wet and sticky. I saw the freckled bridge of her nose, the skin around her heavily lashed eye, one pupil drilled into a gray-sea orb. I felt scared. We were too close—so close we couldn't see each other.

———

ADA PUT OUT HER HAND. It was damp and cold from using the hose on her muddy sandals. "Come see," she said. She tightened her grip, and her short, sharp nails dug into my palm. She led me around the shed to their trailer. "There," she said.

The entire trailer pitched forward, as though searching for something it had dropped. In front of it was patchy grass and a browned, wastefully fat apple core. Paper grocery bags from Carrs were taped over the small windows.

"Climb up there," Ada whispered. She pointed to the stack of cinder blocks that supported the back end of the trailer.

There was room on the block for only half my foot, but as I felt for the aluminum frame of the window, I discovered it was wide open. I wrapped my fingers around one edge to pull myself up.

One side of the brown paper had become untaped from the window, flapping gently. It was darker inside than out.

"Do you see?" Ada whispered from below. Her head touched my knee.

I leaned in. There was a smell in the trailer, like wet carpet or upholstery. As my eyes adjusted, I saw a small steel sink filled with trash—bottles, cans, wrappers, something like grapefruit peels. A bed, faced away. Skinny legs all mixed up. Pei-Pei's hair like a tossed black towel.

I looked under my arm at Ada. She was grinning. "They're always in there," she whispered.

The wan light from the window made part of the mattress glow. Although there was junk piled on the floor around it, the mattress itself was completely bare, without a single sheet or pillow. Pei-Pei was naked. Shadows nestled in the dips of her body and underscored where it rose and lumped. Her hair was spreading, something spilled.

Collin shifted, and I saw he was propped on an elbow,

saying something to her. He was bonier than he was in clothes, his skin less splotchy in the dimness, his face in profile soft and calm. They were awake—and not ashamed.

"You see them, right?" Ada whispered.

My throat clotted. They had a hideaway, where loneliness couldn't nab them. They could rest. They could just rest.

I jumped off the cinder block. I started running, back across the huge, weedy yard to the path. The cotton grass was blooming. The seedpods would split open soon. Ada said how much cotton they released would tell you how much snow to expect come winter. I wanted the yard to explode in white. Ada was hollering behind me. In the woods, it was darker and stiller, and I streaked through it all. I wasn't heading home, though I suppose I was. There was always just this one path, headed one way. I had no choice, really; I was always headed home.

——

WE SQUEEZED in single file through a section of trail where the understory was thick with thorns. Collin was so tall he had to push a drooping branch aside. Huge, barbed devil's club stalks also jutted into the path, and we stepped onto a rotted log to avoid the spreading leaves, big as tennis rackets and spiked along the veins.

"Stop," Ada said. She pointed with the toe of her sneaker to the backside of the log. Nearly hidden in a patch of stinging nettle was a squirrel tail. The hairs were completely matted and the tip was blackened. Collin prodded it with a stick.

"Is it dead?" Natty asked. There wasn't enough room on the log for him, so he hung back.

Collin let loose a horse-like laugh. Using the end of the stick, he began to pick up the tail. When it slipped off, he reached for it with his bare hands.

He shook the tail experimentally, holding it by one end. He pinched the pale nub of something, a bone or tendon, and when he gave it a tug, the tail suddenly curled. My stomach coiled.

"I've brought it back to life for you," Collin said to Natty. He dropped the tail so he could raise both arms slowly toward the treetops.

Natty gawked. The devil's club leaves made an overhang above him, threatening to sink teeth into his scalp.

"I found another one near our mailbox," Collin said. "Bigger than this one."

All those tails. Detached. "Do you think it's our squirrels?" I whispered to Pei-Pei. Being surrounded by so much stinging nettle and devil's club made me itchy, and I scratched hard enough at my neck that dirt or skin collected under my nails.

She shrugged.

But I knew. We had chased the flying squirrels out of our house, and now they were dead.

We followed Collin and Ada all the way to their yard, where we circled their mailbox. A broken window screen leaned against the post. There was a hole in the screen and jagged mesh around the hole where something like a bird or fist had exited. We ruffled the grass to see if anything was hiding in it. Ada opened the mailbox—empty—and closed the dented door as far as it would go.

We could hear their giant dog barking from the backyard.

"Baby's chained up," Ada whispered to me. "Because she left

us. She ran away for a whole week." She pressed a palm hard to her chest.

"Guess something made off with the tail," Collin said. He kicked the window screen. It flopped softly onto the grass, and, maybe because it hadn't made a satisfying sound, Collin stepped on the wooden frame until it snapped.

"Did you really see one?" Ada asked.

"I said I did."

Natty dropped down and patted a spot in the grass. "It was here," he said.

"Actually, it was," Collin said.

A white van ground its way up the steep driveway and parked. Mr. Dolan heaved himself out of the driver's seat.

"What's doing this?" Pei-Pei asked. "Taking the squirrels and leaving the tails?"

"Some sick bastard," Collin said.

"Is it you?" Pei-Pei asked, and they both laughed. Her giggle was soft and thin, almost unrecognizable. She looked strange, too, since she had pushed her glasses on top of her head like sunglasses. I had to think back: How long had she been wearing them like this? Wasn't she nearly blind? I thought of her hunched over the kitchen table with my father at night, and how she had to keep nudging her glasses up the bridge of her nose to see the words on the page.

On his way in, Mr. Dolan paused by the front steps. He stared at Pei-Pei and then at me. A grocery bag hung off his forearm, and he palmed a head of cabbage in each hand.

"Hi, Mr. Dolan," Pei-Pei said.

"Hi, Paige," he said. He stood with his feet planted. "Should I ask what you kids are up to?"

"No," Collin said.

Ada hurried to her father. "Collin found a squirrel tail. Just the tail by itself."

Mr. Dolan gazed into the aspens shading us. "Probably the work of an owl."

He shoved the cabbage heads into the crook of one arm and let the bag of groceries slide down to the concrete step. "Bring it over." He smiled at me. "I'll show you how to tan it. Pull out the tailbone and cure it with salt. Even table salt will do, so long as you're not picky."

"No, thank you," I said.

He shrugged. "It's nice. Real soft." He adjusted the cabbage heads, cradling them deeper in his huge arms. "I saw your mother the other day," he said. "Must've been your mother." He chuckled. "Unless it was some other Oriental lady." He wore a thick sweatshirt that bunched in the armpits. Covered in that plush, heavyweight cotton, his arms and chest looked warm and soft—a place where cabbages would sleep well. "Come through the woods, I think," he said. "I took a breather from the yard work, and there she was, standing right at the edge of our property."

Pei-Pei stepped one foot on top of the other. "Ah," she said. "My mother on the loose."

"I called out. Must've startled her. She ran back into the woods so fast I thought maybe I'd seen a spirit. Think I frightened her?"

"No," Pei-Pei said in a reasonable voice. "She might not have heard you. She's losing her hearing." She made her eyes crumple sorrowfully.

Mr. Dolan scratched his arm where the bag had left a groove.

"Well, tell your mom to come say hello, next time she's wandering by."

"Not everyone wants to stand here chatting with you," Collin said. He pulled Pei-Pei away, across the yard and toward the woods. Natty trailed behind, wading through the grasses. But Ada dropped to the ground beside her father's feet. Her pink knees pointed at me as she sat on her ankles. Mr. Dolan took a step toward the door, and Ada scooted to follow.

"Bye," I said.

She gave me a crooked salute, a two-fingered arc that started by her ear and strayed toward her eyebrow.

"See you later," I said.

She ran her hands over the tips of the grasses and nodded.

"Tomorrow?" I said.

"Okay." She pinched a section of her hair and waved the end of it at me.

I slogged through their backyard. I had scanned every part of it. I knew where there was constant light and shade, and I imagined where the snow might pile high in the winter or thin away first come spring. A stand of leafy aspens grew to one side, their white trunks scarred. Beneath the aspens were ancient roots. That would be a good place. Was that where they had put her mother?

Aboveground, aspens grew and died, but deep below, where our footsteps had no impact, the roots just kept on living, sending up the new trees we saw. The roots were thousands of years old, practically immortal. Wouldn't they have buried her there? But there were no markings I could see.

I entered the woods. Under the cover of trees, the light was paltry, with a cold, briny-blue cast. Natty was tromping alone at the front. Pei-Pei had her arm snaked around Collin's waist and her whole hand shoved into his front pocket. Stuck together, they stumbled along the uneven trail.

Pei-Pei turned around. "Take Natty home."

"You said we were all going home," I said.

"I did say that, didn't I?"

Collin grinned. He took off his cap, scratched hard at his scalp, and put it back on.

I reached up and made a swipe at Pei-Pei's head, knocking her glasses down her face, then dashed away to join Natty. I was leaving her; I would not be left.

Beside me, Natty was practically marching, raising his feet high to clear the thick forest floor. I was grateful for all the noise he made. The scant light began to intensify, and finally we cleared the last thirty yards. We walked along the border of the woods, which had become less distinct as vines and branches grasped at our yard and grasses spurted to the height of Natty's neck. He stopped at the pile of rocks my father had dumped after a job. For landscaping, my father had said.

"Look," Natty said. He crouched over a small, deep well he had formed in the rocks. Resting in it were squirrel tails. A mass of them, or maybe only three or four. I couldn't look for long.

"Did you put those there?" I asked. "Did you touch them with your hands?"

"Yup," Natty said.

"You went by yourself all the way across the woods?"

"Yup."

"When?"

"Yesterday," Natty said.

The day before, Pei-Pei had disappeared with Collin, and

Ada and I had made a game of plucking off all the green spruce cones we could reach. After we'd counted them, she dropped her face into her hands and said, "Now they won't grow into trees."

I gripped Natty's forearm. "Don't do that anymore," I said. "Not by yourself."

By the time we approached the house, it was dark—and dark, in June, meant very late. Past dinnertime. Yet what we had done to be so late, I couldn't have said. Time changed texture quickly in the summer.

The kitchen window glowed. My mother was off-center, standing in front of the sink, and she was examining something in her hands. My father could not be seen. We had left them alone together, for an entire meal and more. What ruin had we caused?

Natty bounded to the sliding door. Watching him, you could believe he wanted to be inside. He banged on the glass and called, "It's locked. You locked us out." No one came to the door.

I stepped to his side and shouted, "Let me in!" We kept pounding, drumming on the glass. Natty was hollering, "It's me! It's me!" When we stopped for a moment, I could hear the sink water running. If we could hear the water, then surely she could hear our racket. But for a long time, no one came to the door.

8

THE NIGHT-LIGHT IN OUR BEDROOM HAD BURNED OUT, BUT I could still see my brother and sister in their beds and even study the way they breathed, the slight rise of their bodies against the stillness. In the summer, the sun never really slipped away. Even in the darkest hours there remained a low gray glow, a residue of light like a whisper.

After Natty fell asleep, Pei-Pei occasionally painted her nails in that faint wash of light, or in the sliver of hallway light that jetted through the cracked-open door.

"Can you tell me about heaven?" I panted. My teeth were brushed and minty, and the words I had been holding back for days were cool in my mouth.

Pei-Pei and I were sitting on the floor against her bed. An acrid odor clung to the air around us. She sighed out of her mouth instead of her nose, impatient but not weary. "What do you want to know?"

"What heaven is."

"It's a place church people go after they die."

"Can you tell me about church?"

"It's a place you go to believe in heaven." She tilted a pinky nail to get at an unpainted strip. "How when we die, we don't really die."

I leaned forward to hold on to my knees, and she pushed me back. "You're blocking my light."

"We don't really die?"

"It's only for believers," she said. "You and me, we won't ever believe. It's too late. You can't suddenly believe after you don't believe, because you'll always know that you're *trying* to believe, and that's a completely different thing from just believing."

I glanced at Natty's bed. He was sprawled across the top half of it, both feet hanging off the mattress. "We won't go to heaven?" I whispered.

"Nah."

"Is Ruby there?"

Pei-Pei twisted the brush back into the bottle before answering. "No."

I held out my hands. I wanted her to cut my nails and use the file on the back of the clippers. I liked the back-and-forth scrape of the grainy metal, that steady, gradual wearing down.

"Wait till these dry." When she blew across her fingers, I smelled toothpaste and something like gasoline.

I picked up the nail clippers and snipped at carpet tufts. "What time is Dad coming home?"

"I don't know."

"Why doesn't he eat with us anymore?" I ran the pad of my finger over the metal file. It felt gritty, like a kind of rock you could find in our yard that flaked when you hit it with another rock.

Our door was flung against the solid stopper. My mother appeared in the light, severe and statuesque. She took a sharp breath and grew even taller.

"Where did you get that? Who gave it to you?" she asked.

Pei-Pei didn't answer. Natty stirred and made a breathy sound. Something, his hand or foot, knocked into the window beside the bed.

"I know you have it. I smelled it in the hallway. Where is it? The paint for your fingernails. Give it to me." My mother's voice was getting louder and more strained.

"Why?"

"Don't speak to me like that." My mother dropped down and swept the carpet with her arm until she found the small bottle. She closed a fist around it. "Tomorrow we'll talk about this," she said. Although she straightened outside the beam of hallway light, I could see the cords of her neck.

"We never talk," Pei-Pei said.

"We'll talk about why you're this way."

"What way?" Pei-Pei said.

After my mother left, Pei-Pei grabbed my wrist. She uncurled the fingers of my hand and started clipping my nails, sloppily and rapidly. "What way am I?" she said. "What way should I be?" She was laughing and cutting past the white on my fingernails.

When she was done, she threw the clippers into the corner and whipped off her glasses. She thrust them in my face. They reflected two gray stripes of light; there were fingerprints all over the lenses. "Are these ugly? Tell me, are these ugly or nice?"

"Ugly," I said.

"Right? Anyone can see that. It's not a matter of not know-ing. She knows. She knows exactly. She found the ugliest ones in the whole store, and wouldn't buy me any other pair."

It hadn't hurt at first, but now the air felt like wires strung into my fingers. I rushed to my bed and pressed my face into my pillow. I thought about crying. But then I heard the crackle of a wrapper. And then a louder crackle.

"I want some," Natty said. His voice was wide awake.

"Me, too," I said.

There was the snap of Pei-Pei breaking her chocolate bar. She came around to our beds. She felt for my hands beneath my covers and thrust a good-sized chunk into them.

We lay on our backs, nibbling chocolate in the dark. My mother had turned off the hallway light, returning us to the low-lit night. I barely noticed the nail polish smell anymore—there was only the wash of sweetness in my mouth. How long had it been since I'd enjoyed any kind of food? It left a coating on my newly brushed teeth.

———

I WOKE to the tips of my fingers throbbing. In the bathroom, I ran cold water over them and tried to numb them. I watched the water envelop my hands before surging into the drain. When I turned around for the towel, Natty was standing in the hallway.

"You're dripping," he said.

I slapped the towel. "Why aren't you sleeping?"

"I got up." He walked the few steps to my parents' bedroom and placed his palm on the door. It opened a little.

"Are you going to sleep in there? With them?"

"No," Natty said, "I'm just going to look at them." He opened the door wider and stepped in, and then closed it so it rested without latching.

Even though I could see in the hazy gray light, I felt my way down the stairs to the den. It seemed necessary to touch something at all times—the wall, the railing, the doorframe, the sofa. At night things shifted and were unmoored.

I was examining a snag of skin on my finger when a movement in my periphery made me whirl around.

Natty stood in the doorway in his bare feet, one leg of his pajamas bunched up around the knee. He jammed a fist into an eye. "What are you doing?" he asked.

"Nothing."

He took a few steps in and dropped down to the carpet, sitting on top of his heels. He was quiet as I rolled his crayons back and forth with my foot, and just as I picked one up between my toes, he said, "Where is Daddy?"

"Isn't he upstairs sleeping? Weren't you just in their room?"

"No, that wasn't him," he said. "That was someone else."

"It must have been a dream."

He stood up, marched over to me, and snatched the crayon from my foot. "I wasn't dreaming."

"Then I don't know what you're talking about."

"Daddy," he said, louder, the edge of a sob bending his voice. "I'm looking for Daddy. Where did he go?"

I took his hands and wedged them into my armpits, then

clamped my elbows to my sides. I had done this last winter. The house had been cold, and the tips of his fingers had been hard as pebbles.

"I'm looking for Daddy," he said.

"Go back to sleep," I said. "When you wake up, you'll find him."

"Will Daddy be back?"

"He'll be back."

He scratched his bare right calf with his left toes, and the movement of his fingers in my armpits made me jerk away.

He laughed. His cheeks popped forward, like scoops of packed snow. Complete strangers used to rub or even kiss his cheeks, exacerbating his eczema and causing speckled red patches to bloom across his face. But no one had come at him for some time.

"Go," I said, putting my hands on his shoulders and turning him around. He tried to sit on the milk crates, but I pushed him out the doorway. I listened to him pad through the kitchen, then up the carpeted stairs.

I don't know if he fell asleep. An hour or two later, or perhaps it was almost dawn, he was back in the doorway of the den. Again I hadn't heard him coming. "What now?" I asked.

"Where's Daddy? And Mama?"

"What are you saying? They're upstairs. Sleeping. Why don't you go back and sleep with them?"

"I don't want to sleep with those people. I want to sleep with Daddy and Mama."

The skin around his eyes was bluish gray. Some of the fine hairs on the surface of his head hovered slightly in the air, charged with static. He stared at me through his long, straight lashes, and I had an image of my parents' vacated bodies slumped in bed. "Stop it," I said.

He drifted up to the couch and put his hand on my arm. "When will they come home? I want them to come home. Where did they go?"

I could tell by the downward crinkles around his eyes and the wide pull of his mouth that he was close to really losing it.

"Where?" he asked in a high, muzzy voice.

"They're upstairs," I said. My voice trailed off, and I coughed to hide it. "I'll show you. Let's go."

Natty crept up the stairs ahead of me, and I shone a flashlight at his butt. It waggled as his small limbs slid up each step, wolf-like. He seemed more at ease than I was, hobbled by a flashlight wedged into my armpit.

From the doorway, I saw two mounds in the bed. As I ran the light back and forth across the room, a tissue sprouting from a Kleenex box cast the shadow of a hand.

"There they are," I whispered.

"That's not them."

"Look. Mama, Daddy."

"That's not them."

I grabbed Natty's forearm, harder than I had to, and led him to the side of the bed. He dragged his feet, and I wanted to hit him.

"Look," I said, but even as I aimed the flashlight at the wall near my mother's face, I could see her sleeping expression was strange—melting. In the weak glow, the cover of the comforter was deeply etched, as though black lava had filled its folds. Where my mother's face was pressed to the pillow, there were wrinkles in skin and cloth, and her skin looked detachable from the flesh, something that could be shed. Darkness pooled inside her upturned ear.

I darted the flashlight around again, trying to illuminate everything at once. Brief flashes of light came back at me: the edge of my mother's wedding ring where she rested one hand on the pillow, the mirror, three dots on the water glass, a curved line on the lamp base, a single piercing point in each of Natty's irises. The curled tag on my father's inside-out undershirt also shone, just before it suddenly jerked. A sound came from my father—not quite a snore, more like a gasp for air—and I pushed Natty into the open closet and squeezed him hard until he started to claw at my chest. When I released him, he said, "Don't be afraid."

I panted in the closet. Some of my father's shirts had fallen off the hangers. I kicked a sweater away so I could stand directly on the floor. The beam from my flashlight pointed up, and there on the wire rack, beside a stack of old shoeboxes, I saw it, though I hadn't meant to, the urn just a little bigger than a soup can. It was dark gray, made of glazed ceramic or polished stone, something with a luster.

I shoved Natty. "What's wrong with you?" I whispered. "Why'd you make me come up here? Mom and Dad are right there."

"I told you it's not them."

I wanted him to feel the same cold pipe that was descending, down my throat, down my chest, sinking itself deep into the soft base of my stomach. "You're crazy," I said. "Don't come near me."

For a while he didn't move or speak. The longer we stood in the closet, the bigger the urn seemed, until it was half hanging off the shelf, about to tip and spill its contents.

"Those people are not Mama and Daddy," he said in a very low voice. "They left her. She was lost, and they left her."

A chill jerked through my torso. In the dark, it was not hard to believe what he was saying, that no one was left in our family but the two of us. Everyone had changed—we didn't know them, and they didn't know us. I hurried out of the closet and out of that agitated room. Natty followed me. When I sat down at the top of the stairs, he did, too. We could hear the tick of the second hand from the kitchen clock downstairs. It sliced the silence into uniform lengths. When I leaned into Natty, he leaned away. His nose was stuffy; I could hear every whistle of his inhales and exhales.

"Natty," I whispered.

When he turned to me, his eyes were small and hooded. "I'm looking for my brother," he said.

I grabbed his hand. It was limp. "No, it's me," I said. "I'm your brother."

His fingers would not curl around mine, but he allowed me to hold his fist. For a long time I clutched it, the end of a life-line, the last tangible evidence I was not alone. I wiped my palms one at a time, transferring his fist between my hands. I felt like I was cradling a peeled egg. In the dark the stairs seemed steep, a tremendous way to fall.

———

THE NEXT MORNING, when we all stumbled down for break-fast, my mother stepped in front of Pei-Pei. "You can eat later," my mother said.

"I'm hungry now," Pei-Pei said.

"The closet," my mother said.

Pei-Pei turned around and walked back toward the stairs. I followed her. She opened the hallway closet, plunged her arms in, and pushed the soft mass of puffer coats to both sides as though she were wading into deep water. She was stepping all over the tops of our piled shoes. She didn't look at me as she squatted. Instead, she reached back out, wrapped her painted fingers around the bottom edge of the door, and pulled it closed on herself. The shoes, I knew, would block some of the light from peeking in under the door. Pei-Pei had once told me that a lunar day was two weeks of sunlight, and a lunar night two weeks of darkness. Our time in the closet, she said, was but a single minute on the moon.

From the kitchen, my mother said to me, "Come eat."

9

I'D SEEN THE XEROXED SIGNS AROUND: SUMMER SOLSTICE SLEEPOUT. A cookout, a talent show, a cover band—all while the sun clung overhead. It never would have occurred to me to go; although it was only ten minutes away, the party seemed as remote and mythological as the kites that flew on Flattop Mountain or the maniacs who signed up for the Midnight Sun Marathon. Only Pei-Pei's persistence could have brought us to such a place.

"But no sleepover," my mother had said.

We stood in the parking lot of the high school. Near the baseball field, a few people had already set up cheery, humped tents. A man on a lawn chair picked at a banjo. My mother sniffed at the aroma of charred meat. She pointed, straight-armed, at the hamburgers and reindeer sausages sweating oil on a grill.

Natty had not wanted to come. I should have dragged him out. Beside me, two children blew bubbles while a third pawed at the air; the shimmering spheres took to the sky in bursts. A few people sat at folding tables and peddled baked items or tiny wood carvings or secondhand tools. When I turned to point out the smiling-sun sugar cookies to Pei-Pei, I found she had already ditched us.

My mother strolled to the short line by the grill, where she squeezed the bagged buns. She inspected the condiment bottles and flicked off a crust of dried mustard. I knew she was suspicious: Were these things really free?

We scooted forward in line. A freckled woman wearing a huge visor slid a thin patty from her spatula onto my mother's plate. She leaned across the table at us. Three red flowers, unsteadily outlined in puff paints, engulfed her T-shirt.

"Having a good time, dear?"

My mother prodded the edge of the patty with her finger.

"You are welcome here," the woman said.

My mother nodded soberly. "You are welcome, too."

At the edge of the parking lot, we brushed aside stray leaves and sat on a patch of grass. I nibbled on the end of my reindeer sausage. The salt shocked my tongue.

"Hurry up," my mother said, "so we can go back for more. Can't you eat any faster?"

I didn't answer because I had caught sight of Pei-Pei standing in an empty section of the parking lot, near a square of pavement roped off on three sides. Although she had left the house in shorts and a T-shirt, she now wore a jean skirt and a sleeveless green blouse. I had no idea how she had accomplished this. She had also finagled her hair into a style called a fishtail braid, a term I remembered because it really did look like a fat fish fillet was stuck to the back of her head, with a snippet of tail at the end.

My mother peered around a truck at the coolers. She crammed the last bite of her burger bun into her mouth, then scurried off to pick out sodas. I watched her root around in a chest of ice and extract one can after another, wedging them carefully into the crook of her arm.

I abandoned my full plate and drifted back into the parking lot. Pei-Pei was chatting with a long-haired boy. He had a violin tucked under his arm, and with his other hand he jiggled the rope between two stanchions. I couldn't hear what they were saying.

I took a few steps closer and found myself standing before a table of Russian dolls. A woman with bleached hair, sun-beaten skin, and a look of fierce melancholy—or heavy eye makeup—appraised me as I opened one set. The bodies were not exactly round, and the dolls nested within one another only because each doll was a great deal smaller than the last. The final one had a botched mouth; the paint had smeared.

As I stood there floating the tiny doll on my palm, music blasted through the parking lot. A girl my age entered the roped-off square, which I realized was a rudimentary stage. She jumped on a pogo stick, stabbing it repeatedly into the pavement.

"Too loud," the woman said. She stuck her tongue out and snapped it back in. It was true the blaring speakers were out of proportion to the drama of the performance. For her finale, the girl jumped in a circle and then over a cinder block. During the scattered applause, the fiddler boy I had seen took her place. With a flourish of the bow, he began to play. He twitched his hand and scratched out chords as he stomped one oversized sneaker.

"You want to buy that?" the woman asked.

I had been standing there a good length of time. I rolled the little doll between my fingers as though considering it. I did like its cheeks, which were very rosy and preposterously big.

"How much?" I asked.

"Ten dollars. But for you, five."

I thought about asking my mother for money. Such a request would be futile, but I wanted to return the favor to this woman who had singled me out for her offer. As I stalled, a slow, rich voice floated over the chatter of the parking lot. I knew this song. I turned to the stage and couldn't breathe.

The woman tipped her head. "That your sister?"

Was it? I barely knew the voice. Gone was the fake whine, the strained growls, her grating mimicry of the songs on the radio. There was no accompaniment. She wasn't trying to sound like anything, so she sounded, very clearly, like herself.

She looked unafraid as she held the mic with both hands. With her hair pulled back into the braid and her glasses off, her face was bare and plain, her eyes pretty and dark. I had not heard the song for such a long time. Her amplified voice warped it, making it less private but also, startlingly, more intimate. A teenage girl caught my eye and smiled. I ducked my head. Other glances came my way. It was obvious, to everyone but me, that I was related to this keeper of strange, lush melodies.

I looked back at my mother, who sat alone with paper plates and soda cans lodged in the grass around her. She was staring at Pei-Pei, too. One hand was lifted in the air as though hold-ing a drink, but the drink itself was missing. Was it surprise at seeing Pei-Pei there? Or did she remember? This song. How Pei-Pei had sung to Ruby.

"A song that they sing when they take to the highway," Pei-Pei crooned. "A song that they sing when they take to the sea. A song that they sing of their home in the sky." I had never once heard the original. When finally I did, decades later, at a low volume in an unloved diner, the entire song had played through before I realized what it was. Pei-Pei's interpretation, it turned out, was very loose—she idled on long notes and kept a languid pace.

Pei-Pei let the last note falter. She lowered her head over the mic as though nodding off. And then it was over. I wished for more. She used to hold Ruby sideways as she sang, and Ruby's legs would flutter in the air, a kind of joyful protest. The kick-ing went on and on, and when it died down, you knew Ruby was asleep. That nourishing sleep.

A boy with a flute tripped onto the stage. I remembered where I was. I set the miniature doll on its fused feet among the shells of wooden bodies. When I rejoined my mother, she opened a can of 7 Up and handed it to me. I took a few small slurps while holding the can perfectly upright.

"Finish this, and we'll each get another," my mother said. We didn't speak of what had happened, or of any memories we shared. When she reached for my soda to check its fullness, she bumped my hand. We both let go, and the can fell over. We watched the liquid fizz and soak into the grass.

Twenty minutes passed before Pei-Pei returned to us.

Breathless, she tugged the waist of her jean skirt upward. She must have borrowed it. "Angie brought an extra sleeping bag," she said.

"Hm," my mother said. I thought she might be preparing to interrogate Pei-Pei about her change of clothes. But she merely studied Pei-Pei's features, maybe for evidence she had really opened her mouth and released those clear, unhindered notes.

"Her tent has extra space," Pei-Pei said. "Oh, just let me stay tonight."

My mother made another noise of half listening. She said, "I used to sleep in a hammock."

"How nice for you," Pei-Pei said.

"We used to tie up our hammocks in a little grove of trees."

Pei-Pei blew air out of her mouth, practically spitting. "Why can't I stay?"

"You can stay."

Pei-Pei stared at me. I nodded. Somehow, it had happened.

She tossed her head. The green ribbon at the end of her braid was loose, about to slip off. "Pick me up tomorrow," she said. "At ten."

After she had bolted, my mother still lingered. Without Pei-Pei around, I felt exposed. Any cover of normalcy we might have had was gone.

"I have never been on a hammock," I said. "And we have so many trees." I couldn't keep the blame out of my voice.

"Think of the weather," my mother said. "Could you lie out here all night?"

"It doesn't have to be all night," I said.

"But that's what a hammock is for."

In her village, she said, there was a narrow strip of trees between a little road and the beach. The fishermen and their families sat in that shade, sorting fish and repairing nets. On hot nights, coaxed by the breeze off the water, they strung up their hammocks. A few lay right on top of the Styrofoam flats they had used to bring in their fish. Bits of tarp overhead defined their temporary living areas. From the trees was a wide view of the ocean, where the lights of the moored boats wobbled on the water.

My father once visited my mother's village during a break from university. When he saw the hammocks, he persuaded a fisherman to loan him one. He and my mother spent a night swaying side by side, suspended in the warm and perfect air, listening to the ocean, the smokers' coughs, the anguished wails of babies.

"It was so exciting," my mother said. She giggled. "We kept asking each other, 'Are you sleeping?' but neither of us ever was."

"But he only visited that one time," she said. She flicked at a leaf beside her. "The ocean did not interest him."

My father had grown up in a rural area, too, but in a landlocked village close enough to Taipei that you could take a train there in the morning and be back by afternoon. What he loved most, my mother said, was the U.S. information center. A big brown building with a library on the ground floor, where my father watched American movies and paged through one English book after another, liking the way he looked reading them as much as the books themselves.

How he adored the *Time* magazines. The bold font, the shine to the paper, the photo spreads in full color. Back then, pages might be blacked out or torn away by censors, or even entire issues banned. That was the real reason he had come to the States, my mother said. He wanted to read the magazines without any missing parts.

"So at least there is that," she said. She stretched her mouth, and I saw now that her smile was as much gums as teeth. "Everything else might tumble down, but at least, at least"— and here she switched to English—"he have his good *Time*s." Then she laughed so relentlessly that I felt I had to laugh, too.

10

ON THE RARE OCCASION WHEN MY FATHER WAS HOME during waking hours, he hounded me to eat. I hid from him, but eventually he came for me. Crouched on the far side of the dresser, I heard the knob turn, the latch dart in, the door open.

"Let's go." My father wrapped his hand around the burl of my shoulder, then pushed me out to the hallway and into the bathroom. He kicked the scale out in front of the toilet. The scale hopped as the rubber feet dragged. "Get on," he said.

I stepped on. I watched the needle jump, tremble, then hover traitorously.

"How?" he said. "Shrinking. You're shrinking."

He knocked the toothbrushes into the sink. As they clattered, he grabbed my shoulders. "You want to starve like an idiot while there's food in the house? Fine. Go ahead." He released me. I stumbled off the scale and into the wall.

My father closed the toilet lid and sat on it. The plastic squeaked as it flexed. "I'm not yelling at you just to yell at you."

He rubbed his knees. "You need to eat more. Who ever heard of a shrinking boy? If you don't grow, you won't have all the things you're supposed to have. Or you'll have to work harder just to get the same things. Every small thing, every tiny thing, like how to hold your wallet and how to scratch your head, you'll have to study and learn. And even then you're not really seen as normal. Even though you are better than normal, you are not even seen as normal. Do you understand what I'm saying?"

I nodded.

"You're the oldest son of an only son. You are passing on the family name. It matters what you do and how you conduct yourself."

"There are a lot of people with our last name," I said.

"That is not what I mean."

My father got up and kicked the scale roughly back into place. As he left, I arranged the toothbrushes in the cup he had toppled. Five toothbrushes that touched at the handles and pointed away from one another. Once there had been six. I pressed my thumbprints into the mirror.

In our bedroom my father knelt in front of the wall, before a spread of butcher paper he had taped up a few months back. "Rules for Long Living" was scrawled across the top in my father's teetering handwriting. Beneath it was a list of actions we had to do every day, compiled from his readings on longevity. Chew each bite at least ten times. Flap the arms upon waking to get the energy flowing right. Eat five dried jujubes. At the bottom, in red pen, my father was scrawling an addition.

"Come see," he said. He swiped his hand across the crooked words. A few letters smeared, sprouting horizontal whiskers. "'Jump for fifteen minutes a day,'" he read.

"Jumping," I said.

He raised his hands. "Up and down. It makes your bones and muscles stretch. It encourages them to grow."

"Just me?"

"Yes."

"Why do I have to jump?"

"Think of it as, why do you get to jump? Think, why am I so lucky, that I can still grow?"

"I don't want to grow," I said.

"Don't say that," he whispered. He patted the floor, searching for the pen he had dropped, keeping his panicked gaze on me. "Don't say that out loud."

———

HOYT STAMPED HIS BOOTS in our doorway and then stepped right on top of the plastic slippers my mother had laid out for him. The soles of his boots were so thick he probably hadn't noticed. It was a Saturday and the first time he had come into our house, maybe the first time anyone had—I couldn't recall a single repairman or utility worker. "Suey, this is the narrowest, skinniest house I ever been in," he said. "From the front it looks like a two-by-four."

My father laughed, a whinnying sound. "A tour," he declared, as though the idea had just struck him. All morning we'd been shoving things under our beds, behind the sofa, into cabinets and closets. Books that didn't fit in the crates were crammed in the freezer and oven. My father had hauled stacks of cardboard to the garage and tossed two cases of expired vitamins onto his truck. His enormous collection of pristine

Time magazines, usually boxed up, was on display—a pile on the kitchen table, a few on the counter, a stack on the bathroom floor, and even one on each of our beds.

My mother grimaced at Hoyt, her attempt at a smile. The rest of us took in the spectacle of the first guest in our home. We had seen him only from a distance. Close-up, he had hair all over his face—and feathering the back of his neck—and he was big. The top of my father's head was level with Hoyt's collarbone. Hoyt felt his bigness, too. "You're all as little as Suey," he said. He laid a heavy hand on my head, and I was afraid he would push me into the floor like a stake.

Natty said, "Suey."

Hoyt bent over and boomed in his face. "Your pops."

"My pops."

"'Cause Sue's a girl's name and I can't pronounce his first name."

"Tour!" cried my father.

Natty slipped his hand into Hoyt's. He'd never been so familiar with strangers before. As we trekked up the stairs, Hoyt was overly careful as he led Natty, turning around to check that he'd made it up each step.

We peeked into my parents' room, the bathroom, our bedroom. I walked behind Hoyt, who was so heavy he left temporary footprints in the carpet. He liked to touch things. He trailed a finger along the wall, and in our bedroom he scratched at the butcher paper. I was afraid he would stand there and read it. But he was more interested in the arrangement of beds. "All together like that?" he kept asking. "They're practically sleeping in one bed."

Pei-Pei had pushed our beds together to create more floor

space for practicing her angry dance moves. The fused bed filled more than half the room. She said, "You should've seen it before. It looked like an orphanage."

In the kitchen, my mother set out tea and sesame crackers. "I thought these would be sweet," Hoyt said, talking around the cracker he'd jammed in his mouth. He took a seat at the kitchen table, and the wooden chair creaked.

"Just wait," Pei-Pei said. "We're going to bake cookies."

Natty mimicked Hoyt and slid a whole cracker into his mouth. He had to force it, and it stretched his cheeks. I could see the exact form of the cracker. He stood behind Hoyt's chair, fingers wrapped around two back spindles, blinking panicked, shiny eyes.

My father, Pei-Pei, and I slipped into the other chairs.

"Not much yard," Hoyt said, nodding toward the window.

My mother leaned over the table. She held the back of her hand to the clay teapot to check if it was hot enough.

Hoyt shifted in his seat, listing to the left so he could see the far window in the den. "Not much there, either." He paused, and when no one responded, he gestured at the closer window again. "But you could get a deck back there."

My mother perked up at this. "Or fence. Fence the best. I tell him, build the fence"—she slapped my father's shoulder—"but he lazy. Or he don't know how to build the fence. Maybe you teach him." She gestured vaguely outside.

"You don't need a fence," Hoyt said. "You don't have any neighbors."

My mother swatted at the hair in her face. "Fence is good for children," she said. She turned and walked to the sink.

Hoyt leaned back and dangled his arms toward the floor.

He tilted a chin in my father's direction. "The Bonner lady's almost come around," he said.

"Push it closer?"

"Yeah. Figure we'll save a couple hundred, with the piping and trenching. Plus the half-horsepower pump instead of three-quarters."

"She agree?"

"I'll get her there. She thinks her kids are going to fall in. I told her, 'Lady, even if the well was a mile away, your kids could still fall in.'"

My father said something about a submersible pump that had been struck by lightning.

"I'll talk to him," Hoyt said.

"No, I will."

"He still of the mind he can keep it there?"

My father shrugged.

"I'll convince him to pull it," Hoyt said.

"No, I am talking to him."

"I'll just drop by and have a quick chat."

My father pushed his chair back. He stood at the sink and ran his hand along its edge, then in one swoop he pulled down a bottle of clear liquor from the cabinet above. He pinched together two plastic cups from the drying rack and clapped them down on the kitchen table, where they made a hollow sound.

Hoyt chuckled. "Man gets straight to the point."

My father unscrewed the cap and tipped the bottle twice, splashing out two portions.

"Jesus, that smell. What is this?"

"Baijiu. Chinese for white wine—"

Hoyt took a gulp.

"—but it's not wine."

"Fuck me. What is this, Chinese Drano? Is this going to make me blind?"

"Pretend it is water." My father tipped his cup back and emptied it. "Or you want beer?"

"Nah." Hoyt swirled the liquid in his cup, and I recognized his expression. I felt it myself at mealtimes; he was gathering will.

I wanted my father to tell Hoyt about his childhood. I wanted to hear it again. He had grown up in a brewery village. The whole town smelled like burnt bread and soured oatmeal. When he was a boy, a huge vat of beer had ruptured and spewed a river of lager down the hill, and people brought pails, bins, pots. My father had dragged over the wooden tub his family used for bathing.

"Everyone drinks this in China?"

"I think so," my father said, though no one in our family had ever been to the mainland. There was a ban on traveling there from Taiwan, and on phone calls and mail as well.

"Down in one," Hoyt said.

"Yes." My father was pouring again.

"I'm going to hold my breath."

My father hit Hoyt's cup with his own and drank. "Too strong? I have beer."

Hoyt snorted, which triggered a coughing fit.

As they worked on the bottle, my mother stood in the kitchen, unsure of where to go. She touched the handle to the fridge but didn't open it. She walked a few steps to the drying rack and started putting away the cutlery, though it was still wet.

"Am I going to be able to drive after this?"

My father was pouring again.

"My cousin, he got a second DUI, and now he gets around on his lawn mower."

My father traced the lip of his cup with a finger. "The well casing," he said. "I do everything right. Not my fault it cracked."

"Sure."

"I do everything right. You know this. I need you write a—a document for court—say I do everything right. Steven, he won't do it. He say he never see the install, he say, 'That's all you guys.' But you see it. You did the grouting."

"Hey, now," Hoyt said. "It's not the grouting that's the problem."

"I know—"

"Well, what's going on with the insurance?"

"He say no coverage for subcontractor's—for subcontractor's"—my father slid his jaw forward—"negligence. Poor workmanship." He swept a hand in front of his face as though clearing something away. "But it's not—"

"Hey, I didn't come out here to talk shop." Hoyt hooked his elbow over the back of his chair. "Look at your nice family, and here we are, going on like this." He palmed the side of Natty's head. "This one's starting kindergarten?"

"Yes," my mother said.

"Sweet boy," Hoyt said. "And this one?"

"He just finish grade five," my mother said.

"Five? You kidding me? He's almost as small as the little one."

"I not kidding you." My mother took a few quick steps to

the table and stood beside Hoyt, so close to him it looked like she was about to investigate the dusky roots of his hair. "I work at his school," she said.

"That right? You teach?"

"Crossing guard."

In fact my mother had only subbed for Paula, the teary-eyed, frosty-lipped lady who limped us across the intersection outside school. For three weeks, while Paula recovered from a surgery to reposition a toe, my mother worked a half hour in the morning and a half hour in the afternoon. She wore a neon-yellow vest and held a stop sign in front of her like a longsword, poised to make a downward slice.

"Yeah," Hoyt said. "Sure. Crossing guard."

"Keep children safe." Layered over her turtleneck was an old hoodie of Pei-Pei's, unzipped, and she tugged on the bottom corners of it. Her eyes were getting huge. "If someone don't drive safe, I remember license plate number."

"An important job," Hoyt said.

"Nobody walk until I walk," she said. "I walk first. Protect the children behind me."

Hoyt gazed up at my mother. Her hands were up by her throat, and if she lowered one just a few inches, she could grab his large, geological nose. "It's a good thing," he said, and when my mother did not move, he mumbled, "a marvelous thing."

I ran my half-eaten cracker around on the vinyl tablecloth. My father sat low in his chair with his legs spread and his arms falling away from him.

"Let's go see about that fence," Hoyt said, and stood up. My father straightened, nodded, and grabbed the liquor bottle by the neck. Then Hoyt bent down to kiss Natty on top of his head, right on the whorl from which Natty's hair grew clockwise. And Natty let him.

They left through the front door so my father could yank on his shoes, and soon I saw them walking up the slope of our patchy side yard. My father was on the far side, and for a moment he disappeared completely behind Hoyt, so that I couldn't find a single hand or shoe that belonged to him.

Pei-Pei tossed her head back; her glasses slid down her forehead and came to a crooked rest on her nose. "The cookies," she said to my mother, and got up to switch on the oven. "First, preheat." We weren't permitted to use the oven except in winter months, when what was wasted in energy could be used as heat. But on this night in late June, my father had asked Pei-Pei to take charge of what to serve to Hoyt, and she had chosen thumbprint cookies. Such a choice. I knelt on my chair to get a better view. Sometimes it seemed to me that Pei-Pei knew every corner of the world.

My mother heaved an unopened seven-pound sack of brown sugar onto the counter. "I don't know why you can't just use regular."

"Because it says brown!" Pei-Pei wailed. She flattened the recipe on the back of the Hershey's bag and underscored the words with her fingernail. "You didn't have to buy so much of it. But we have to follow it this time. I'm going to do it myself."

She put Natty and me to work unwrapping the Hershey's kisses, but a few candies in, Natty began rolling the flimsy foil wrappers and paper flags into tight, wrinkled beads, which he flicked across the table at me.

"Stop that," I said.

"Get out," he said.

"What?"

"Leave." He flicked another bead, and it hit me on the chin.

My mother pressed herself against the wall, just past the edge of the window frame. She craned her head to peek out. Through the window, I could see two figures in the backyard. Their hands were in their pockets and their legs were swallowed up by dark grass. Above their bowed heads was the jagged silhouette of treetops against the coppery sky.

Pei-Pei opened the sack and dipped a measuring cup in, packing the brown sugar so hard that the plastic handle bent backward. She dumped it into a bowl and slapped my hand when I tried to break the fragile shape with my finger. As Pei-Pei scanned the recipe, my mother returned and stared into the bowl. For Pei-Pei's birthday last year, my mother had made a pound cake. She kept murmuring, "What a thing, a cake made from a whole pound of sugar," shuddering at the audacity of the granulated sugar as it poured smoothly out of the measuring cup. In the end she had tripled the flour. "This is bread," Pei-Pei complained, and would not take another bite even when my mother whapped the back of her head. My mother picked up the whole loaf from the top and flipped it, feeling its heft, and said, "Someone should make a cake for me, since I've raised you for another year."

As Pei-Pei reached for the butter now, my mother shouted, "No!" Pei-Pei froze, but my mother was looking at the wall clock. It was nearly seven in the evening. "No," my mother wailed. She unhooked the phone from the wall and jabbed at the rubber buttons. While she waited, she wrapped the phone cord around her fingers, weaving it in and out, like a string game

I'd seen Ada play. Suddenly she jerked and expelled a flurry of Taiwanese. "Hello? Hello? Yes, I'm the daughter. I know. I know. But—how long did they wait for me to call? They didn't wait too long, did they? Heavens. I don't know, I just—we had a guest, we were preparing—I know it's Sunday morning there. It wasn't chilly while they were waiting, was it? No, I know it's too late now. I'll try again next month. Tell me, how did he look? Did he look like he's been eating? I know they waited a long time. I know I made them wait."

As my mother continued her chatter, I became aware of a chemical smell filling our kitchen. I took a long sniff. Pei-Pei looked straight through me for a few seconds before slamming down the can of baking powder, which wheezed up white dust. She dashed to the oven, wrenched open the door, and pawed at the books as they tumbled out.

I strolled over and picked up a paperback. The edges and corners were toasted brown. As I riffled through the warm pages, they crackled. At my feet was a glossy softcover book; its plastic laminate had taken on a whipped, raised texture. I squatted and put my face close to it, inhaling the burnt electrical smell a few times and holding my breath until I felt the sweet forward creep of a headache. The kitchen glowed yellow, and Natty hopped off his chair. He scrabbled at the sliding door to the yard and pulled it open just a foot, maybe less. He turned sideways and slid through it like a coin through a slot.

The floor squeaked beside me, and my mother's slippered feet came into view. "What happened?" she asked.

"I forgot," Pei-Pei said. She was kneeling among the books with her arms outstretched. "When I turned on the oven, I forgot about the books."

"Ah. I forgot, too," my mother said. "There's no real harm."

Pei-Pei's head stayed fixed, but her eyes slid up to appraise my mother.

My mother touched the side of Pei-Pei's face, her ear, her jaw. Her hand lingered in the dark cavity beneath Pei-Pei's hair. Then she picked up the book I'd been smelling and laid it to the side. As my mother quietly stacked books, Pei-Pei remained kneeling. With a shock I saw my sister was crying. She had cut her own bangs recently, exposing her thick eyebrows with their downward twists. The nose pads on her glasses interrupted the flow of her tears, diverting them toward the corners of her mouth.

I grazed the tops of a few books with my open hands. "You can still read them," I said. "Every single one of them."

She nodded, took off her glasses, and swiped at her face with her wrist. I glanced from my sister to my mother, who was trying to nudge a stack of books in line so they shared a perfectly straight edge. Was it possible, to realize only now something simple about people you saw every day? They looked alike. Their expansive cheeks and pointed chins, the wide hollows beneath their eyes. The nonexpression on their faces, beneath which a hundred other expressions lurked.

When my mother finished, there were five stacks of books as high as my chest. It was astonishing, how many books could fit in an oven.

"Where will we hide them?" Pei-Pei asked.

My mother leaned back and rested her head against the sink cabinet. "Oh, just leave them." She squatted on her heels and palmed her knees.

"Dad wanted it to be clean in here."

When my mother rolled her head from side to side, the cabinet behind her clacked. The door hinge was loose.

"I guess there isn't anywhere to put them," Pei-Pei said. "If he wants them put away, he can figure it out himself."

"Show some respect," my mother said, in a voice so weary it seemed to have traveled up from her bent, burdened knees. "He's your father."

———

WE HEARD THE STAMP of Hoyt's boots again, and then he was taking long sniffs and barking out laughs. "A book burning? And you didn't invite me?"

Pei-Pei shoved her glasses up into her hair while my mother looked toward the closed front door. "Where—"

"Suey's still outside, seeing to something or other. I'm on my way. Just wanted to say good night."

"Good night?" my mother said. She used the counter to pull herself up. "But my husband . . ." When she ran out of words, she took a careening step toward Hoyt. I was afraid she would grab his shirt.

"We're making cookies," Pei-Pei said. She pointed to the bowl on the table.

"Don't mind if I do." He walked to the table, peered into the bowl, and dipped his finger in, bringing a dollop of batter to his mouth.

My mother gasped. "There is raw egg."

"How I like it best." He scooped out a larger gob and chewed it.

I caught a glimpse of my father's figure through the far

window of the den. He was walking down the slight slope of our side yard, catching himself every few steps, as though the ground had gone soft.

"There he comes," Hoyt said. "I already said my goodbyes, so I'll get going."

Hoyt was out the door in seconds; his boots were already on and he moved fast. Almost impossibly soon after, there was the sound of his van bouncing over the gravel, and then my father was standing in the open doorway, looking in at us.

The oven was off, the batter was raw, and my mother, Pei-Pei, and I stood in front of the lolling tongue of the oven door, surrounded by stacks of heated books.

"You couldn't manage it," my mother said.

My father didn't move to take off his shoes. The front door was still open. So was the back door, I knew.

I inched my way to the sliding door and peered out. A chill rushed boldly in. There was no sign of Natty in the yard. The sky had turned drab, as though mixed with batches of ash. Where the woods began, there was only a stripe of darkness, with a pale glow at the opening of the trail. When you stood at that entry point, I knew, you sensed something waiting for you in there. Some days it was a foreboding, and some days it was a kind of comfort, a promise of company.

"All he has to do," my mother said, "is write a piece of paper. It's worth nothing to him. How could you not manage it?"

My father only shut the door. I stepped between them, into the wide doorway to the kitchen. I gave a tentative jump.

No one spoke. Then my father said, "Again."

I raised both arms and jumped higher.

"Touch the top this time," my father said.

"Touch it!" my mother shouted, and when I turned around, I saw the full roundness of her eyeballs, eyelids pared back.

I jumped for a long, hard minute until something soft hit my leg. It was a roll of toilet paper with a long tail. Pei-Pei was chortling into a clump of wadded tissue.

In the voice he used for joking, which sounded like despair wrapped in laughter, my father said, "You can't stop jumping until you touch it."

I jumped. I wrenched my neck back to see how far I was from the header. It wasn't even close. I doubled up, curling over a stitch in my side.

"You can't stop—" My father broke into a long cough that turned phlegmy at the end. "Keep—jump—jumping."

"Go!" my mother cheered.

"Taller!" my father bellowed. "Grow taller!"

My jumps had slowed, and my toes barely left the floor. My extended arm was heavy and drooping. I was aware of some grit or gravel flecks sticking to my bare feet, perhaps carried in on the underside of Hoyt's boots.

I saw my family's blurred faces around me, flushed, as though they were jumping, too. And then something buoyed me up. In my head was a voice urging, Higher, higher, touch it, and my fingertips could sense the proximity of the piece of wood they'd never before touched. I burst from the floor with one hand up, then the other hand, then both hands, high as I could and trying for higher, driven by the certainty that if I were ever to touch the header and attain this triumph, this would be the night to do it.

Suddenly there was Natty, watching us from outside, from

the other side of the glass. Where had he been? What did he see? Natty, who saw strangers in us and kinship in strangers. I jumped harder. I never did touch the top, but Natty slid in through the gap and pulled the door closed, sealing our house again. And eventually my father bent over to take off his shoes for the night.

//

THE OPEN FRONT DOOR LET IN A GUST OF SLANTED RAIN from the July storm. Pei-Pei kicked off her dress shoes as she ducked in, and my father barreled in just after her, shaking water onto the floor. He writhed until his overcoat slid off. That morning he had excavated it from the very back of the closet, and now the damp wool released a musty stink from its heap. My father picked up Natty and whirled him around until Natty's smile was spun away.

"You're making him sick," my mother said.

"He likes it," my father said, panting, "don't you?"

Natty grinned by baring his teeth. Then his head flopped back as though his neck were made of rubber tubing.

I watched my father's feet as they danced. They veered back the way they had come. Midspin, he stumbled and caught himself by smacking one hand against the door. He straightened and made a swatting motion with his free hand, batting off my mother's gaze.

Meanwhile, Pei-Pei peeled off her own coat. Her hair was coiled up in a giant bun. Beads of water sat on it.

My father's knee buckled, and he laughed. "Do you feel that?" he cried, supporting Natty's head with both hands. "Our brains are all stirred up. They don't recognize the world when it's still. They are saying, I thought chaos was the only truth!" He squeezed Natty's cheeks, checking their firmness or reality.

My mother draped my father's coat over the end of the banister to dry, then looped the hood of Pei-Pei's coat over the doorknob. The storm was so loud, you wouldn't have known the front door was all the way closed. Water splashed against our doorstep as though trying to crack the concrete and dent the earth beneath.

Upstairs, Pei-Pei pulled her pants on under her skirt and then shimmied out of it.

"How was it?" I asked.

"It's over."

"What's over?"

"It was just a room with a table. The chairs were plastic."

"What did the judge say?"

"There was no judge."

"Was the boy there?"

"Just pictures of him." Pei-Pei slid a tie out of her bun, and a massive swoop of hair fell out of it. "He was white. Really white, like cream cheese. Maybe it was all the nosebleeds—he had no color left in his face. He looked like a piece of paper after something's been erased."

"And that's our fault?"

Pei-Pei shrugged. "That's what their documents say. The other side's documents."

"What do our documents say?"

"We don't have any documents."

I sat on the edge of our large, fused bed. This mattress section was Pei-Pei's, and it sagged more than mine.

She told me about the room. Across the table, in a neat row, had sat three men and the boy's parents: a woman with a silk scarf that barely knotted around her ample throat, a mustached fellow who kept wiping the sides of his fisted hands on his pants. There was no judge, she kept saying. There was no one to make us do anything. Not a one. "So it's a mystery," Pei-Pei said. "A real puzzle." When they scooted the papers across the table, my father had picked up the pen.

"It makes you think about what he did." She turned her palms up to study them. "And about that boy. His face. Like the inside of a pear, so soft it comes apart in your hands."

She rose and stood at the dresser, facing the wall. On the drive there, she said, our father had kept calling it a waste of time. Just laughable, he said. "And now I see," Pei-Pei said. "He's one person, and then he's another." She picked up a comb. "Or he says he's one thing, but the whole time he's actually the opposite. You can just flip everything he says about himself. Top of the class? Best in the village? A genius or angel no one else can see?" She raked her hair. I could hear the long scrape against her scalp and the flick when she ripped through a tangle.

Our parents' words floated up the stairwell and through the short hall, as clear as if they were at our door.

"How much? Tell me how much."

"I don't report to you."

"So it's a lot."

In the silence, Pei-Pei muttered, "Define 'a lot.'"

"Can we afford it?" my mother asked.

"Define 'afford,'" Pei-Pei whispered.

"Ten thousand? Twenty? More?"

"It's not all at once. It's broken into payments."

"What did you agree to?" my mother screamed. The sudden noise made me grab my own arms. Her voice was wretched, like the screams of a lynx we had once found in the woods.

"We better get down there," I said.

Pei-Pei made a sucking sound through her teeth. "For what?" she said.

I wondered if my father was still holding Natty. Like a shield.

"Any amount is too much for us," my father shouted, "and not enough for that boy. So we are all punished—that's how it works."

"How it should work," my mother said, "is that you take it all—every punishment you deserve—and leave us be."

Pei-Pei sat down beside me on the very edge of the bed, and our combined weight sloped the mattress forward, so that we had to plant our feet against the urge to fall. The lynx we had found had been lying on its side against the rotted remnant of a trunk, swiping at air with one massive paw as though fighting off ghosts. There was red—blood—and a beard hardened into points, but we were already leaving before we ever really saw it. What was wrong with it, what might have brought it to such a state, what it might be calling for. Once we heard the sounds, throaty and strained, human, pleading, we were backing away, we were gone. It was just after the summer solstice, when the sunset endured until sunrise. I knew the creature would have no cover and no rest.

———

MY FATHER made himself scarce again. Soon there were just two moments of each day when my father's presence in the house was felt, and if I slept too deeply, or too long, I would miss them. First, as morning broke, I could hear him leave: the front door pulsing open and closed, the snap of the lock, the thud of the driver's door, and the low, hushed rumble of his wheels crawling rock by rock over the gravel and away, to wherever he was looking for work. Or hiding. At night, if I stayed up very late, I could hear the sounds in reverse. The truck creeping back in, my father slinking home. It got to be a kind of lullaby, sliding me into a flurry of broken thoughts, then the blankness of sleep.

The storm kept up, and the longer we stayed in the house, the less energy we had to keep ourselves entertained. After dinner, we drifted to the den and listened to the fragmented radio on Pei-Pei's boom box. No one bothered to flip on the lights. I sat on the couch with Natty at my feet. My mother leaned against me, though there was an armrest on her other side. Pei-Pei sat with her legs folded on a metal chair and twisted her hair. The radio droned about falling oil prices. The recession. The typhoon sweeping into the Bering Sea, hacking up the ocean near the Aleutian Islands so waves jumped fifty feet high.

When we heard about the fishermen tying down their boats in Dutch Harbor, my mother said, "Once I rode my bicycle ten kilometers in a typhoon wearing two layers of garbage bags and a shower cap. The roads were flooded, and the water was almost up to the chain."

Pei-Pei said, "Ten kilometers isn't far. It's, what, five miles?"

Outside, the wind flung the rain around in strange patterns. Behind the rain, we could hear the thrashing of the spruces, an army of trees rasping as they reached for our back door. By the end of the storm, I imagined, all the trees would be scoured and bare, and our house would be entombed in needles. Natty used his crayons in the dark, and when I saw his drawings later in the dismal light of day, they scared me with their chaos. A bowl-shaped bulge formed in our bathroom ceiling, and through the center of it, water began to drip.

"Here we go," Pei-Pei said. "It's coming in."

Someone, it must have been my mother, pressed a piece of duct tape over the leak. Water seeped through anyway, and the edges of the tape became unstuck. The whole house began to feel damp. From the window of the den, we checked often on the growing lake in the side yard and the lines of rain agitating its surface.

When finally the rain began to let up, my mother said we should go to the store to buy sealant. She drove slowly, navigating around fallen branches that had been dragged partly off the road. Near a cluster of branches and logs, we saw a man bent over a chain saw. My mother stopped and rolled down the window. "You are working hard," she said.

The man tried to brush sawdust off his sleeves and pants, but the wet residue clung to his clothes. "Thing ran out of gas," he said. "Can't hardly blame it, though." He swept his arm in a half circle. "Been at it all day, and I've barely made a dent."

"Can I have some of this?" my mother asked. She nodded at the chaotic pile of logs.

"What for?" Pei-Pei said from the backseat.

"We're not supposed to give it away. Supposed to save it, for the burn barrels around the rink."

My mother nodded.

He shrugged. "But who's keeping track? Why not, I say."

My mother jumped out of the station wagon to open the tailgate and stand rigidly beside its extended wing. The man hauled sectioned logs over, one chunk at a time. Each time he loaded one, we felt the whole car sink.

"I thought I saw lightning last night," the man was saying, "but it wasn't lightning at all. The power line was down, and the transformer exploded outside my house. Jesus, what a storm. You ever see a bigger one?"

"Yes," my mother said.

When she climbed back in, my mother turned around and looked at the three of us. "Free firewoods," she said, and started up the car.

"For what?" Pei-Pei said. "Our daily campfire?"

My mother just kept driving. The asphalt, tree bark, raw wood fences—everything was wet and several shades darker. Where sidewalks were drying, they looked stained. Standing pools of water reflected soupy sky. Water droplets hung on the undersides of things. From inside the car, we scanned the drenched wreckage. A shed smashed in half by a tree, a dented van, a cat picking at the gray flesh of something that had once been alive. My mother hit the brakes. She rolled down the window.

"No," said Pei-Pei. "No, Mom, don't."

"You are working hard," she said.

Pei-Pei let the side of her head hit the window. Anyone who bothered to look would see only a swath of black hair plastered to the glass.

A boy about Pei-Pei's age scratched his nose with his pinky nail. He was not holding any tools, but there were split logs at his feet and his hands were crusted with dried mud, so it seemed he had done something substantial.

"So many firewoods," my mother said.

"Yeah," said the boy. "My dad cut it up."

"Give some to me," my mother said.

———

AT NIGHT, I began to listen for the sounds not just of my father returning home, but of Pei-Pei sneaking down the stairs and out the same door. If I bothered to crawl to the window, I would see a short, wan beam of light in the yard, swerving back and forth, scanning the edge of the woods and hovering around the start of the path. Then the light would shrink to a faint dot, which would disappear in a gulp of the woods.

After Pei-Pei left, Natty's sleep mumblings frightened me. I didn't like to be the only one to hear them. The first scrambled words sent me flying into the hallway. One night I huddled near the bottom of the stairs.

At one or two in the morning, it was dim but not quite dark. I saw my father's shoulders through the narrow strip of window as he worked the front door lock. When he came in, he nearly tripped on me. With one hand on the wall, he said, "It's you."

He sat on the step below me and faced the door. Beside

him was a dark spatter on the linoleum—his shadow. He was sitting so low he was nearly in a squat, his knees at his chest.

"You should sleep," he said, his back curved, talking to his knees.

"Why?"

"I don't know. Because that is when you will have peace."

"I don't think so," I said.

"Well, you're right," he said. "That is not how it is at all."

I put my arms around his neck. My wrists on his chest were damp. One of us was lightly sweating.

"Shall we go?" He leaned every which way as he straightened to a stand.

I hung on his back. "Go where?"

"Out there." He extended his arms in the direction of the window and the gravel road beyond, then wrapped them behind me. He bent his knees so I could reach down and unlock the front door. "You're light as a tissue," he said as he dropped me to the floor. As we stepped through, we might have left the door open behind us; it was that kind of night.

A month ago, my father would not have needed to switch on the headlights. Now, in late July, twilight had turned murkier. There was still a remnant glow from the sun, which hovered just below the horizon. But it was a marbled gray light, without brilliance.

He drove so fast it seemed we would plunge beyond the weak thrust of the headlights at any moment. There were no other cars on the road. I could measure our speed in the black flinching trees we passed. I thought of Pei-Pei on her journey across the woods with her veering flashlight, and I couldn't help but imagine we were moving in the same direction, and that we would meet.

On a downhill, with the road dropping away and the sky swelling before us, my father said, "The stars will be back soon. I haven't seen a single one for months. Have you?" He sank his foot on the gas.

I didn't know how to answer, since I hadn't been looking for them. In the gaps between the trees I could see the mountains. I could feel them, too, solid and stuck and envious of us.

"Yesterday, meteorites hit some houses in Japan," he said.

"Hm," I said.

"I'm trying to talk to you."

At an intersection surrounded by wooded and overgrown lots, a stop sign caught our lights and gleamed, and my father braked hard. He let his foot up, then braked again, so that we were thrown forward as he said, "That boy. All of that, that mess. It wasn't because of me."

I put my hands on the dashboard. We had driven so fast, but we had outrun nothing. "But if it was because of you—" I began.

"It wasn't. It wasn't my fault."

"But if it were your fault . . ." I had trouble finding words. I glanced at the empty glass of the side mirror and around the interior of the truck cab. I barely recognized it. Had there always been so many knobs on the dashboard, had it always looked like a flight deck? At school once, a freak onslaught of freezing rain made birds drop out of the sky, stunned, and they waddled stiff-legged and dim-witted on the lawn.

"You think it's my fault, too."

"I mean . . ." I didn't know how to say the rest. That if it were his fault, we would be the same. That there would be two of us. That it would be a cherished thing, to be at fault together and not condemned alone. I became aware of an immense pressure where the seat belt dug into my sternum. The whole band was tight.

"You've got to know this," he said. "Listen to me this once. Your father had nothing to do with it."

My throat ached. "Okay," I said. We were stopped in the middle of unoccupied, shadowed land. Just yards away, the trees began to mass.

My father cupped the side of my face with one hand. Warmth leeched into me, and my throat knotted closed. I heaved once with my private sorrow. His palm was wet but he didn't move. I was crying, but only water came out of me. "I know, I know," he said, his voice a gritty song. He didn't know. He didn't know. But I rested my whole heavy head in his hand and thought, Carry this for me.

"It was the room, that cursed room," he said. "The chairs were too low. The air was too dry. The table was long and scratched with the marks of other people." My father removed his hand from my face and pressed it on top of his own head, as though trying to keep the memory from expanding. The ghost of his handprint was cold on my face.

"Once we entered that room, you see, it was over. It was their room, not ours." Gripping the wheel now, he shifted and straightened. "And when has a room ever been ours?"

I felt for the latch on the glove compartment, and when I found it, I just grasped it without opening it. It was a place made exactly to be held.

He began driving again. Maybe it was the jerk of the truck,

or maybe I moved of my own volition. The glove compartment opened. At the sound of the unlatching, my father shot out an arm, and I saw his bare flesh at the same time I saw Ruby's urn. A metal knob on the lid and the glazed curve of the vessel shone under the puny bulb. The urn looked like nothing else we owned. It was simple, and it was beautiful.

"I haven't—I just put it there yesterday," he said. He thought that I needed an explanation. That if he had been driving around for weeks or even months like this, that if it had given him a kind of company, I would have thought any way about it. All I comprehended was that my sister fit inside a jar that fit inside a glove compartment. I closed its door.

"I wasn't going to do anything with it," he said. A few silent miles later, he said, "Actually, I was."

We turned onto the highway, where the occasional steel pole sprouted a halo of orange light. The trees vanished on our right, replaced by blank expanse—the mudflats and waters of Knik Arm and Susitna River—and the steady ombré mountains far behind them, still scarred by snow.

"Your mother wants to take her back to Taiwan," he said. "But Ruby was born here. This is all she's ever seen. This. These mountains, this sky."

As the highway cut inland, we entered a corridor of trees. It widened and narrowed and the trees stretched and shrank as we passed through Eagle River and came to Anchorage. Still my father drove, through the empty streets, and then we were on a highway again.

Finally we stopped at a small park: a stock-still swing set, a wooden bridge that breached from the ground. The only other vehicle in the lot was a truck with a makeshift, windowless camper—just screws and plywood. My father pulled up the brake and jumped out. I followed. He held the urn with both hands as he forged ahead past a crooked sign and onto a freshly paved path, where the smell of tar still lingered. We walked until the path curved. Thirty yards ahead, the asphalt petered out into a long, wide strip of compacted gravel and dirt. It was framed with wood on the sides, and metal bars were spaced along it like half-buried railroad ties. A small excavator and loader had paused there, sad and stooped.

He stepped off the path and onto the grass. A few long strides would take him to where the grass dwindled and the mudflats took over. "I'm going to put her in that water," he said.

It was a long way to the streaky water of the inlet. The flats looked wet. I searched for the rock where my mother and I had stood before a lonely whale, but that stretch of Turnagain Arm, wherever it was, was lost to me.

"Your mother wants to leave the country," my father said.

"Will we all go?"

"No one is going. Not one person in this family is leaving." He held up the dark urn. "We're going to put Ruby in the water there. And then we can never leave this place." He jabbed his chin toward the water, and I began to walk. I listened for his footfalls behind me. His steps on the soft ground made no noise, but I felt his presence like a hot wind. I kept moving my feet; if I stopped, he might trod on me.

"The ocean," he muttered, "is a magnificent place. Your mother lived by the ocean all her life."

"I already know that," I said.

"I will always remember the time I visited her where she grew up. Her friend took us on a speedboat, and we flew. The water became solid, and we banged against it with the bottom of the boat, hopping across the sea.

"Look at this," my father said, and when I turned, he threw one arm loosely into the air. "So much sky and not one star." As we left the path behind, we also ventured away from the fallen logs and rocks and stunted trees, until what remained before us was a low, soaked plain, the faded shapes of mountains, and as much stone-colored sky as we could take in.

"You think it's right that they stopped the space shuttle program? That they just cut it off? You think it's right to give up like that?"

"Well, it's dangerous," I said. I stepped over a wide, shallow rivulet of milky water. My heels dug into the silt. "People died."

"That's just the thing," he said. "People died. You can't just walk away from it."

The land around us was so flat, and so close in shade to the mountains and sky, it seemed we were tottering on a thin bridge—all around us were infinite openings to dive into void. In winter, I had glimpsed this shore from the road; the mountains were white, the mudflats were frosted, and the edges of the inlet were crowded with chunks of ice knocking about— but still the takeaway was gray, gray, gray. Day or night, snow or sun, nothing could change that essence.

My father shouted behind me. A beast-like noise. When I looked back at his figure, he was nearly my height, his legs cut off at the knees. The mud was swallowing him. I ran over just as he shouted, "Not too close!" When I stopped, my own shoes disappeared and I felt the earth suctioning my feet.

"Get flat," he said, "get low." But I had already fallen when the ground clamped onto my feet. It was trying to absorb me.

My sweatshirt was cold, maybe damp, where it pressed into the silt. I used my elbows to drag myself toward ashier, harder mud, barely aware of my father pawing and pawing several feet away. The mud was tugging on my shoes, and it took all I had to squirm loose of it.

"Get me something, some sticks," he said.

I lay on my stomach, panting. My father was in danger. The sky spun as I listed to my feet and stumbled back to the path. My head throbbed. I scanned the length of the path in front of me, but all I saw were twigs and logs. I attacked the largest tree, barely bigger than a shrub. It whipped back and forth and slapped its leaves together as I tried to break or twist off a branch. For a few long minutes I wrestled with it, my heart fluttery with exhaustion, the edges of the world warping in. I couldn't manage it. The branch simply bent in every direction. When I let go of it, the tree looked no worse for its thrashing.

My father yelled something, but the words were gummed up.

"I can't find anything!" I shouted back, louder than I had ever screamed. My failure was thunderous.

I ran back to him, a touch more slowly than I had run away. The only thing left to do was to try to pull him out, but how could I manage that?

"Don't get too close," he said, and when I was a few feet away I saw he was clawing the ground with his fingers, raking tracks into the mud as he strained in vain to pull himself out. "Stay back," he said. His motions were slow, his voice quiet and grim and compressed with effort. Suddenly he stopped. "It's very cold."

I lay down on my stomach and stretched my hands out to him. Either I would save him, or he would pull me in. But my father did not touch me and instead began a strange slithering with his upper body. Was this what dying looked like, this wrenching, this struggle?

And then he was beside me. He flipped over onto his back, one hand heaving on his chest. For a minute he didn't speak. Then he said, "I couldn't lift my legs. I couldn't get them out."

"I know," I said, though I had gotten only a small taste of that strange, inhuman tugging and that seeping cold. But I knew what he meant. Something had tried to sink us. Something stronger. We had not prevailed against it—we had been spared.

Without moving, he said, "We have to get up. It's not safe here." He continued to gape at the sky.

A long time later, he rolled over and pressed himself up to kneeling. He reached for the urn, which lay on its side with the lid off. A tuft of clear plastic stuck out from the opening. With the lidded urn cradled again in his arm, he turned to gaze at the water. We were perhaps just past halfway from the path to the edge of the inlet. The liquid had a different sheen from the mud, both brighter and blacker, it seemed.

"Let's go back to the car," he said, and nestled the lid in its place. Something about the primness of his gesture, or the way he wiped his hands on his thighs, delaying, irked me. Everything he did was full of excessive effort and care, as though his bones were held together by thread.

"You can't do anything," I said. He looked at me, surprised. I had never spoken to him like this before, but I found that it was easy. The words were already formed and only had to be released. "You sure know how to talk," I said, "about the things you'll never do." I snatched the whole cold urn. "You wanted to leave her here, didn't you?"

I held the urn with two rigid hands as we stared at each other. He did not move. I dropped the lid to the mud and pulled out the dusty bag. It was knotted but came undone easily. It was intolerable to me that she had been kept inside this plastic; I hadn't known until now. My father watched as I held the bag by a corner and, with a hard flick, dumped everything out. I didn't want her in the water, I didn't want her washed away. I wanted her mired. Stuck here. The mudflats were hungry. They would take her, and they would keep her.

I avoided looking at the coarse pile, at the shards and fragments that tried to announce themselves. I didn't look at the water or the sky in the warped twilight. Somewhere, there was a moon.

I thought of the way Ruby ate. "Like a man," my father had said. She ate with more enthusiasm than even he did. She used both hands at the same time, shoving in food though her mouth was already full, her face awash with simple joy and abandon. How I missed her. No one else ate like that.

My father lowered himself gently to his knees. I waited for the ground to react, but it didn't. He garbled some kind of prayer lost to the wind. When he tried to get back up, he seemed to lack the strength. He put his hands on the silt and, with a great push upward, added, "Or at least not be forgotten." We brushed our arms and legs, a futile gesture against the sticky ashes, and turned back to the path.

12

THE PHONE RANG OFTEN. IF WE ACKNOWLEDGED THE sound—"Not this again," or "They sure don't give up"—whatever my mother was doing would become loud and sloppy. She would shove the kitchen chairs against the table so hard that the whole table skipped, or clean the den by flinging all of our belongings into a small mountain; her anger changed the topography of the room. Pei-Pei picked up the phone just once, while my mother was at the store, and said it was a man with a lisp. He was from the bank, and there was an urgent matter at hand.

Soon my mother stopped going to the mailbox and sent me instead. "Quick," she said. "Don't let anyone see you." I ran so hard, I kicked up gravel behind me. Who was watching us, and from where? The clearing across from our house had turned wild with foliage and weeds, and it would make for a good place to hide, if someone had an inexplicable interest in us. Just inside the open door, my mother waited for me, hidden except for the outermost fringe of her hair. Week after week, I handed her envelopes that had bent in my fist as I sprinted, and she slipped them unopened into a deep kitchen drawer.

If my mother was avoiding incoming calls, she made up for it by generating what seemed to be hundreds of outgoing ones. She was trying to reach someone to ask after her father. She sometimes held the phone away from her ear, and we could hear the faint, endless ringing, like echoes of the more urgent rings that plagued us when the phone was on its hook. Five thousand miles away, as well as here, the world resounded with pleas.

The edge of the woods flamed magenta as the last flowers on the tips of the fireweeds bloomed. School was just around the corner. Reagan announced that a replacement shuttle for the *Challenger* was in the works. My father must have been happy about that, but I hardly saw him.

The salmonberries had just become edible, terribly late this year. Two weeks ago, the green, tight berries had become tinged in red around the drupelets, as though the seeds were seeping blood. Now, finally, half of them hung fat and vermilion on the shrubs, among masses of serrated leaves. We paused by the bushes to snack on patches, and sometimes I pulled a plastic bag from my pocket and filled it for my mother.

One afternoon, Collin held a twig out to me and said, "Will you eat this?"

"You want me to eat that?"

"Yeah. Will you?"

"No."

Ada knocked it out of his hand, but he only opened his other hand to show us a small spruce cone. It hadn't lost its seeds yet; its scales were flat and overlapping. "How about this?" he said.

"You eat it," I said.

Collin took a large step off the trail to strip a tab of bark from a birch.

"This," he said. "You'll eat this, won't you? Fry it up with some oil?"

I glanced around for help. Pei-Pei was giggling, and Natty had run off again.

I gave Collin a shove, but he barely moved. Though he was skinny, he still towered over me, and I made a note to go for his knees next time. If I could get them to buckle, he would go down. And I would step on his face.

"Just now I felt a little pinch," he said to Pei-Pei.

In a fury I trampled off the path and regretted it instantly. We were due home soon, and in the late summer the understory was flourishing and high. I had to squeeze between shrubs, climb over fallen trunks, and mind the cow parsnips, and all the while I could hear Collin laughing with Pei-Pei, who grew stupider with his proximity.

There was one massive patch of cow parsnip I avoided by walking a huge half circle around it. Earlier in the summer, they had sprung clusters of miniature flowers—all angelic. Their toxins were dormant, activated by sunlight; once you had brushed the stems or the big, floppy leaves, they lay in wait until you ventured out from the shade. Then they scalded you. When Pei-Pei's legs had broken out in blisters and curdling rashes, I had helped her rub them down with ice cubes.

I didn't know where I was headed, and was not entirely sure I could find my way back to the path. For fifteen minutes I walked what felt like a straight line, as it grew darker and denser in the woods. I stopped to toe the exposed, sprawling roots of an ancient spruce. Piles of pine cones lay between them.

Stripped of seeds and scales by squirrels, the cones were just bare cobs.

In the wind was a murmuring, and when I looked up, there was Natty, perhaps eight trees away to my right. He was gazing up at the crown of a spruce with a long, silvery scar, and the intonation of his voice suggested he was asking questions. I couldn't make out his words. As I watched, he moved to another tree. He peered up, circled it, spoke in the same searching way, and moved on.

Even as I moved closer to him, his words stayed indistinct. I had the sense he was speaking in some veiled forest language of undertones and hums.

"Natty," I said.

He paused and glanced over his shoulder at me. Among all those trees, he looked imperiled, something left behind, left to chance.

"It's time to go home," I said.

He began to make his way over, slogging across the spongy ground. He sank and rose as though climbing in and out of low ditches. When he was within arm's reach, the laces of his sneakers caught on a thorned vine, and he stumbled a little toward me.

He stood on his toes and put his face very close to mine. As he spoke, his breath had a strange, adult kind of odor, as though something had been festering in his mouth. "I'm looking for Ruby," he said. His eyes were huge. Maybe it was the angle of his face, turned up to gaze above my head. His thick lashes curved toward the sky. Both my mother and father had often said he was a very pretty boy. It was hard to turn away.

But I turned away. Everywhere, there were trees straining,

driving themselves upward. They fought to break through the canopy, only to have their crowns beaten scraggly by the wind. I focused on my shoes, with their dirty laces neatly tied and tucked. In the darkening woods, you had to keep your gaze close, lest you catch a glimpse of something bigger than you could accept. Darkness in the woods was like a raw, grave wound. You wouldn't want to look at it, you wouldn't want to know how big it was.

"We've got to go," I said.

"All right," he said, and turned away. He began walking in the direction of the path, and I followed a few paces behind. He was only five, but then again, he was just a month away from six and knew the woods better than maybe any of us. He didn't turn around to check on me and seemed to have forgotten I was there. Or he knew I was there, but it wasn't of any consequence.

When we returned to the path, everyone was gone except Pei-Pei.

She fussed over us. "Look at you both. What is this stuff? Where have you been?" She smacked us all over the shoulders, back, and chest, making needles and bits of dry leaves jump from our clothing. "Come when I call," she said, and rubbed the back of my head so that I would know she was sorry.

"We didn't hear you," I said.

"Then you went too far in." She pivoted on one boot and raked her hair back with her hand. She sighed. "Homeward."

As we started our last journey of the day, we were blasted by a wind. It carried the chill of the glaciers it had swept. Natty's hand was light and dry in mine, like a piece of balsa wood.

When we burst out of the forest into the blue-lit clearing of the yard, I suddenly saw how narrow our house was, just as Hoyt had said. Piled on the foundation that jutted out from the ground were two slim stories and a steep-roofed attic, like a block balanced on its end, waiting to be toppled.

The lights were all off. We banged on the sliding door. A minute later, my mother lifted the side of the curtain to peer through the glass at us. Or perhaps she was taking in her own reflection in the large pane of glass, tall enough to display her rumpled person, from her socks and slippers up to her puffy hair. When she tried to slide the door open, it caught on the tracks.

"I don't want to go in," Natty whispered.

Pei-Pei smirked. "I know what you mean."

With no real hurry, my mother tried the door again, and it slid open just enough for us to squeeze through. "Come in," she said. "My stray children."

As we filed into our dark home, my mother tapped each of us on the shoulder, as though counting us. Pei-Pei, then me, then Natty, who flinched at her touch.

———

DAYS BEFORE SCHOOL BEGAN, we returned from the woods to find my mother digging by the sliding door. In late spring, a few old potatoes had sprouted in our cabinet, and she had chopped them up and planted them along the house. Stalks had grown out of the ground, unfurled leaves, and turned bushy. By late summer, the stalks had started to die.

She sank a long shovel behind each plant and stamped on

the shoulder of the blade. She used it as a lever to turn up a great heap of earth, in which we could see pale gems—flashes of buttery potatoes churned into the black soil.

"They're so small," my mother said, kicking at a fallen plant. Sweat glued wisps of hair to the sides of her face. "What have they been doing all this time instead of growing?"

Natty and I knelt and collected the potatoes with our hands. Some were still attached to the roots, and others were hiding by themselves in the loose dirt, which simply had to be brushed away. They were the size of golf balls and shooter marbles, all miraculously whole, and we uncovered them like artifacts. I shivered at the thought of them growing in the ground, enlarging, quiet and unseen, until there were five or six to a plant.

My mother leaned on the shovel. "I received a letter," she said. "Your grandfather is dead. He died almost four weeks ago."

A letter? I would have been the one who brought it in from the mailbox—an envelope stashed with news of death.

Natty dropped two potatoes from as high as he could reach, and when they fell into the bucket, they sounded like rocks.

"So we can't visit him anymore," she said. "We waited too long."

I stuck my hands into the dark, loose dirt.

"I missed my last phone call with him. And I couldn't reach him after that. He wanted to hear your voices, but he didn't get his wish."

Natty wiped his neck with his dirty hand. "I dreamt that he came here."

"Did you?" my mother said with a tremble of a smile. "That is a good dream."

"Yes," Natty said. "I showed him these potatoes." He tilted the bucket toward us. Four potatoes rolled to the front.

"How wonderful for him," my mother said.

I did not tell her that lately Natty had been calling certain kinds of thoughts dreams. Before we fell asleep now, Natty liked to inform me, "I'm dreaming I can hear my heart inside my ears. I'm dreaming I can't turn it off."

My mother released the shovel, and its handle disappeared in the grass. She bent over and let her head hang as she gazed through the space between her legs. The woods would have been flipped—trees stabbing down, nothing to step on but air. She sat and rolled an oblong potato between her hands. "But why are these so small? These lousy things. They won't even feed us for a day."

Natty swirled the plastic bucket around so it made a rumbling sound.

"It's this place," my mother said. "It's not a place that allows them to grow the way they ought."

I threw three potatoes at the bucket, and two of them went in. I reached for the lone potato in the grass, but halfway through gave up.

———

ON THE NEXT MONDAY we woke to the anxious bleeps of the alarm clock, and with that small and sudden violence, school began. There were new classes, some new clothes in the halls, one or two faces I had not seen before. But it was the same trapped seats and the need to be wary. There were a few true differences in the sixth grade: in the classes where we were allowed to choose our own desks, Ada kicked her legs beside me. Also, I discovered I could run. As kids began to jog past me on the road that looped our school, my skin would flash hot and cool. Maybe it was my daily practice of sprinting all the way to the mailbox at the entrance of our gravel road. Or maybe I just learned how to put everything I had into it, the surge. I found I liked it there at the front, where I didn't have to look at anyone. For a full minute or two, I was weightless. But the moment I finished, it all caught up with me. My legs hurt, my chest burned, and the air was too muddy for my lungs. When I made a sound like squeaky shoes, the gym teacher asked, "Are you having an asthma attack?" He sent me to the nurse, who said, "Just don't run so fast." Soon weeks had slid by.

It must have been different for Natty, for whom every small occurrence was new. The kindergarteners were assigned to one of the portable classrooms, a trailer decked out with thin carpet and faded posters. The room was vigorously heated, and if you looked in the windows, you could see a few rows of small, sweating, red-cheeked children. Beside this classroom was a set of portable bathrooms, and when I visited them on the way to the bus, I saw Natty outside, motionless on a half-court below a basketball hoop. The cracks in the concrete were newly patched, a web of gray filler spreading through the puddles from the morning rain. Natty stood with his foot on the edge of the web.

"What are you doing?" I asked.

As I spoke, three boys standing at the far sideline skittered away. From what I had glimpsed, they were a few years older than Natty. And much bigger, probably bigger than I was. Natty still didn't move. A suffocating sadness landed somewhere between us, folding us both into it. I nudged him in the direction of the buses. He started to walk, the way a man who has never seen snow might wade through several feet of it, not knowing what it was or why it was impeding him.

I sat with him on the bus. At the Qwik Stop, I said, "Here we go," and together we descended the rubber-lined steps and walked the ditch along the road. It was very warm and humid out, but I had to tell Natty to take off his jacket.

When we got home, there was a piece of paper taped to the door. At the top, the words "Notice to Quit" were printed. Who had noticed what, and who was quitting? I was afraid to touch it. The rain had pasted the entire sheet flat against the wood, and it looked as though it would disintegrate if I tried to peel it away. I scanned the clearing across from our house. Someone had stood right here, on our doorstep where so few had stood.

That night, lying on my stomach in the dark, when it felt like the house had taken an inhale and swelled on all sides, and there was more space in which to say things, I opened my mouth. "Pei," I said, "someone taped a paper to our door."

Pei-Pei's blurry figure beside me shifted. "I know," she said.

"Do you know what it means?"

"I know what I think it means." Pei-Pei's voice was more uncertain than it sounded during the day. There was a depth to her voice, of something suppressed.

"What?"

Instead of answering me, she rustled her way out of her blanket. As she sat up, the fabric fell away from her, so that she emerged from its soft, dark mass, stripped to her core.

"What does it mean?"

She reached over and put a hand on my forehead. It was a

strange touch—not at all like my mother, who, when feeling for a fever over and over, made you sense she was beckoning one. Instead, it seemed as though Pei-Pei were passing something on to me, palm to forehead, some kind of immunity or resilience. It stilled me. I sank deeper into my mattress.

I was almost asleep when she said, "It's happening soon."

"What's happening?"

"I think our house won't be our house anymore."

In the warm nest of our massive bed, formed from our three individual beds, I thought this a silly statement. At that moment we were burrowing deeper under our shared blankets—stowed away in our beds, in our room, in our house, which was filled with no one's troubles but ours.

13

AFTER MY FATHER HAD STACKED MY PARENTS' MATTRESS, the kitchen table, a few folding chairs, and several suitcases and crates in the bed of the truck, he began shoving things into the foot wells. His packing became half-hearted. Nothing more would fit in the truck, and we'd sold the station wagon. In the den, my mother unbuttoned the canvas cover of a couch cushion and slipped her hand in to feel the velour. The glimpse of maroon was a shock; I had forgotten there was a different fabric underneath.

At the store, Pei-Pei and I had been allowed to choose the couch from two options. My parents had eased it into the house with newspapers wedged between the rails and the tight doorway. My father held one end inside the front door, and my mother was outside, and for a long time they were frozen in that halfway state for fear of damaging it. From behind the stack of cushions in her arms, Pei-Pei kept saying, "Just push it," like a taunt. When finally it was in, and set in its place, we fought to sit on it, to see how different it felt in our home than at the store. It did feel different. Then all six of us managed to squeeze onto it, someone holding Ruby, and probably Natty, too, and Pei-Pei declared that our house was all right.

"Are we going on vacation?" I asked.

From the doorway my father whispered, "Yes, vacation."

Pei-Pei grabbed my hand and yanked me around the corner. In the kitchen, the cupboards and pantry were open, and two brown grocery bags squatted on the floor, nearly splitting, jammed with cereals in rolled-up bags, stale pretzels, and other half-consumed snacks that had been languishing in the recesses of the cupboards.

"Have we ever been on vacation?" she asked.

"No."

"Use your head."

"My head says vacation."

For two weekends every summer, the Dolans drove to the Kenai Peninsula and came home with coolers full of fish to stock their freezer through winter. It got hot down there, Ada said. Not the river water, which was iced by glaciers, but the air. It heated you past your skin. I wondered where the weather took this turn—maybe where the highway hooked around the tip of Turnagain Arm. We had driven south along the inlet before, but only up to the ghost forests. The coastline there had sunk during the Good Friday earthquake, and the spruce forests had guzzled salt water and died. Decades later, the silvery skeletons of those trees still stood, petrified by salt and leaning drunkenly, some nearly horizontal. It might be there, in the bewitched space where trees defied time and gravity, that the world shifted.

"I want to go fishing," I said.

"When has anyone in this whole house ever mentioned fishing?"

"I just want to go."

Pei-Pei shook my arm so my whole body wobbled. "What's wrong with you?"

My father leaned against one side of the doorway and said, "Don't fight today."

"It's not my fault," Pei-Pei said. "When people are idiots, we don't do them any favors by pretending they're not."

"Don't call your brother an idiot," my father said, in a voice so weary it suggested he believed I was an idiot, too. But then he asked me, "Where do you want to go on vacation?"

"Fiji," Pei-Pei said.

"Kenai," I said. "Seward."

"All right," he said. "We'll go."

Pei-Pei's nostrils shrank and flared as she contemplated my father. Finally she said, "I'm done with you," and pushed past him. She kicked the closet door on the way to the stairs. We heard her rapid, ascending thumps.

My father's neck was shining with sweat. He wiped the side of it with his wrist, then did it again and again. With Pei-Pei, just a certain phrasing, a certain inflection, could make you wonder what was so repulsive about yourself, and how to get rid of it.

"Where are we going?" Natty asked. He had come in from the front yard, where he'd silently watched the procession of furniture and crates to the truck. "I don't want to go any-where."

"A little vacation," my father said. "You know what that means? It means we're leaving home to have fun."

"I want to stay here."

"Well," my father said, "you've never been anywhere else, but you'll see." He put his hand on Natty's head.

"No," Natty said. "I won't leave."

My father scooped him up and tipped him sideways. Natty was too old to be held like that, and I waited for him to kick his way down. But he turned limp. With the pad of his thumb, my father rubbed a spot in the very center of Natty's forehead. I could almost feel the pressure, or the memory of that pressure, on my own head. I turned away from their exchange.

In our bedroom, Pei-Pei was kneeling on her bed with her face smashed into the mattress. She took deep breaths, as though trying to smell something all the way on the other side of the bed, underneath it.

"What are you doing?" I asked.

She jerked up. "I forgot to grab this." She jammed her loose, lumpy pillow into her lap. Her whole face was red from how hard she had pressed it, practically suffocating herself. She turned away and began to sort through scraps of paper at the foot of her bed—notes from her friends, saved school programs, candy wrappers with some kind of meaning. I did not have such things, whose worth was a thrilling shared secret.

I stood at the window. The fireweeds edging the driveway looked blighted as they spit ruined cobwebs from their brown stalks.

"You still think we're going on vacation?" Pei-Pei asked.

I nodded.

She shoved a few scraps into her pocket. "Get out," she said, no longer with malice, and flipped a thumb at the door.

On the way, I put a hand on the wall, on top of the sun-bleached butcher paper with my father's childlike scrawl. It crackled at my touch. When I gave the edge a tug, it came down easily, the tape apparently ready to give in.

Pei-Pei followed me down the stairs. The front door was wide open, and my mother was standing on the first step, taller than my father. He bent to pick up the book Natty had left in the doorway.

"Why won't you answer me?" my mother said.

My father opened the book. It was a hardcover about flower arrangements, pulled from a library crate.

"Is it time to go yet?" Pei-Pei asked. "Aren't we all packed?"

"No," my mother said. "There's something I can't find."

My father turned a page and smoothed it. It was cool and glossy, I knew, with pictures of artificial flowers being stabbed into foam.

My mother whipped around, barely aware of Pei-Pei and me, and charged up the stairs. I followed her into her bedroom and the big closet, where she started pulling shoeboxes off the shelves. When they tumbled down and the lids fell off, familiar yet miraculous objects landed at my feet. Things I hadn't seen in years, that had stopped existing for me, were rematerializing. A shirt with a faded tomato that all four of us kids had worn. An ice-blue teething toy in the shape of a pretzel. The past was taking shape on the floor.

"She's gone," my mother said.

It dawned on me then what she was looking for. And that she would not find it.

My mother spun around in the closet. "For the garbage," she said. "Everything is for the garbage." Half of the clothes had been removed from their hangers, and my mother finished the job, yanking what remained and flinging it to the carpet. She reeled into the ravaged bedroom. Bundles of old clothing had been excavated from under the bed and opened, spilled in heaps like snowdrifts.

My mother lurched to the top of the stairs. She hollered down, "What did you do with her? Don't lie to me."

Pei-Pei was still standing at the bottom, and the back of my father's figure was visible through the open frame. I took a step down and stopped.

"Where is she? Where is Ruby?"

My father did not turn to look at me. Pei-Pei gave me an astonished look, then hit my father in the shoulder. "What is she talking about?" Pei-Pei said. She hit him again. "What did you do?"

The longer my father stayed silent, the more he incriminated himself; even I saw someone past the question of forgiveness. As he turned slightly toward Pei-Pei, he leaned to one side, as though his spine had grown crooked. The sparse hairs of his sideburns were unruly. His thin waxed-cotton jacket was zipped all the way closed. He looked like a man who was on his way out because no one wanted him to stay.

"Tell me now or you will regret it," my mother said.

"What's going on?" Pei-Pei asked.

"He wanted to leave her here, in this place he thinks is so grand." My mother breathed rapidly into my head. I felt moist heat on the back of one ear. "So he threw her away."

"Threw her away?" Pei-Pei's voice was strained. "What does she mean?"

My father finally closed the book and turned around to face

us, though he wouldn't meet my eyes. "Our time is up," he said. "We have to go."

"Tell me," my mother said. "Will I find her in the house?"

My father worked his mouth in a way that hollowed out his face. "No."

I was the first one to move. "Vacation," I said, and tore down the stairs and out the door. The sudden whiteness of the sky stung my eyes and stopped me in my tracks. Clouds coursed past our house and appeared to be converging behind the clearing.

I turned to the driveway and with dismay saw Ada standing right on it, a few feet from the truck where our furniture was piled helter-skelter. She held one good stick in each hand. Probably one of them was meant for me. I couldn't run back inside; she had already seen me. Her mouth was slack and partly open. She stared at me, and then at my father, and then at me. Her sticks drooped to rest in the dirt. The front door had been wide open. What had been said? In what language, in what tone? What had she understood?

I didn't want to go anywhere near the truck; I wanted to disown it. But I made myself keep moving. "We're not free today," I shouted at her, spending all the gaiety I had ever had. "We're going to Seward for vacation." I scrambled into the cab of the truck and slid into the bench seat in the back. After my father climbed in, I waved at Natty urgently.

He squatted beside the step and jammed his chin into his hands.

"Come on," I said.

"I won't go," he yelled. "I won't."

———

WE DROVE SOUTH, toward the ghost trees. On our left, the familiar yellow and green mountains of the Chugach range swelled and dipped. Dark, dense shadows passed over them, so it seemed a fleet of airships might be sailing overhead, but when I looked above, there were only unremarkable clouds.

It was the distant mountains on our right, across the inlet, that we didn't know, and it was this range I studied as we wound around Turnagain Arm. These mountains were blue and brooding, still splattered with snow. They had been cheated of sun and warmth and gentle slopes on which grass and wildflowers could grow and stain the ground with color. Constant landslides had left them cragged.

Natty was crying, but he was so quiet that my parents might not have known. Drops hung on the edge of his upper lip, fattening before they broke.

When we reached the ghost trees, my father pointed out the remnant of a collapsed house. It was surrounded by a marsh that had formed when the earthquake had sunk most of the town. Only the caving top half of the cabin was visible. "Roof," he said, and cleared his throat as though more words were coming—but it was a false alarm.

I began to chatter. I tried to forget Ada. As my father took an unannounced detour off the highway, I pointed out everything we passed. The railroad crossing. The hawk perched on a broken branch. Far off, the waterfall of blue ice suspended mid-cascade down a mountainside. As we drove along the curving spur road bordered by aspens, the ice came in and out of view.

Eventually the road forked, and the route we took ended right at the massive frozen waterfall, which spilled jaggedly into a lake. I read the sign aloud. This cold blue mass was Portage Glacier, and the lake was eight hundred feet deep.

"See that? Eight hundred feet, it says. How long do you think it would take to sink to the bottom?" I was just talking, just making sound. It wasn't until later that night, when I closed my eyes and tried to sleep, that the fact of the lake's depth caught up to me and disturbed the pumping of my heart.

The brand-new visitors' center was closed and the restrooms were locked. A hard wind cut through the valley. We passed around some snacks while my father moved the table and crates around the bed of the truck. From inside the cab, we heard a great deal of scraping. When my father had finished clearing space on the large mattress, my mother went out and fastened a tarp over it. We brushed our teeth and washed our faces in the cold, low stream of a drinking fountain. While my face was wet, my mother ran back to the truck to look for a towel, but by the time she returned, my face was dry and chilled. Everything took three times as long as at home, and by the time we were all done peeing in the shrubs, it was well into night.

In a mass of blankets and towels, my mother slept with us. My father dozed practically upright in the driver's seat, leaning on a pillow over the steering wheel. That he avoided sounding the horn all night seemed only to confirm his weightlessness, his inconsequence. "No one would even believe me," Pei-Pei said the next morning. "Our whole family in the back of the truck."

When I said, "Not the whole family," she gave me a confused look.

For hours I lay stiffly, trying not to bump Natty, who was curled into my side. His fist dug into my ribs. My mother's arm extended over his head and into my territory. It didn't touch me but I sensed it there, her hand somewhere near my neck. The tarp that sagged over us made a darkened space, and I was glad for it. There had been too many stars out and no moon to keep them fixed in the sky, to keep them from whirling. But even with our view cut off, it was impossible to erase the feeling of the unoccupied parking spaces around us. So many freshly painted rectangles and no cars. To one side was an empty building, to the other, empty roads. I thought of sinking, with eight hundred feet to go. The cold air hurt the back of my throat.

14

THE NEXT DAY, WE CAUGHT GLIMPSES OF THE KENAI RIVER from the road. The opaque river coursed with water so turquoise, the trees and surrounding land seemed faded. My father pulled off into a small dirt lot, and we sprang from the truck. As we approached the bank, we could see fly fishermen casting with their thin, curved wands, trying to enchant fish out of the water. Though most toed the bank, a few stood, splendidly, right in the glimmering river, dipped to their waists. Behind them, on the other side of the water, was a small stand of Sitka spruces and two mountains heavily patched with snow. Some of the fishermen wore puffy coats, but where we stood on solid ground, the air was warm. The heat, the turquoise water, the glinting sun—they were swallowing us into a different world. I could almost believe what I had been selling. We were on vacation.

We stood captivated. It wasn't long before a fisherman on the bank shouted. His rod was deeply curved, and the tip of it trembled. He reeled the line in, stepping into the river so the water sloshed around his waders. The hooked fish skipped in a zigzag pattern that approached the bank. Just a few feet from where we stood, the fisherman trapped the fish against the ground with his hands. As it flopped, he cut its gills, which bled.

"A bonanza," said his friend, who raised a bent arm to recast.

The first man tinkered with the fish's mouth.

"String her up," said his friend. He gave a jut of the chin to a murky area in the water. I followed his gaze to a dense school of big silver fish swimming close to the bank. But when the fisherman tied a string to a tree and released his fish into the water there, I understood that these were dead fish, all of the fish they had caught, being iced in the river.

"Salmon," my mother informed us, pronouncing it "saulmon," but the fisherman squatting by the tree understood her. He said in our direction, "It's a good morning for silvers."

My father echoed, "A good morning."

"Got a line to wet?" he asked my father.

My father hunched over and contorted his face into a smile that showed no teeth. He nodded to the fishermen and ushered us away, back toward our truck with its jumbled contents.

In the lot my mother picked up a small dip net leaning against the clunky bear-proof garbage bin. The handle was snapped off, and the net was separating from the hoop.

"Don't think you're bringing that with us," my father said.

"Why are you raising your voice?"

"There's no room for more junk."

"It's not junk." My mother rubbed the uneven end where the handle was missing. "We don't need that part." She turned the net over. "And this is nothing. I can tie it with floss."

My father stormed to the driver's seat. "You should listen to me," he said. "Someone should." My mother followed, holding the dip net against her hip and swaggering a little.

We climbed back into the truck and drove on. We hit a beach at low tide, walked along the snaking edges of the wet sand, collected kelp and a few intact shells, and turned around again. Everyone was saying gas prices were low, low, low, falling, falling, and we drove wastefully, exploring forks in the road and backtracking. In Soldotna, we found room for our truck at a campground, mostly RVs parked along a dirt loop, their elaborate wings and extensions creating outdoor dining rooms furnished with folding chairs and card tables.

My mother could not stop craning her neck, for she was curious about what people ate, and how, and this must have been the most access she had ever had. Pei-Pei and I were more preoccupied with hiding our own dinner, corn and Spam straight from the cans, supplemented with handfuls of the yellow kelp that my mother had made us gather on the beach. The kelp didn't taste bad—a little briny, a little pickly—but we hid it in our hands and nibbled at it so that another kid watching us might have assumed we were popping M&M's or Reese's Pieces. Although there were several hours of daylight left, many of the RVs had fires going on the side, and Natty kept asking for his own. He hadn't talked much all day, or maybe at all; now he sounded like a caveman, or a primitive creature bargaining with the gods. "Make me fire. I want fire, too."

"All right," my mother said. "Ask someone to help you. I saw lots of dead branches in the woods between the outhouses and the river."

"Where are you going?" I asked. She had one arm through her winter coat and had pulled on her boots without my noticing.

"I'm going to catch some fish."

My father chortled. "With that piece of trash?"

My mother slid her lower jaw forward and held his gaze until he scratched his nose and looked away.

"Can I come?" I asked.

"It'll be dark soon," she said. "Too dark for you." She stepped up onto the rear bumper of the truck and leaned over the tailgate. "I just need to find the flashlight that works."

After she left with her dip net, Natty and my father worked on gathering wood by the river. It took six or seven trips for them to heap together branches and break them down. Dead leaves still clung to many of them, and when the fire caught, the leaves flamed individually before the fire settled into the wood. We each wrapped a blanket around ourselves, except for Natty, who shared one with Pei-Pei. They sat on a rock that seesawed beneath their weight. She lifted her arms so the blanket made wings around them and said, "This is the story of a boy who disappeared from a camp near a river."

Inside their pupa, Natty wriggled. His fingers curled around the edges of the blanket. He peered out with one eye. "And they found him?" he asked.

"I guess you could say they found him," Pei-Pei said. "They did find a few pieces that belonged to him. The smallest part was his tonsils, which looked like two peas stuck together."

"All right," my father said. "All right."

I asked him how many fish he thought my mother had caught by now.

"I used to catch fish, too," he said.

"You?"

Outside his house, he said, there had been a series of drain channels that fed into a deep trench. After storms, he could climb a fence with friends, jump into the overflowing trench, and catch tiny fish with a mesh strainer. He kept them in a jar, but they never lived beyond a few days, so he started feeding them to his neighbor's turtle. The turtle always ate them in the same order: tail, head, body.

When the blaze crept onto the large branch that jutted toward me, I could feel the jumpy heat on my face; it alternated with the cool breeze. I fell asleep with my elbow on a rock. My father must have added wood, for I woke a few times to a greater warmth and let my blanket fall away.

I woke to the sound of sizzling. My mother was soaked, and her sleeves were dripping water onto the fire. The flashlight was shoved in her chest pocket, the top of it sticking out to illuminate a diagonal stripe across her face. "Success," she said. She hugged a bulging plastic bag to her stomach. The top handles had stretched and ripped, and the wind lifted them like flimsy ribbons.

"Did you go for a night swim?" Pei-Pei asked.

My mother's laugh bounded away from her. "I'm not afraid of a little water," she said. "Water is afraid of me." She was shivering.

My father threw our wool blanket over her head. "Dry yourself," he said.

She shook it off. "I want to prepare the fish."

"I'll do it."

"You don't know how to clean them."

He rustled a leafy branch at the fire, creating a great plume of smoke.

"I caught five." My mother crouched and turned the opening of the bag toward me, as though showing me the face of a bundled baby. "One of them is very big. Don't you think I did pretty well?" My mother started laughing again. "There are bears," my father said. "You should care about that."

My mother continued to speak only to me, but a touch too loudly. "You should have seen me in the river. I could have caught enough to fill the whole truck, but I only brought one bag."

With a knife, my mother gutted the smallest fish, a trout, she said. She balanced a frying pan right on top of the fire. The bottom of the pan blackened almost instantly. Soon the smell of crisped fish wafted around with the breeze. When we peeled bits of the meat from the pan, we found it unevenly cooked, but my mother said it was fine, the fish was fresh, it was practically still alive. "This is the way to eat it," she said. "Not frozen and thawed and frozen and thawed until it's been dead for longer than it's been alive."

"Come eat," Pei-Pei said, but my father would not. Three empty beer cans sat in a neat line by his feet, and he held the precious fourth one with both hands. In the truck I slept next to his stash of liquor and beer, and I knew it was diminishing.

I wanted the RV families to see us, eating our fish by our fire just as they had. But they were asleep or watching TV, their windows dark or flickering blue. They saw us only the next

morning, cooking another fish on a dirty pan for breakfast, the
fire practically buried under ash, while they were milling around
with their coffee mugs and clean plastic bowls of cereal. Soon
they had all driven away, on to another site or off to the river
for the day, and we were the only ones left. My mother set two
chairs in the sun and rigged the long handle of a shovel between
them. She cut the remaining fish into strips and salted them,
then hung them from the handle to dry.

My mother triumphed again several days later when our
father drove us to Ninilchik, where razor clams lived unseen.
The clams burrowed quickly—some of them were the size of
bananas, each one a perfect digging muscle—and only my
mother seemed to know exactly where to sink her shovel so that
one big thrust of sand would throw the surprised clam onto
the surface of the beach. The more clams my mother dug up, the
closer my father drifted to the water. Finally he stood in it to
his shins, his bare feet likely numb. I was sent to retrieve him.

I tapped his back. "We're done. Let's go."

"Go without me," he said.

"Come on," I said. "It's time to go home."

He whirled around with a look of devastation. "Go where?"

That night we feasted on the huge clams, boiled right in a
pot of rice. My father ate around the clams and shoveled heap-
ing spoonfuls of rice into his mouth, barely chewing before he
swallowed.

"I have this for you, my Natty." My mother giggled over her
cupped hands, then opened them slowly to reveal the circular
plastic piece shoved into pizzas, the thing that kept the box from
sticking to the cheese. "A tiny table," she said. "A table for snails
and crabs. You can put it in your castles of sand."

Natty took it from her and held it by one leg. We had lost track of the days. Someone should have given him a pad of clean, thick paper to draw on. One whole week had passed, and it was his birthday.

———

ONE EVENING, my mother decided she wanted to cut her hair. She made a racket rustling around in our crates for the scissors, but it was a weeknight and the campground was almost completely vacant. Four sites away were a single truck and its attached trailer, and a few sites after that was an old RV with a missing door. Farther down the loop, near the outhouses, a pair of tents had been staked into the dirt. That was all. Scraps of litter from the weekend blew around.

"Where are the scissors?" my mother sang. She had not slept the night before.

"You were the last to use them," Pei-Pei said.

My mother giggled. "That's true. My hair is growing so fast. The fresh air, the sea. It's good for our bodies."

"If that's how you want to think," Pei-Pei said.

"How could it not be?" My mother gestured at Natty and me. "Look at their hair. They look like girls."

By the time she finally gave up on the scissors, it was nearly dark. We all followed the weak and trembling ray of my mother's flashlight to the outhouses. Pei-Pei washed our spoons and forks at the faucet labeled POTABLE. I stood brushing my teeth behind her and spitting toothpaste in foamy clumps on the ground. My father spent a long time in the single working stall, and then we all took turns. The wind picked up while we waited.

When we returned to our site, my mother dashed to the truck. Beside it, tossed on the ground, were two of our crates and their contents. Our table was upturned, and my father lifted it to check if it was broken. My mother jumped the flashlight from item to item: my coat, my sister's underwear, a can of peaches.

My mother ran back to the path. Her head swiveled left and right. "They must be close," she said.

"Forget it," my father said. "I don't think they took anything."

"There isn't anything to take." Pei-Pei picked up a pillow and dusted it off by whacking it.

My father climbed into the truck bed. He knelt as he tidied the mess. Every few minutes my mother or Pei-Pei made exclamations, discovering another belonging that had been touched, opened, or tossed aside by someone we didn't know. My father produced no sound. After everything had been put away, he climbed into the driver's seat and placed his hands on the steering wheel. His dim figure stooped forward as he faced a thick cluster of trees straight ahead.

The rest of us lay on the mattress, and sleep was slow in coming. I kicked at the space to my side. There was more room there now. I reached out and touched nothing but the cold metal of the truck. My father's stash was gone.

My mother had the most trouble staying still, and the entire truck jolted and trembled as she jiggled each leg or knocked into furniture. The leaves swished in the trees. They were louder now than they'd been before, though they were not the problem. Finally my mother slept. Very late, at two or three in the morning, I heard snapping branches and a peal of cutting laughter from the river.

15

WE STARTED THE DRIVE BACK. WITHOUT DETOURS, OUR
journey was startlingly efficient, and soon we were approaching
Portage again. At a gas station, Pei-Pei and I were allowed to buy
a large bag of Cheetos while my father filled up. A girl with
honey-colored hair gave us change and told us to stop at Bird
Point to watch the bore tide, which was sure to be ten feet high
that day. "Low tide in Anchorage was around two today, and the
wind is blowing"—she stepped around the counter and squinted
at the bent tips of three little spruces in the parking lot—"west.
So it'll be early. I would get there before four, to be safe. It'll be
a good one today, I know it. I saw the moon last night."

"Does she think she's a witch?" Pei-Pei whispered as we
stepped out of the store.

In the back, we smeared orange streaks on each other's arms.
Every time Pei-Pei passed the bag to me, she said, "Hail,
Cheeser." The wind made a ripping sound beside her, though
the window was rolled up as far as it would go.

At Bird Point, we stopped and stood on a cliff. Jittery aspens fluttered on one side of us. The undersides of the leaves were a paler green than the tops, and as each leaf twisted on its stem, the trees flickered. Below us, a cluster of trees had turned gold, a suspended shower of coins. We waited a long time in the gusty wind.

"She was wrong," Pei-Pei said. "The witch was wrong."

"Have faith," my father said.

"I don't," Pei-Pei said.

When the bore tide came, we were so far above the water, it looked like nothing more than a length of white yarn. The line was pulled taut and then bent out of shape as a leading point formed. Seagulls hovered over the froth at the tip of it, where there must have been fish caught in the turbulence.

"Marvelous," my father said. All five of us gazed down at the thin line of foam.

The bore tide was formed by the outgoing tide of the inlet crashing against the incoming high tide from the ocean, creating a surge of water that could travel for thirty or forty miles down Turnagain Arm. It headed in the opposite direction of our travels, and my mother watched it silently as though wishing to follow.

Across the inlet were the cold blue mountains that held on to snow. We had driven into them and back out, but they looked no more familiar now. Small clouds hovered above their peaks, as if they'd spoken but we had missed what they'd said.

AS WE DRIFTED through Anchorage, my mother clung to the grab handle above her seat. Pei-Pei and Natty were not wearing seat belts, and they huddled to one side of the truck with their hands clamped between their knees. They looked like hostages.

The diminishing sun turned the thin clouds sulfurous. We had driven more in the last two weeks than in my entire lifetime. A road was just a feeling now. Of being stagnant in the midst of motion. Of things rushing to meet you and then fleeing.

Without warning, my mother grabbed my father's arm, and we all careened to the left. We went bouncing off the road, across the shoulder, and into a huge patch of daylilies.

"They're blooming so late," my mother marveled. She ignored my father's sputtering. She bent over to grab a pot wedged beneath her seat. Outside, she squatted and riffled through the flowers, searching for long, yellow buds, which she pinched from their stems. Cars were few, but the six or seven that passed by were enough to make Pei-Pei screech—about what people should and should not do in broad daylight, and how we were animals, escapees, clowns.

My father rolled down the window. "People can see you." His words were short and sharp, as though additional speech had been hacked away.

"Drive," Pei-Pei urged. She kicked the back of his seat. "Now's your chance. Do it. Do it."

My mother stood and tipped the pot to show us it was only two-thirds full. "If you all help," she said, "we can fill an extra bag." She tapped my window, but I didn't respond. I was sinking into the bench seat, softened from driving all day, every day, without any destination.

"Get in," my father shouted.

My mother wrinkled up her whole face from her forehead to her chin and climbed into the passenger seat. She hugged the pot over her lap.

As we approached the gravel turnoff to our house, my father sped up instead of slowing. He took the turn so hard I caught air, and somewhere behind us, crates slammed against one side of the truck bed. We came to a haphazard stop in the driveway, with two tires disappearing into the weed-engulfed lawn.

We sat processing the fact that we were home. My father was the only one moving; he ran to the front door and then back to the truck, and in my daze it seemed as though he were playing a game by himself, tagging arbitrary surfaces. A frenzied game, to prove to onlookers he was having a good time, the best time, he was fine on his own. As he unlatched the tailgate, Pei-Pei and I opened the passenger doors and fell out of either side. It was difficult to straighten my legs, and the gravel beneath my sneakers shifted and stirred.

Pei-Pei put her arms around Natty to pull him out and said, "I think you need a shower."

My mother was still sitting in the passenger seat with her seat belt on. When I opened her door, in addition to the flowers I could smell the staleness of the cab, like sheets that had sat damp for days.

"I'll stay here awhile," she said.

"Aren't you tired of the truck?"

"Yes."

"Don't you want to go in?"

"No."

My father rushed the house with a hammer. When he reached the door, he took a swing.

There were several more cracks as my father hit the doorknob, then a duller, heavier sound as he missed and struck the door again. We left our mother and approached. There were two half circles on the wood, like a giant's fingernail imprints.

"Step away!" my father yelled. The back of his neck was very brown and sun-damaged, and it was the scaly texture of his skin, more than anything else, that made me retreat.

"They changed the locks," Pei-Pei said.

My father grunted. "See if that can keep me out."

"You can get us back in?"

"Of course," he said. He flipped the hammer around with one hand and began to use the claw end on the doorknob plate. "It's easy if you know how these things work in the first place."

Eventually he worked the claw under the plate, but even when he had wiggled the knob loose, it wouldn't come all the way off. He yanked the knob toward himself, and it slid out an inch, but the knob on the other end held tight.

"Maybe pull a little harder?" Pei-Pei suggested.

My father straightened and raised the hammer to the side, then took two swings so wild, Pei-Pei stumbled off the step in alarm. The knob and other metal parts clattered onto the step. A screw bounced off the cement into the grass.

My father nodded in satisfaction, then tilted his face to gaze at a spot above our heads. He thirsted for our praise. We took in the door; it was covered in gouges and scratches.

My father stuck his fingers straight through the hole where the doorknob had been and pulled the door open. Natty darted past me. I stood in the entryway. Our house had been raided. Our junk—gone. As I drifted from the empty den to the empty kitchen, I saw that a few stray objects remained. Already they seemed like artifacts: a mostly empty bottle of rice wine in the cabinet, a shoelace, the dead ficus tree. Two books lying face-down in the corner of the den that must have slid off the crates. Natty would be glad for them. *The Amateur Aquarist*, with its photos of aquarium pumps and vibrant fish, and *Automotive Mechanics Volume II*, full of diagrams.

"They still work," my father said, flipping the lights on. He toggled the switch back and forth. It was hard to see the change in the broad daylight. I left him to find Pei-Pei and Natty.

Even more than the downstairs, it was a shock to see that our bedroom was completely bare. Pei-Pei stood where the dresser had been. She chewed on the knuckles of her fist, then examined her teeth marks on her skin.

"I found something," said a small voice from the closet. I opened the door wider and found Natty squatting in the very back corner and looking snug in the tight space. He was pinch-ing something between his fingers and holding it up to us. It may have been the only item left in the room: a green plastic house from Monopoly, dug out from between the closet wall and the carpet edge. He sat there scratching at the tiny chim-ney, so small I had never noticed it before, a little blip that might as easily have been a manufacturing defect. It forced me to re-call how, when I could convince Pei-Pei to play the game with me, Natty and Ruby would line up the houses and hotels along the side of the board, fixated on their own unfathomable game. Ruby would sit on her shins with her feet pointed in opposite directions, breathing out of the side of her mouth.

"I see," I said, and backed away.

From the window I saw my father carrying a box toward the house, a cardboard flap hinging up and down in front of his face. A minute later, he reappeared to unload a crate from the truck bed. My mother's figure still haunted the passenger seat. The clouds were stuck in the darkening sky, the wind was on hiatus, and it seemed to me that nothing was in motion out there except my father, who was single-handedly trying to fill the empty house back up.

On his hands and knees, Natty emerged from the closet. He was grinning. He didn't care that our room was completely empty, or that there was nowhere to sit. He was where he wanted to be.

When I looked out the window again, the truck was gone.

I went downstairs. "Where is my mother?" I asked.

"Getting groceries," my father said.

"What groceries? What store? How long will she be gone?"

My father paused with his knee under a crate.

"Is she really going to the store?"

"Where else would she be going?" he asked, but he knitted his eyebrows together and then released them, his expression wilting.

"Is she coming back?" I asked.

He put the crate down with a thunk, and I saw that he did not know.

She did come back. She hugged the big pot with one arm, and in her other hand was a clear plastic bag of pork bones. The bones were thick and neatly cut, and they sat in a little blood.

My mother simmered the bones for hours. My father set up the kitchen table and folding chairs. He slid a few things into the cupboard. We sat around the table, and Pei-Pei sank her head onto her arms. We had returned. This was our old kitchen with its jaundiced light. It wasn't just that it was emptier. It felt smaller when it should have felt bigger. The air was stale and thin, full of every exhale we had ever taken here. At the stove, my mother added the daylily buds to her soup. She lifted the lid and leaned her face into the billows of vapor.

"Where are the spoons?" she asked.

No one offered to find them. My mother dipped our bowls straight into the pot and placed them, wet, in front of each of us.

"Eat," she said. "Then we sleep."

Eat and sleep, I thought. All I could foresee was more eating and more sleeping, and the struggle to eat, and the struggle to sleep, on and on, without a wisp of hope for more.

My mother leaned way over and nearly kissed Natty as she blew at the shimmering dots of oil in his bowl. "Go on," she said to him. "It's cool enough."

When he still didn't eat, my mother started in on her own soup. "It's good," she said. "So good. It reminds me of when I was your age." She bared her teeth. "Doesn't it taste just right?" Her eyes flashed above her tipped-up bowl.

It was the first time she had spoken to my father in hours. He reared up, brought to life. He gasped. "It's just right, just right. I feel like I'm there." He seemed to be in pain.

I nibbled on the end of a flower bud, then lifted it to examine it in the light. The buds were long, slender, and closed, with a little nub at the bottom where they had been attached to the stem. They had a turnip-like flavor with an odd stringiness and crunch, a texture like thin asparagus or mushroom stems. I could hear my mother's teeth working the fibers.

When all that was left in our bowls were the bones and a protein film, my mother and father stared at the remnants and seemed to see something in them. Their bodies were slightly swaying. Maybe all that exuberant posturing really had transported them. To a different place, a different time. A table in a dark, oily room with a packed-earth floor. Dim lights that flickered from voltage sags.

"Things are changing," my mother said. Her voice was different when she spoke only to him and without discernible anger. Less musical, less inflected, almost serene. It was rare to hear this voice of hers, and I strained to fix it in my mind. "There's an opposition party now," she said. "It's a good time to go back."

"Are you kidding?" my father said. "In another year they'll all be jailed as Communist spies."

"How do you know?" she said. "We're not there. Things are not frozen in place just because we left." She sounded so reasonable, so dignified, so unlike herself, I found myself nodding.

My father stood up. "I won't talk about this anymore."

Like that, the voice was gone. She snatched Natty's bowl, then mine, then lunged across the table for Pei-Pei's. "It's time for bed," she said. She turned away from us all and looked at the dark den with its single mattress and its promise of watered-down sleep.

16

CHILDREN IN THE MIDDLE, PARENTS ON THE OUTSIDE. OUR arrangement kept Pei-Pei from sneaking out at night. But I liked it exactly like this, pinned between Pei-Pei and Natty. Three stacked blankets weighed upon us. My father said we had to conserve what propane was left in the tank, so we turned the furnace on for two hours after dinner, and flipped it off again as we dug under the pile of blankets. It surprised me how warm Natty was, and I worried he was radiating more heat than he should, the smallest of us, giving away all he had.

In the morning, the sun assaulted us. The windows were naked, and the light blazed through. Someone stirred, shifting us all into wakefulness. My mother sat up with her hair thrust to one side, and Natty rolled back and forth over his spot in a fight to hold on to sleep. He peeped at us from two barely open eyes, then shut them tight. Wariness drew his features together.

School, with its orderliness, felt foreign. I wasn't sure what

Natty had said about our absence. Most likely nothing. But maybe his silence had been strange and thick. Mrs. Reardon, a third-grade social studies teacher who wore skirts above calves that curved outward, began to follow him around. She shuffled beside him to lunch or class or the buses.

In the evenings, Natty sometimes piped up to speak of her. "Winnie makes jelly from fireweed, and she's going to bring us a jar to try." He might have been the only student ever to call her Winnie in the history of our school, though she requested it every year, of every new batch of students. When they were together, Mrs. Reardon looked ecstatic, and Natty looked, amazingly, like any other kid—shoelaces untied, mouth moving as words tumbled out, scratching a dirty spot on his neck.

"Winnie says there used to be bears in our woods," Natty said.

"She's a loony," I said. She wasn't even his teacher, and I didn't know what she was doing with him. That she would profess to know our woods—these depths we had entered daily and still did not know—irked me.

Still, he continued to speak of her. The sun was setting at seven, and we spent more time in the dark. My father didn't like us to use the lights; he was afraid someone would see. Before bed we relied on flashlights, and when the batteries died, we used fat candles with tunnels melted down the center of them so that even when they were lit, they barely glowed. Anything Natty said in those hours seemed infected by another presence; his voice and face trembled, and he even occasionally laughed, a disembodied sound.

Eventually the candles ran out of wick and nights ran colder, especially by the windows. The old woodstove we'd never used, with its dual possibilities of light and warmth, rose to sudden prominence. After a few attempts that smoked us out of the house, my mother conquered it. We celebrated her triumph with genuine joy. Into the stove went the first of the firewood my mother had collected after the record storms in July. We made them last longer by also throwing in twisted newspapers, twigs, cardboard boxes, and anything that looked suggestible to the idea of burning.

The refrigerator was off, but we stored food in there anyway to keep out the ants. During the last hard rain, they had taken refuge indoors, teeming along our kitchen windowsill and the baseboards. We used to have a vacuum with a long plastic nozzle that I would point at trails of ants, and though they dispersed in all directions, I was good at chasing them down. Now our vacuum was gone, and Natty used his thumb instead, like a love stamp. He was too slow; more ants came. Pei-Pei and I were hyperaware of them, brushing off our arms when we felt the slightest tingle, jumping up and shaking out our legs for no real reason. When I gazed at the blank walls of the den, I saw crawling specks, but upon closer inspection, nothing was there at all—just the agitated ghosts of the ants Natty kept squashing one by one.

"I found where they're coming in," Pei-Pei said. "There's a hole under the window that you can't see unless you put your head right on the floor."

"Who cares," my mother said, "if they're not biting. And even the biting ones won't kill you." She was in a good mood because she had overheard a conversation at the Qwik Stop. Septic tanks were mysteriously failing all over Anchorage, which meant work for my father.

"I care," Pei-Pei said. "I'm getting out of here."

"Take your brothers. They're soft as boiled turnips."

As we put on our shoes, Pei-Pei whispered to me, "Don't think I'm going anywhere with you."

"Are you going to find Collin?"

"No." She kicked me in the shin with the toe of her hard shoe. "You don't know anything." Though I managed to keep from wincing or rubbing the spot, I knew it would leave a bruise.

Outside, she hurried toward the gravel road.

"Where are you going?" I called.

She made a shooing motion.

I thought of following her, to see which way she would turn once she reached the big road. But I wanted to see Ada. It had been weeks since we'd played outside, such a long time. "Come on," I said to Natty, who was struggling to pull the door closed. In the end, he left it ajar. We tramped the weeds down in the side and back yards, then found the subtle parting in the long grasses. As always, it invited us to enter the woods.

———

WHEN WE ARRIVED, we found Collin and Ada in their yard. Collin held Ada's shoe high above her, and when he saw us, he threw the shoe onto the roof of the trailer. It landed upright on its rubber sole.

Their enormous dog, Baby, chomped on a flattened soccer ball. A mutt with some bullmastiff in her, she was as tall as Natty and probably three times his weight. Natty reached out, and Baby dropped the ball to lick the back of his hand. One taste seemed to make her a fanatic; she placed a paw on his shoulder and gave his face a rapid washing.

"She's friendly," Mr. Dolan said. "Don't be scared." Just a minute earlier, he had waved at us from the window. Now he had materialized in the cold grass in sandals and shorts that exposed his massive bare legs. His ankles were the size of coffee cans.

"He's not scared," I said.

"I meant you." Mr. Dolan showed his small, neat teeth.

Ada stood on one foot, the other leg folded, like a waterbird.

"I saw your ma a few weeks ago," Mr. Dolan said. "She came through the woods and out our side. She was holding a colander full of grass."

"Chives," I said.

"You really ate them?"

The way he asked it made me unable to say yes, so I rolled my feet from side to side.

Mr. Dolan planted his leather sandals in a wide stance. For the first time I noticed he was missing the outer two toes of his right foot. I stared at his incomplete foot.

"Vietnam," he said.

I forced myself to focus on something else. Their sprawling dusty blue ranch house spun out a rope of smoke.

"Would you believe I lost the toes on two separate occasions?" He guffawed.

I made a noncommittal sound. Without Pei-Pei and her social graces, I didn't know how to stop Mr. Dolan from nosing in with his distressing, unanswerable questions.

"You're not Vietnamese, are you?"

I imagined him pointing a rifle at me. Perhaps he was imagining it, too.

"No," I said. "Not even a little bit."

"I didn't think so."

To avoid Mr. Dolan's translucent eyes, I kept scanning the yard. A snowmobile with a shattered windshield was languishing in the grass. Collin picked up a broken table leg in the middle of the yard and swung it.

"You guys don't have the build," Mr. Dolan said. "It's all about wiriness, like whether you could climb a tall fence and how fast. You guys are small and skinny, but you're not wiry that way."

I nodded.

"Why don't you two stay for dinner? Let's get you fed."

Natty looked at me with his huge lashed eyes. Of course he wanted to stay. At home, our meals had turned the corner from unappetizing into something dancing on the edge of edible. Canned beans stir-fried with dried fish. The remnants of differently shaped pasta and noodle packages boiled together, with ketchup as sauce. My mother's wrath when we stared at the food was silent but heavy in the air; we hunched under the weight of it.

"We just have to be home before dark," I said.

"We eat at five-thirty," Mr. Dolan said. "I'll give you a lift home. Want me to give your folks a ring?"

"No," I said. "No, no."

At dinnertime, Mr. Dolan came out to fetch us. He said something nonsensical about letting meat take a rest, then led us around a small deck. Underneath it, in the shadows, was a pile of long wood planks and what appeared to be ten or fifteen ladders. I didn't know why someone would need so many ladders. It wasn't as though you could string them together and climb somewhere far away.

Up a short set of unfinished steps was the deck, which I had never set foot on before. It was overloaded with bikes and skateboards and snowshoes and other riches that had been shoved against the wood railings. Smaller items had tumbled to the floor, in the manner of a rockslide, and left only a little path to the sliding doors. Beside the glass doors, I couldn't help but touch the polished curve of a helmet hanging on the end of a hockey stick, like a head on a spike. The helmet wobbled. Collin poked me in the back with the table leg before dropping it on the deck with a clatter. He pushed ahead of me and I heard him say to his father, "Do we really have enough food?" Behind me, Ada put her hand between my shoulder blades and gave me a tiny push in.

Upon stepping into the house, my skin prickled with the pleasure of the extravagant heat. It was so early—before dinner—and the woodstove was already ablaze. My arms and legs marinated in warmth. My nose began to run, and I kept sniffling, but I didn't want to ask for a tissue.

A slight asphalt smell was overpowered by a food smell, a kind of soggy, squash-like odor, as though frozen vegetables had been steaming all day. The living room we had entered was carpeted, and on top of the carpet were two rugs, faded to dull pastels and trampled smooth. A fat sectional took up one side of the room, and immediately Ada flopped onto the center of it, sinking deeply into the cushions and blankets. She was still missing one shoe. On the bottom of her dirty sock was a heart.

As Mr. Dolan reached over to latch the door, I stepped out of his way into a loosely gathered curtain. I was afraid to walk onto the rug in my sneakers, and also afraid to take them off. I had to use the bathroom, but I didn't want to ask where it was.

"Set the table," Mr. Dolan said, and with a mumbled protest Collin walked through the doorway to the kitchen. A drawer rasped open and silverware chimed.

Mr. Dolan heaved himself onto the couch beside Ada, saying, "Well, I'll just rest my legs for a second." With a hiccup of the springs, he sank so far down that Ada tipped over into his lap.

On the other side of Ada, Natty took off his jacket, revealing an old T-shirt of mine with a coyote wailing at a crackled moon. Ada took hold of Natty's bare arm and kneaded it. From where I stood, they looked like puppies, nuzzling each other, propped against the languid body of their mother. All three of them lay in a nest of soft, worn cushions and textiles, just a few feet away from the hot woodstove. I wanted to pile on top of them. I wanted them to pile on top of me.

"What are you doing?" Mr. Dolan asked. His hands were clasped atop his belly.

I stepped back and hit the glass door.

"Come on," he said. "Join us."

I stared at the waxy undersides of his arms. His sleeves were rolled up, and when he motioned at the couch, he turned one hand and revealed a pelt of hair growing on top of his forearm.

Collin came to the doorway and pointed at me with a serving spoon. "Table's set," he said.

With great effort, Mr. Dolan pushed himself back up. We followed him to the dining table, made of a rich, dark wood.

Out on the deck everything was a jumble; inside the house, I began to understand, there was order and arrangement, a mind or presence—maybe their dead mother's.

In the corner of the dining room was a cabinet displaying miniature porcelain animals. The glass door had its own lock, which impressed me. The back wall of the cabinet was a mirror, and in it, on the lowest shelf, I spied the reflection of three elephants facing one another, midconsultation, the largest no bigger than a quail egg.

Our class had gone to the Alaska Zoo last winter and watched two elephants playing. The little one, an orphan, kept swirling her trunk in the snow and then whipping it up, sending sprays of powder through the air. "Elephants grieve," the docent had said, and I had studied them for signs of distress. Their skin was hatched and creased, and their large, thin ears hung from their skulls like tacked-on towels. Maggie had recently come from Zimbabwe, where her whole herd had been slaughtered. Annabelle, the older elephant, was the very first animal of the Alaska Zoo. Back in the sixties, a grocer had won her in a contest by selling the most Chiffon toilet paper.

I stood with my hand on the back of a chair while the Dolans settled into their seats. Would they let me hold the elephants? How would I go about asking such a thing? Were they very precious, to be locked behind that glass?

"No, not there," Collin said.

I let go of the chair. I couldn't tell if he was joking. He watched me without blinking. Even his legs, which always seemed to be kicking something, were still.

"Don't sit there. Can't you see there's no place setting?"

"Try this one," Mr. Dolan said, nudging a chair out with

his foot. When I was slow to move, he said, "No one's sat in that chair for years."

"Oh," I said.

"It's all right," Mr. Dolan said. "Chairs are meant to be sat in. Only, there's a place for you over there."

"He can sit wherever he wants," Ada said.

"Yeah?" Mr. Dolan said.

She turned to me. "You can sit there," she said. She spoke in a slow, high-pitched voice, like an older child speaking to a younger one, or someone healthy speaking to someone sick. She lifted a large tumbler to her face so that I could see only the edges of her jaws, her temples, her forehead. The glass was completely full of water, but she drank it all without stopping. Her throat pulsed.

I wrapped my fingers around the back of the chair. I didn't know what was taking me so long to get settled, except that I was a little frightened of the food on the table. A whole roasted chicken with shining skin, a bowl of softened vegetables—green beans like smashed fingers, baked potatoes half unwrapped from their foil casings and exposing their freckled skin. I knew I wasn't up to the task before me. Natty was already reaching for the largest potato. Three Dolans sat across the table, watching me with their identical blue eyes, clear as cellophane.

———

DURING THE MEAL, the small window in the dining room darkened quickly, obscuring the view out. Soon it reflected the small chandelier, whose five or six spots of light gleamed wetly in the glass. The window looked like a porthole, holding back an entire black ocean, and I had to pee.

"What do you usually eat for dinner?" Mr. Dolan asked.

"Oh," I said, "the same thing."

"Chicken?"

"Yes, chicken."

"How often do you eat chicken?"

I shrugged.

"Every day or once a week?"

"I don't know," I said.

"What kinds of vegetables?"

"All kinds."

"You eat three times a day?" Mr. Dolan asked. He kept wiping his hands on the same paper towel, which softened as he worried it.

When I didn't answer, Collin offered, "Paige doesn't eat lunch."

"She eats lunch," I said.

"She just sits by herself and doesn't eat anything or do anything."

That didn't seem right to me, though it was impossible for me to contradict him in his own house. But Pei-Pei had her friends.

Collin shoved a huge forkful of chicken into one side of his mouth and gave me a lopsided grin.

"You still go to school?" I said, even though I knew he did.

"He had to repeat," Mr. Dolan said.

Collin scratched his neck, and his nails left red lines on his skin.

"What do you eat for lunch?" Mr. Dolan asked.

"Bread," I said.

"Bread?"

"A sandwich."

Ada waved a drumstick bone in front of Baby.

"Don't tease her," her father said. "You know she can't eat that."

The dog's drool splattered onto the floor. She extended a massive tongue that was pink on top and almost purple on the underside. I felt my stomach lurch.

"Ada loves that stupid dog," Mr. Dolan said. "Named her herself when she was three."

"She's a guard dog, for Christ's sake," said Collin. "You should've let me name her."

"When their mother died," Mr. Dolan said, "Ada slept in the basement with her." He rubbed her head. "Didn't you? Right on the floor."

Ada adjusted an elastic in her hair. She gave me a strange, molded smile, like a curved line drawn in mud. I thought of our intimate whispered conversations in the forest, her face so close to mine I could feel the little gusts of her breath.

"For weeks I had to bring food down there," Mr. Dolan said. "And a space heater. Because it was November."

Collin leaned back and stretched his legs out. His nostrils flared. "It was November, so they put our mom's body in a freezer."

"That's a joke," I said. I took too big a gulp of soda. The bubbles hissed at the base of my throat.

"It's true," Mr. Dolan said. "They even close the cemetery from November to May. The ground's too hard to dig."

I tried to burp, but nothing came out. I wondered if Mr. Dolan would really drive us home, or if we would have to take the woods, which would be inky now. I sat on my hands and tried to forget the woods, as well as the wringing pressure of my bladder.

"It used to be they'd pre-dig graves in the spring and summer, then cover them with a sheet of plywood. But bums started sleeping in the pits for warmth."

"Let them sleep," I said.

"Good point," Mr. Dolan said, "but it's not just a hole in the ground. It means something to people." He cut a slice of chicken with very precise motions of the knife. "Anyhow," he said, "we know what it's like to lose someone."

Without looking up, I considered the warmth of the house, everything layered and soft. Mr. Dolan's firm orb of a stomach, which looked like it would support you if you leaned on it. The expanse and heft of the wooden table, how there was so much space for a meal.

"How long has it been since your sister died? Almost a year? I wanted to tell you, we were sorry when we heard it. Everyone was. We would have paid a visit, but we didn't know you then. We didn't want to be a bother."

Natty was sitting still with his hands palms-down on the table. I thought of him frozen under the basketball hoop at school. I was afraid he would find some kind of permanent stillness.

"My parents don't want us to talk about it," I said.

"Is that right," Mr. Dolan said. Suddenly his skin looked thin and loose, as though he had released a drawstring somewhere behind an ear. Beneath that skin, I thought, was skull.

Thick bone, empty sockets, teeth set in the jaw like kernels that had dried on the cob.

"Talking doesn't usually hurt," he said.

"It hurts me," Collin said. He had cleaned his plate and was slumped on his elbows, mouth hanging open and his face slipping lower and lower between his hands.

"When their mother died," Mr. Dolan said, "their aunt came to stay. Their mother's sister. That was a good thing, too. You got family? Aunts and uncles and grandparents?"

"Yes," I said.

"Who've you got?"

I didn't know much about my father's side. His mother had died young, and he didn't have any siblings. His father had died of liver failure. And maybe also overexertion, my father said, which was his funny way of saying that he'd been beaten a lot as a child. There was only an aunt now on my mother's side—one single living relative.

"We have an uncle in Texas," I said. "And three aunts in Florida. And two grandparents in California. And cousins. Cousins in all those places." As I went on, I saw the image of a U.S. map populating with our family members. I felt myself panting a little. There were so many of us. A pushpin here, a pushpin there, and yarn strung around to connect us. A big pin in Alaska, so that even though we were practically hanging off into the ocean, with a whip of islands trying to dash away, we were tethered, too, fastened to other people.

"Your family likes it hot," Mr. Dolan said.

"What?"

"Florida, Texas, California. Those are hot places."

"Yeah," I said. I stabbed my fork into the remaining half of my potato. I was afraid to look at Ada.

"You been to any of them?"

"Florida," I said.

"Never have been myself. Did you like it?"

I conjured up the hottest place I knew. On the last day of third grade, we had gone for a hike in the Chugach Mountains. The sun baked the rocks around us so that the ground radiated heat upward while the sun scorched us from above, and my classmates, it seemed, started going mad, like fish in an over-heated tank. Someone picked up a stone and licked it, and someone else curled up on the ground and could not be budged. I stepped off the trail, and when I looked up, there was a Dall sheep perched on a ledge, staring down at me, its horns twisted into curlicues. It moved a black hoof. Rocks and loose dirt skidded down. I had the impression it had cursed me. And perhaps it had.

"I didn't like it," I said, and then stood up. "We need to go home."

"Now?" Mr. Dolan said. He craned his head to check the clock beside the doorway. "It's only six. You haven't eaten much. There's still dessert."

"That's okay," I said.

"It's chocolate cake."

"No, thank you."

"He says, 'No, thank you,' to chocolate cake." Mr. Dolan shook his big, rueful head, his arms hanging limp on each side of his chair. "Another can of fizzy?"

"No, thank you."

He rolled himself a little from side to side and pressed hard on the end of the table to thrust his whole mass upward. "Well, maybe you can take something home," he said, and lumbered into the kitchen.

"I guess I'll get my own dessert," Collin said, scraping his chair all the way back to the wall before he followed his father out.

From the kitchen came the sounds of cabinet doors closing. I sat down again and ran the back of my spoon along the length of Natty's bare forearm. He still didn't move.

"Natty," I said. "Get up. We're going home."

I stood up beside him and lifted the back of his chair to tip him off. But instead of catching himself, he fell to the floor, knocking the empty chair aside. The crash brought Mr. Dolan in. He was holding a half-full grocery bag.

"What happened?"

I held Natty up by the armpits. "Just a game that we play," I said.

"Oh," he said. "I thought something had happened."

"I didn't hurt him," I said. "He's fine." Natty was getting heavy, so I let go of him, and to my relief he stayed standing.

Mr. Dolan glanced at Ada and then gave his bag a little shake. "This is just something for you to take home." He was speaking quickly. "I'm almost done. Let me finish up here, and then we'll get you on the road."

Before I could respond, Mr. Dolan had wheeled around and reentered the kitchen. I heard Collin say, "You can't just throw everything in."

In the dining room, Ada and I couldn't seem to find anything to say or do. I hoped desperately it was a symptom of her house and its hazy, yellow-lit rooms, and not a permanent shift between us, though it felt like one. She was looking at me very seriously, sucking on her upper lip. Ever since we had come back, I had often turned during class or at lunch to find her studying me or whatever I was holding, wearing, eating.

I walked over to peer at the porcelain elephants. Their ears and tails were taut, and their black eyes gleamed.

"Do you want one?" Ada asked.

I was appalled. The elephants formed a defensive huddle, and I imagined her mother had placed them carefully in that exact arrangement. Even to disturb them seemed profane.

"No," I said.

"You can have one if you want," Ada said. "No one will notice if you take one."

Separate them? They understood loss. You could even see it in the incline of their heads, the droop of their trunks.

Mr. Dolan rustled in with a bulging grocery bag on one hip. Jutting out the top was a box of cereal and a bag of potato chips. "This is for you to take home," he said.

Though I didn't look at her, I could feel Ada leaning forward, sliding her elbows farther over the table. Had she asked him to do this?

"That's all right," I said. My cheeks flamed.

"Just go on and take it home," he said.

"It's okay," I said.

Mr. Dolan shifted the bag, and I saw a sleeve of Ritz crackers. I began to salivate at the thought of their salted surfaces.

"You might as well take it," he said. "Otherwise I'd have to unpack it again."

My hands hung loose in front of me. He wanted to give the

bag to me, and I wanted to take it. But there was some kind of block.

"Well, I'll just put it in the van," he said.

He shambled toward the front door, and we followed him. With our shoes already on, we drifted easily from indoors to outdoors. Mr. Dolan slid the van door open for us with one hand, and after Ada, Natty, and I had climbed in, he set the grocery bag on an empty seat. He shook out his arms as though he had been carrying something much heavier, like a sack of rubble.

When he started the engine, the radio came on. "Have you heard this?" Mr. Dolan asked, backing the van down the driveway. "The snow lottery. Five thousand dollars."

Although dust covered the lower half of the van's white frame, the interior was clean and empty. The seats were covered in beige velvet, with worn patches in the vague two-comma shape of rear ends. A canvas organizer hung from the back of the driver's seat, but it held only a Kleenex box and no trash.

As we drove on, Mr. Dolan tapped the steering wheel and said, "Tickets are two dollars each. And I'll tell you this for free—winter's coming early this year. You can see it in the pine cones—they're twice as big. And we got the termination dust weeks ago. The first real snowfall, it's going to be early, it's going to be this month. Consider that a free tip."

He turned off the radio and told us about the snow lottery's official machine: an arm with a bucket attached to it. When snow had filled the bucket to a certain weight, the arm would fall and trigger a clock to stop. It was all rigged up somewhere downtown, high enough that no one could mess with it.

We turned onto a dirt road. It was so narrow that if you

didn't take the turns just right, you would swipe a tree, maybe lose a side mirror. But Mr. Dolan followed the curves without apparent thought. A few branches clawed at the windows.

"My thinking is the chances are pretty good. It's not like the Ice Classic, where you haven't got a real shot. That one's got so many bets, they hire ninety people every winter just to sort them. Of course, the jackpot was almost two hundred thousand last year. You know about the Ice Classic, don't you?"

"Uh," I said. I turned to Ada, but she just sat beside me with her hands in her lap.

As we drove, I stared at my own hands in the last vestiges of light, the woods pulsating on one side of the road. My fingertips felt swollen. When you didn't pee for a long time, my mother said, all that urine seeped into your blood and poisoned you.

By the time we turned onto our gravel road, Mr. Dolan had told us all about the huge lottery to guess when the Tanana River would melt. Every winter the town of Nenana built a huge tripod with a flag on it, and placed it in the middle of the frozen river. When the river broke up enough to carry the tripod one hundred feet downstream, a cable tied to the tripod would trigger a siren and trip a meat cleaver that cut a rope that pulled out a pin to stop an antique clock. And everyone would gather on the banks to celebrate.

"You can buy tickets at pretty much any bar," he said. "Or Carrs." The headlights swung to illuminate the pale crushed rock of our gravel road. The van bounced deep into a gully, then reared up over a hump.

"You can drop us off here," I said.

But Mr. Dolan finished the turn. The front tires kicked up gravel. "I'll take you up the driveway."

The light was on in the back of the house; I could see the small glowing circle of the doorknob hole. I knew that if I crouched, I could look through the hole all the way to the kitchen, where my mother might be eating dinner. She would be contained perfectly in that circle. It was only when you opened the door that she would become life-sized. It was tempting to delay that moment.

When I jumped down to the driveway, Mr. Dolan put his hand on me. It covered my whole shoulder. "Tell your folks about the snow lottery. It's smaller."

"The chances are pretty good," I said.

"That's right." With a jovial flourish, he shoved the grocery bag into my arms, while Ada hung halfway out the open van door and raised one somber hand. Her hair was tucked behind an ear on one side, and the other side hung straight. She looked neat and cautious and unrumpled, and I missed the other version of her. She pulled the door closed.

Natty and I stood thigh-deep in the grasses to watch Mr. Dolan back out of the driveway. The bag was so heavy it was slipping, and I let it slide to the ground. Mr. Dolan's thick arm hung out of the open window, and he slapped the side of the van in farewell. As he turned, the headlights painted a yellow arc onto the colorless gray shrubs of the clearing.

I could barely get up the step. The groceries were cumbersome and my bladder was so full, the slightest movement caused a twinge. We entered the house to find my mother barreling toward us. I shoved the grocery bag into the stairwell—I didn't want to explain it—then stepped into the entryway to meet her full-on.

"Where did you go? Who was that? Why didn't you come

home?" In my mother's hands were a sneaker and a house slipper, though she herself was barefoot. "I waited hours for you,"
she said. "Why didn't you come home before dark?"

"Why do we have to?" I said.

"Don't talk to me like that. Because you are a child."

"I'm not." My voice cracked as I said it. I didn't feel like a
child—what did that feel like?

She whirled blindly toward the open closet, where there was
a small heap of shoes and coats, and above it, a bar. All of the
clothes hangers had been taken away, along with any jackets we
had left behind. "I didn't know where any of my children were,"
she said. She waved her arms into the empty space and grabbed
at nothing. "Four children, I had once. Tonight I didn't know
where a single one was."

I thought once more of how I alone knew Ruby's location,
and how cumbersome that knowledge was, big and water-
logged. "Here are two of us," I said, swinging an arm to include
Natty, who I saw just then was sitting on the second step,
rummaging through the grocery bag out of my mother's
sight.

"Yes, yes, here you are," my mother said. She rubbed her
hands on the thighs of her corduroy pants, as though trying to
calm herself, but her voice got higher and higher. "Nobody came
home," she said. "So I didn't cook. I was just waiting."

"We already ate," I said.

"Where?"

"At a friend's," I said, the way Pei-Pei used to, as though she
alone could know what that meant.

"That's good," my mother said. "I don't need to cook." She
had put one slipper on and begun an odd, injured shuffle into

the kitchen. She called over her shoulder as an afterthought, "Close the door." I heard the sink water come on.

As I pulled the door in, I could see back through the doorknob hole to our dark yard and the gravel road, and beyond it, the clearing that was softened with a layer of seed heads suspended over the tall grasses. Where had Pei-Pei gone?

A warmth spread around my crotch and down my legs and the relief was so immense that I couldn't—or didn't want to—stop. When I was done, the smell of urine was unmistakable, and a puddle on the floor was spreading with a mind of its own.

I stepped into the closet and took off my pants, underwear, and socks, then thought in the dark about the question of laundry. For a long while I stayed there, squatting on our coats, mustering willpower. Then I streaked out, past Natty who was putting a Reese's Peanut Butter Cup in his mouth, up the stairs, and into the hallway bathroom, where I threw my clothes under running water in the bathtub. I went to find new pants, then returned to finish the washing job.

While I was wringing my sweatpants out over the tub, Pei-Pei stepped into the hallway and wrapped her fingers around the doorframe. "What are you doing?" she asked.

She had come in so quietly that my mother had not heard. Without the knob and latch, the front door was very quiet—it made only a soft swoosh upon opening. No car had dropped her off, or at least I hadn't heard tires on the gravel, or an engine cutting out or starting.

"Mom's looking for you," I said. "She's mad."

"Mad or"—Pei-Pei pulled all the skin around her eyes back with a spread of her fingers, and her eyes popped—"mad?"

"Both."

"But why is it wet downstairs?"

I looked at my sweatpants, twisted in my hands, and was too tired to make up a story. "I peed on the floor."

Pei-Pei nodded slowly. "What's with the cookies on the stairs?"

"From the Dolans." The reminder of the groceries made me sag and sit down on the cold, hard side of the tub.

"I'm going to dig in."

"Didn't you eat dinner?"

"No." Pei-Pei leaned farther through the doorway. "But I found a job." Her cheeks were flushed. "It's a lot easier to find one in the summer than now, but I managed anyway. I did it."

"Oh," I said.

"Four dollars an hour," she said. "Four hours a day, six days a week—that's ninety-six dollars a week." She was swinging from the doorframe.

"What's the job?"

"I'm a helper."

"What does that mean?"

"Well, what does it sound like?"

"You don't know what the job is," I said.

She shrugged. "I know it means helping people."

"Help me," I said.

"All right," she said, and entered the bathroom. I thought she was going to sit beside me and flick my face, or elbow me in the stomach. Instead, she took my pants, wrung them out further, and spread them over a towel to dry. "There," she said, and patted me on the chest. And I did feel helped.

17

THE FIRST DUSTING OF SNOW CAME IN OCTOBER. IT VAN-
ished in a day and was replaced by a cold mist. Pei-Pei began
her after-school job—watching over a man who forgot things.
It was easy, she said. She sat next to him on the couch, and together they flipped through his hunting magazines. She read
to him about caribou and ptarmigan and rifles with equally
pretty names. When he wandered toward the front door, she
ran ahead of him and politely blocked the exit. Meanwhile, his
wife picked up the cellophane candy wrappers he trailed in his
wake and cooked dinner by dumping jars into pots. The three
of them ate in front of the TV, usually pasta without any meat.
Every day was a repeat, Pei-Pei said, enchanted.

It sometimes seemed on long afternoons that Pei-Pei had
left our house for good. But every night ended with Pei-Pei
bringing home the *Anchorage Daily*, rescued from the trash. We
pored over it by the stove, the words so dim they melted into
the gray paper. There were treasures to be found: a traffic dispute

that escalated until one man beat another with a twenty-six-inch auger drill bit, or a sidewalk encounter that left a man shot between the ribs with a crossbow. Big, crucial chunks of information were missing, and later we filled them in. Pei-Pei whispered reenactments of the brawls as we lay beside each other, wide awake in our family nest on the floor. "I know you stole my musk ox," she said, squirming closer to me, speaking so softly only I could hear. Prodding me with a finger, she said, "Who you calling a girl when I've seen you sit down to pee?"

When we were done, we twisted the papers tightly and threw them into the woodstove, where they flamed brightly, then blackened, joining the drifts of fine gray ash and unsettling clumps.

———

IN THE WOODS, the chill of the air was unmistakable, that sharp warning: *winter*. At our favorite spot, the tree I thought of as having saved Pei-Pei's life—the squat spruce—continued to prop up the trunk of the fallen tree. But it was a changed thing, splitting down the center and abloom with thousands of pine cones. I didn't recognize the display for what it was: a massive, last-ditch effort to shower down seeds. Death was at hand for the overburdened. In the sunlight, the cones were marvelous, gold or copper at times, like ornaments hung by a madman.

Ada said she'd looked out her bedroom window the night before and found a halo around the moon. Bad weather ahead. "We won't be able to play tomorrow," she said. "And maybe for a long time yet."

Natty and I dug shallow holes, and Ada dropped her treasures inside: a hair elastic, a root beer candy, a piece of dried skin from her lip. Then we filled the holes back up with dirt, watching the offerings disappear. But Ada's heart wasn't in it. Her eyes kept twitching toward me and away. She wasn't any good at it. Didn't she know I was the one who had always done the watching? I noticed every one of her glances.

Natty stepped farther down the path, into a grove where the alders were thick and low. He knelt and stabbed a pointed rock into the dirt, and soon we could hear him scrubbing the ground.

Ada asked, "Are you all right?" Her knees pointed inward. I knew she was probing me about something larger than this moment in time. One of her barrettes was barely hanging on, dangling like a pull cord as she eyed me.

I swiped my face with my forearm and flicked my hood up to cut off part of her gaze. It made a plasticky crunching sound. Soon it would snow, and the woods would be too cold for us. Today might be the crossover day—the day before our long winter confinement. Were we doing enough with it? I scraped a stick into the earth and created a short, narrow trench.

"Is there anything you need?" she asked. "What do you need?"

"Oh, everything," I said, and laughed—then winced at the grating sound. The wet air settled over our faces and shoulders, and we breathed the chill into our lungs. I pressed harder on my stick. It snapped, and I worked with the longer of the two pieces, using it like a pencil, rewriting the same line over and over.

Ada lowered herself to a squat beside me and studied the trench I was making. "You can keep digging if you want," she said. She pulled the lining of her pockets out. The fabric was thin and nubby. "But I don't have anything left."

It made me sadder than it should have. I laid the stick down.

We fell into a clotted silence. The mist thickened and seemed to curdle above our heads. Finally Ada kicked the loose dirt. "Let's go see what he's doing," she said, tossing her head in Natty's direction. Thirty yards down the path, he was frantically digging below the alders as though on the brink of an archaeological find. He had put down his rock and was pawing. The only sound I could hear, apart from the hushed rustling of the woods, was the spattering of dirt and stray rocks on the leaves of the understory. I followed her.

The alders on this part of the path grew in the shape of wide funnels, muscling back the spruces that wanted to shade them out. We had to stoop, for the branches forked into one another, creating a low canopy of woven branches. They were encrusted with lichens, and through them I could see sky, or rather fog, moving like a conveyer belt.

At our feet was a small crater, nearly a gallon in size. Soil was backsliding into it. I wouldn't have thought Natty could dig a hole this big, and so quickly. I stuck my hand in, pressing on the cool soil at the bottom of it. The hole gave me a strange feeling. That something belonged in it.

"It's raining," Ada said. She dabbed her forehead with her thumb and showed it to me, but all I saw was a fleck of dirt. Then a single droplet tapped the ground beside my feet.

"Winnie says it's going to rain all weekend," Natty offered.

"Or snow," Ada said. She had inherited this from her father—premonitions about the weather, or at least an insistence that what she had were premonitions.

Natty paused to look at the sky. "Winnie says we shouldn't eat snow."

I lifted my hand from the hole, and the two of them worked on widening and deepening it. Ada hit a root and carefully scraped around it with Natty's rock, then dusted it as though excavating a human bone. She ran the pad of her finger along its length.

Natty chattered. "This hole is getting big. Really big. What will we put in here?" He raised his eyes to me and rubbed his nose, smearing snot across his upper lip.

"No," I said. I clenched my hands in my coat pockets. "I don't know. How would I know?"

As he resumed his pawing, Natty said, "Dirt is made of dead plants and animals."

I could hear Mrs. Reardon's inflections in his voice—the melodramatic range of tones. It was an unnatural way for any child to talk, but for Natty, my detached, tight-lipped brother, it was sickening.

"Not just dead animals," I said. "Dead people, too."

He flicked his eyes at me. "Oh my," he said mildly. Another of her phrases. That fake, liquid voice. It made me want to expose the part of him that was really him. The part that was soft and raw.

I stepped forward, just across the hole from him, and shoved him so hard he sprang backward and fell. Why had he dug a hole sized for Ruby's urn? The very place for her to rest—he was right—it was here. I staggered off-path into the thickets. I thrashed at the leaves around me, sweeping my hands over the thorns and toxins and inviting the small dangers of the understory to come to me. I parted leaves and trampled stems and found myself in a tight clearing, encircled by shoulder-high weeds that appraised me.

That cool, quiet hole. Ruby had always liked small spaces. More than once I'd opened the cabinet under the kitchen sink to find her hiding there, a bag of onions or potatoes in her arms, her short hair mussed. How long had she been waiting? Twenty minutes. Thirty, even. It wasn't that she was unusually patient, but that she thrilled at being found—that sudden burst of light, that screaming rapture.

As I stumbled back toward the path, I saw Natty had not moved from where he had fallen. He lay supine with his hands spread open, as though trying to catch the rain that was falling more consistently now. Every five seconds or so there was a drop, on my shoulder, on the toe of my sneaker, in the exact center of my scalp, drilling into my skull.

He pressed himself up to sitting and looked at his palms. Damp soil clung to them but he didn't wipe his hands. His eyelids looked dark, almost bruised.

"Get up," I said.

He did, slowly and unsteadily.

"Ruby's dead," I said.

"I know," he whispered.

"You know? What do you know?"

"Daddy carried her away. You were dead, too. I saw it. But then you came back. You came back without her."

I felt the force of his accusation. It made me sway on my feet. It was worse than what he was saying. I hadn't abandoned her, I'd killed her.

"She's dust," I said, spreading my fingers apart in the air. I wanted him to know—I wanted someone to know—that her ashes had stuck to my skin and worked into the weave of my clothes. "She's nothing," I said. "Dirt. Your dead animal dirt."

In the gloom he stood frozen, crinkling his eyes at me.

"She can't come back," I said.

He squeezed his hands together, like a heart seizing.

"Not ever," I hollered.

He pivoted on one boot and almost fell. Ada and I watched him shuffle down the path, his brown coat and brown pants becoming very small until he was gone. For a time she said nothing. Finally she said, unnecessarily, "It's starting to rain."

I felt myself deflating; what was left was guilt and shame. I could go after Natty, but he wouldn't want me near him.

"Let's wait it out," I mumbled.

"All right," Ada said, and scooted to a spot just off the path, where the alder branches overhead were thickest. She said nothing about my outburst.

I thought of her dissolved, haloed moon. I didn't know why she stayed. I busied myself taking off my coat and spreading it on the ground. Though I tried to smooth it with the underside of my arm, it retained its clumps and ruts.

Once we sat, I examined the stinging yellow spines in my palms.

She took one of my hands in hers and angled it for a better view. "You have to get them all out," she said. "You can't leave bits in there."

She adjusted my hand until it was three inches from her face and began to pinch the thorns with her dirty fingernails.

"Does it itch?"

"Maybe."

"Does it or doesn't it?"

"It didn't until you asked."

When she was done examining my palm, I leaned forward to hold my knees, and she brushed my back in a strange, slow rhythm. It was achingly sweet. The whole surface area of her palm swept back and forth across the drifts of my shoulder blades. I thought I recalled my grandfather—just a sliver of a memory. A hot, quiet night, a cupped hand thumping me hard on the back to loosen phlegm and make me cough. A buzz came from the dim fluorescent light, and I lay on my stomach in his lap. Or was it my father? It may have been my father, in a long-ago time. When things fell into place. When there was no fronting. When people said what they felt because what they felt was very easy to say.

Our legs didn't fit on the small spread of coat, and when we moved, the pine needles piled up, as though we were making snow angels in it. There were stray bits in Ada's hair. We smelled like wet earth.

Ada said, "I'm cold." She pressed herself closer to me. Dampness was creeping from the dirt through my coat, which was too old to be completely waterproof. I felt it soaking into my pants. My skin prickled all over; I wanted to put my coat back on. But then we would have to stand instead of sit, and standing was a step away from leaving.

As the drops merged into streams and stirred up the understory, I gazed up at our roof of sticks. At our sides the alders were bushy, leafy, and spotted with catkins, but the branches above us were bald. There was no foliage to shroud us. Where was Natty now?

I thought of how we slept on the mattress in the den, all of us pressed into one another. Pei-Pei's hair tangling around my fingers, her knee digging into my shin and creating a slow bruise. I often threw an arm to my side to check that Natty was there. But the solid feel of his ribs, the sharp point of his hip, the tendons of his wrist—it wasn't enough. I was always checking and checking.

Ada wriggled beside me and her eyes were so close to mine, her irises looked textured, almost etched. I felt she was waiting for me to say something important, but I couldn't manage it. A root or shard of rock dug into the side of my thigh. "Maybe it'll stop soon," I said.

Her thin sweatshirt was soggy. As she leaned further into me, I could tell that all of her muscles were clenched. She was knobby in the arms and legs but soft in the stomach. Behind her was a thick clump of ferns; raindrops clung to the feathery shoots.

"I don't think so," she said, wiping water off her face. More rain replaced it, running down her forehead, over her eyes and cheeks, dripping off the ends of her hair.

Even as she shivered, she asked, "Do you want me to stay?"

Yes, I wanted that. The rain and mist, they hid us away. "You can go," I said.

I watched as she crawled away from me to straighten in the tallest part of the bower. Her sneakers squelched. Her pale face gleamed in the constricted light. Watching her lift one foot and then another, hunched in vain against the cold, made me convulse in recognition. Cold—she was cold, and I was cold, too.

"Storm's coming," she said. "Go. I'll send Natty on home when I see him." She waved at me by scratching the air with her fingers. With that, she set off, for that warm place of hers, full of lived-in smells and those soft, overlapping rugs, where adults tried to lighten your burdens. She scrambled away.

———

I WAITED for ten or fifteen minutes, but Natty didn't come, so I trudged on home through the corridor of trees. The spruces offered some protection, but where the rain splattered through the boughs I got pummeled. Breathless and dripping, I slid the back door open and found our house empty. I closed the glass door and stood perfectly still, and soon I could distinguish the sound of rain from the water running through the pipes; my mother was taking one of her swift evening showers.

Upstairs, I peeled off all of my clothes and stood shivering in the empty bedroom. I knew I wasn't supposed to leave wet things on the carpet, but it hardly seemed to matter. I found my long johns in a heap in the closet, put them on, and pulled a dry sweatshirt on top. When I looked out the window at our cheerless, washed driveway, I still felt cold.

I waited for Natty in the kitchen. I toed the small puddles I had brought in. Through the water-smeared glass of the sliding door, and the yard full of rain, the visibility was so low I couldn't even see the woods. I focused on a spot just a few feet away; surely Natty would appear there any moment, charging toward me with his small hands shielding his big head.

When my mother flipped on the light, I had to put my face right up to the glass to see anything outside. Behind me, she toweled off her hair, commented on the thick rain, and started dinner. She chopped cabbage on a little plastic board and simmered the leftover bone of a pork shank. When it was boiling, she dumped in a cup of rice and handful after handful of cabbage. The house filled with steam—a warmer dampness than before—and an earthy, meaty fragrance, with just a hint of sourness that reminded me of decay in the woods. The lid rattled on the pot, and the window above the sink fogged over. My nose started to run. At six o'clock she said, "Go get your brother."

"Dad's not home yet," I said.

"We're going to eat first, just us. Go get your brother."

I shook my head.

She slapped the backs of her wet hands on her pants and jerked her head to aim a look of threat at me. "Go."

"I can't," I said.

"What are you saying?"

"Natty's not home."

She shook her head. "But he came home with you."

"No."

"What?" She jammed a hand into her hair. "But it's raining," she said. "And it's dark."

I didn't respond, and in the silence we listened to the rain drumming on the roof and aluminum gutters, flicking the windows, assaulting the already sodden ground.

Suddenly my mother grabbed me roughly, her fingers finding the soft parts of my shoulders. "Is it the truth? Really? You left him alone out there?"

"No, he left me."

"How long? How many hours?"

"I don't know."

"One? Two?"

"One," I said, thinking it was definitely more than two.

"Where is he?"

"In the woods, maybe. Or at Ada's house." The second possibility had just occurred to me, and I latched on to it. "Ada said she was going to send him home, but he must have stayed over there because it was raining so hard."

"Tell me her phone number." My mother bumped the sack of rice on the counter as she moved toward the phone, and kernels scattered across the floor. It was not unlike the sound of the rain. I had a sudden image of hope: instead of rain, seeds were falling outside—a downpour of tiny, dry seeds.

"Her number," my mother said.

It stunned me that she thought I might know anyone's phone number. "I don't have it," I said, ashamed.

My mother knelt to dig in the lower cabinet where we used to keep the phone books, but of course it was empty; like much in our house, they had been taken.

"Your father has the truck," my mother said. She sat at the kitchen table to think. "He should be home soon."

The soup cooled on the stove. The window above the sink unfogged, and a viewing circle into our dark yard expanded. I stayed in front of the glass door imagining the scene that would unfold at the Dolans' house—my mother banging on their door in her corduroy pants with the faded knees, a coat three sizes too big zipped to her throat, her hands lost but gesturing inside the sleeves. Without any kind of greeting, she would stick her head into the house and shout for Natty, a strident, jay-like call.

As we waited, my mother spoke to me only to say, "Your brother, your little brother."

I glanced at my ugly reflection in the glass, then leaned forward until my forehead touched it and I could see the dark rain again.

When my father came home, my mother sprang up and said, "What took so long?"

He had nudged the front door open and was stamping his muddy boots on the concrete step. His hood was up, but his face was wet. His gray pants had turned black. He squinted at my mother in surprise, and then at me. "I just finished," he said. He had found a small job working on a small septic tank, and my mother had been all relief—a job, a job.

"Don't take your shoes off," my mother said.

She grabbed my shoulder again and said, "And you. You'll stay here."

I nodded. I certainly didn't want to go with them to the Dolans' house.

My mother said to my father, "Natty is gone. We think he's on the other side of the woods."

My father rearranged his hood and his face retreated into it. "Why?" he asked.

My mother turned to me. "Yes, why," she said.

After they left, I fed the woodstove in the den—we were nearly out of firewood. I turned off the kitchen light again. My stomach growled, and I eyed the shining pot on the stove. The sky was rapidly changing color, like the tea my father used to steep, black leaves uncurling right inside the cup and staining the water darker and darker still. Soon I couldn't see a thing, even pressed up to the glass.

Every sound caused my chest to seize: a pop from the woodstove, a leaf scratching the concrete step outside. I became convinced that the phone, which for months I had been warned not to touch, would ring. If it rang, should I pick it up?

A long half hour later, Pei-Pei came in holding her dripping hair off to one side. "An umbrella would've been good," she said. She took off her coat and peeled off her socks, leaving the wet donuts by the door. She said, "That was a real long day." Though her sleeves and pants were wet, the *Anchorage Daily* tucked into her waistband was completely dry, and she tossed it onto the kitchen table. She planted herself on a folding chair, placed her arms on the rests, and settled back with the to-do of a very large man. I sat at her feet, more glad she was home than I knew how to show.

"I'm soaked," she said. "I'm freezing." Her cheeks were flushed. "Where is everyone?"

"They're looking for Natty," I said. "I left him in the woods."

From her throne Pei-Pei surveyed me. I lowered my head. She and I had both let Natty play by himself in the woods before, but never at night. And we had never come home without him.

"They're looking for him where?"

"At the Dolans' house," I said.

Pei-Pei frowned—for the same reason, I was sure, that I had. She hugged one knee to her chest and asked, "And is he there?"

"I think he's there," I said, but my voice got a little scrambled in my throat.

She reached down and pulled on the neck of my sweatshirt, then wiped her glasses dry on the thick fabric. She sat back, and I waited for her judgment. Finally she said, "He wouldn't be across the street, would he?"

The clearing? "No, I don't think so," I said.

"That pond is huge right now. You could slip and fall in."

None of us knew how to swim. "He's definitely not there," I said.

She put her glasses back on, and her eyes focused again. After she studied my face, she said, her voice a little lighter, "Well, don't worry." She reached for the newspaper, opened it, and handed the local section—the best one—down to me. I spread it over her feet and on the floor. We read quietly under the kitchen light, and she didn't mention Natty again.

When my mother finally returned, she shot through the front door and came at us, her shoes squeaking on the linoleum. "Is he home? Is he home yet?" Her eyes jabbed at our surroundings, under the table, behind the counter, into the crackling darkness of the den. My heart knocked against my ribs and I scooted back from Pei-Pei's feet until I was partly under the kitchen table. The front door was open, and my father appeared in the rectangle of rain.

"He wasn't there?" Pei-Pei asked.

"No," my mother said, shaking large quantities of water off her coat right onto the floor. "I looked for him in their house."

I tried not to imagine the scene—my mother running through the sprawling rooms while the Dolans stood in one place and watched—as she went on to explain how they'd searched the yard, thrashing the large bushes and peering under the deck, even stepping into the trailer. There was only garbage inside, my mother said with a disgusted swat.

"What?" my father called from the entryway. "What are you saying? Should I come in or not?"

"We need to call the police," my mother said.

The emptiness in my stomach felt raw, everything scraped out.

My father walked halfway to us and stopped. "No," he said, echoing my only thought.

"We have to," my mother said.

"No one is calling anyone." My father took a few more steps in. His boots were cleaner than my mother's.

Ignoring him, my mother strode toward the phone, but in a sudden rush through the kitchen, my father overtook her and knocked the receiver from her hands.

"What are you doing?"

"Don't call." My father grasped with both hands at the swinging receiver. "Just—don't call. We'll look for him ourselves."

"Who will? You will? You?"

My father caught the receiver and held it against his chest. I imagined someone on the line listening to his skittish heartbeat.

"Give it to me."

"I'm telling you, we'll find him."

"Give it." My mother clawed for it, but my father turned away.

"Can you see in the dark?" she asked. "Can you see the whole forest?"

My father hunched over the phone.

"There isn't time for this. The police will find him."

"Don't you see? We can't call anyone."

"Listen to me."

"No, you listen to me. They don't understand us." My father's voice swelled. "They see only half of us. You know what they'll say? That it's our fault. It's all our fault." In the cold, still air, wisps of his breath materialized before his face, but they immediately dissolved—they didn't have enough substance.

"Every minute—you count them," my mother said. "There's another. It's yours. Only yours."

The off-the-hook tone blared over and over, and my father clutched the receiver tighter to his chest, trying to muffle it. But we could hear it clearly, the alarm.

"Can you live with that? Can you add it to your list? Along with—"

"Don't—" my father said, and thrust a hand out: Stop. I couldn't tell if it was a command or a plea.

"—the death of your daughter?"

"No, that's not—"

"You said it was just a cold. No hospital, you said."

My father mouthed some silent words.

"Even when it got worse—when they both got worse—you said it was just a cold. When anyone could see it was more than that." My mother was crying, but she wouldn't acknowledge it by wiping her face.

My father wrapped the phone cord around one wrist.

"You killed her."

I pressed the side of my face to the cold floor. Wasn't she talking to me?

"My daughter, my daughter, my daughter," she said.

My father lurched away, still holding on to the receiver, and the cord snapped loose from the wall-mounted base.

When my mother stepped toward him, he shrieked. "Don't come any closer," he said. He bumped against the kitchen sink.

"Give me the phone."

My father shoved the receiver under one arm and patted the counter until he'd found the cleaver on the cutting board. The rectangular blade looked enormous when he held it in the air. Shavings of cabbage were stuck to it.

"I said don't come near me," he said.

"And what are you going to do?"

I remembered the crunching sound the knife had made when it sank through the head of cabbage. My father was holding the cleaver loosely by its wooden handle, and the blade glinted as his hand trembled.

When my mother leaned forward, poised to take another step, my father suddenly took three swings in the air with the knife, defending a small half circle in front of himself. The blade passed so close to my mother's face that I stopped breathing.

"Put it down," Pei-Pei said. She sounded bored, but she was sitting on the edge of the folding chair, about to flip it. She rose.

My father looked at her, then whirled around so he wasn't looking at anyone. He leaned far over the kitchen sink. He still held on to the cleaver, and the phone was wedged in his armpit.

"I'm leaving," Pei-Pei said. "I'm going to find Natty." She pulled her coat back on.

"Me, too," I said, my voice dry and whispery. It didn't matter where we were going.

My mother pointed a bent finger at us. She said, "When you go out there, you two stay together. Hear me? Take the path and stay together. I'll search the woods." Her chin was wet and shining. Her low, broken voice still echoed in my head. My daughter, she'd said. I couldn't go back to a time before I'd heard it.

"No, you take the path," Pei-Pei said. "We know the woods better."

I could feel my blood pumping, sending a surge of hot fear to my throat. What was she saying? The truth was, we didn't know the woods at all. We only knew the path. Once you stepped off of it, there was no telling what you'd find. All those sagging trees heaved down at you; things were unloosed beneath their wings.

My mother said, "We don't have any flashlights that work."

"It's all right. The moon is out."

Pei-Pei took me by the elbow. She snapped my coat off the back of a chair and slid open the back door, then yanked me out into the yard.

The rain had stopped. The cold air held the smell of trampled grass and spruce. The moon was an egg yolk, bright and ready to break. Although it shone on the upper reaches of the trees, I knew it wouldn't even graze the gobs of darkness beneath.

"Can't we bring some kind of light?" I whispered to Pei-Pei as she tossed my coat over my shoulders.

"What kind of light?" she asked, and slid the door closed behind us. "We don't have any batteries."

"A torch?"

Pei-Pei ignored me. I had one arm through my coat when she started off. I glanced back through the glass door into the lighted kitchen. My father had disappeared. My mother was packing a meager bag at the table: water, blanket, paring knife.

"Wait for me!" I shouted. It seemed Pei-Pei couldn't get out of our yard fast enough; she was nearly at the entrance of the woods. The blur of trees took shape as I raced toward them. I had never been inside the forest at this hour. But I knew Pei-Pei had; I had seen her from the upstairs window as the trees received her. I took one last gasp of air, as I imagined she had done, then leaped through the soft barrier of grass and plunged into the dark.

18

GLINTING POOLS OF WATER HAD OVERTAKEN THE TRAIL. AT first we danced around them. By the time we veered off the path, our shoes and socks and pants were drenched and we were tromping straight through anything that hit us below the knees—ankle-deep puddles, disintegrated tree trunks, feathery horsetails, and unidentifiable wet, slapping things.

We shouted into the mass of forest for our brother. Pei-Pei's calls were questioning, and though I tried to mimic her, I couldn't keep panic out of my voice.

"Natty?"

"Natty! Natty!"

"Natty?"

"Natty! Natty!"

We sounded like blind creatures trying to echolocate. In fact, we were practically blind. I could see only Pei-Pei's outline and the silvery puffs of her breaths. In the spaces between trees, I sometimes caught her expression, and though it was dimly lit by spare glances of the moon, it was piercing in those flashes. Her straining neck, dark hole of a mouth, and eyes that sought to see the whole woods at once.

The trees took up more space at night; their shadows added to their volume. I was afraid of the softness of my steps. Beneath our shoes there was none of the crunching and snapping I was used to, only mush. We were weightless, we had no impact.

When I tripped, I barely felt it; thick mounds of duff softened my fall. As I pawed at the wet ground to get up, the missing-children posters inside the Qwik Stop appeared in my mind. A teenage boy, a nine-year-old girl. They had been pasted to the wall since I could remember. Their fixed and knowing smiles.

"Natty?" Pei-Pei called, her voice swelling. She no longer seemed to be addressing Natty at all, but rather the woods, asking for his release. She shivered like a flame tussling with the wind. When she turned to shout into another patch of darkness, her hair flung out and lashed my face. It stung. Her hair was stiff, maybe frozen. I remembered how wet it had been when she had come in from the rain.

"Are you cold?" I asked.

"No," she said. She shut her eyes, and I thought I saw her eyelids twitching.

"Just a little longer," I said. High over us, the forest canopy was listing, and we could hear the individual boughs shoving one another.

Pei-Pei grabbed my hand, and we ran deeper into the woods. It all looked the same, looming tree after looming tree.

Pei-Pei stopped in her tracks. The cold air cut up our breaths.

Pei-Pei put her hands on her thighs and looked straight up. "Natty!" she screamed. "Please!"

Immediately it was silent again, as if nothing had happened. The woods would swallow anything we unleashed.

"Come home!" I hollered. "Don't you know we're looking for you?" But the harder I shouted, the more false I felt. I was the one who had chased him away.

Half an hour passed, maybe an hour. Each time we stopped to yell or catch our breath, the temperature seemed to plunge a few degrees. We were soaked from brushing against all those wet leaves, and maybe from our own sour sweat. Our lungs were raspy. I could feel my whole body trying to retract from the cold. My jaw was tight, and it was hard to form words.

Stubby branches jabbed at us. When Pei-Pei's coat caught, she gave it a yank until we heard the whole brittle branch snap off. In a frenzy she took off her coat and balled it up.

"Put your coat back on," I said.

"Put your coat back on," she said, mimicking me, or maybe it was my mother she had heard in me.

"It's freezing," I said.

"No, it's not," she said. "It's hot from all the running."

Pei-Pei stumbled. I couldn't be sure, but we didn't seem to be running in a straight line, or making any kind of systematic pattern. We were more like a kite in a storm, reeling through the woods, carried by a greater force.

My fingers and ears burned, blasted by chill, and I longed for very simple things: a hat, mittens, socks that were not wet.

Pei-Pei kept falling. It took her longer and longer to get back up until, finally, she stayed on the ground.

"Get up," I said. "Where's your coat?"

She swept her hands around her, hitting needles and leaves and decay. "I don't know," she said.

I turned a full circle to scan the woods, but in the dark there were only expanding shadows. I grabbed Pei-Pei's wrists and gave them a pull. "Let's go. Get up."

"Oh, no," she said, flopping heavily until I had to drop her arms. She muttered something I couldn't make out. She was slurring.

"What?"

"I said it's all fine. All of it." She wrested off her sweatshirt and tossed it to the side, then lay all the way down in the nest of needles. Her white T-shirt glowed dully. Beside my foot was her collapsed sweatshirt; I could see through the neck hole to the black ground.

"Get up," I said, but she didn't respond.

When I knelt and pushed her shoulder, she said, "Stop it."

"Then move," I said.

"It's too hot."

"That's not funny." I gave a small kick to her ribs, but she still didn't budge.

Minutes passed, then more.

"Please," I said.

"Mmm," Pei-Pei said.

I kicked her harder, then harder still, but got no response. I couldn't leave her there, but I knew we couldn't stay. The only thing I could do was scream Natty's name in one place, tottering as I tried to throw my voice in every direction. How far did it travel? Fifty feet? Sixty? My throat hurt, and I longed for something to drink. For rest, for warmth. As I grew more desperate, I started to shriek, "I'm here! I'm here!"—more to reassure myself than anything else. For this was where things ended. This unknown swath of forest. Ruby, Natty, Pei-Pei—they had always been on the brink of vanishing.

When I bent to spread Pei-Pei's sweatshirt over her torso, the sky lit up. Through the spaces between the lurching trees, I glimpsed something on fire above us. I raced to a cluster of alder trees, where there was a break through the spruces and a rare view of sky. A burning object was moving across the firmament, much larger and slower than any meteor I had ever seen. For a few seconds it seemed to hover, perfectly still. I watched, gaping, as pieces broke off and flared, trailing red and blue tails of light. All of this happened in utter silence, the stillness of the lower forest perfectly unbroken, so that I couldn't help but clutch my head and think, in a wave of white-hot terror, that I had gone truly mad. A UFO? A Russian missile? A permanent crack of my mind.

Was this how it had looked when the *Challenger* exploded? I was reliving the disaster I had missed—a punishment for sleeping through it all, for having skirted the liquid terror of it.

Parts of the forest were lit, as though the world had frozen in place mid-flicker of lightning. Thirty yards away, I could see Pei-Pei with her arms flung out on either side of her. I spun around to take in the entire empty forest. No path. No life, not even a startled owl or darting squirrel.

The skin on my cheeks tingled feebly—it was all the feeling my body could muster. This, I thought, was the right moment to pray. I closed my eyes, then closed them tighter. But there was no one and nothing. I returned to Pei-Pei, who raised her open hands in the air, her fingers arching back. Her palms shone a strange shade of blue.

"Finally, it's morning," she said, bringing her hands together, receiving something invisible.

My heart slowed just a touch at her words. "You see it," I said. "The lights."

"Morning," she sang, and hummed a tune I'd forgotten. In a rush I remembered just how often she used to sing, and how that music was gone now.

She broke off. "Finally," she said. She inhaled and then let a great breath out in twenty ragged pieces, as though daybreak were something she'd been waiting for all her life. The sky darkened once more, settling into a shade blacker than before.

"It's not morning," I said. My heart was clenching almost painfully. Something was wrong with the sky.

I squatted in front of her and pulled on her arms until she was almost sitting, but when I released them, she fell back again like a stuffed doll. I wrapped her limp arms around my neck and tried to hoist her onto my back, but I couldn't get her off the ground. I turned around and jammed my arms beneath her torso and legs, straining to lift her. She barely budged. She was too heavy; I was too small. Ringing in my head was the voice of my father: "You need to eat more. Do you understand what I'm saying?"

I couldn't move my sister. In the empty woods I had a long, wrecked cry. No one was watching, no one was listening. No one knew a thing about us.

The cold added resistance to my every movement. It was difficult even to bend my knees. I lowered myself gradually, like a decrepit man.

I sat beside Pei-Pei. I knew it would be hard to get up again. I closed my stiff eyelids and thought of home. Was anyone there? I thought of the clearing in front of our house. Natty wouldn't have played there. He wouldn't have fallen in.

I sat until my limbs grew heavy and numb. My head hung and I half slept. The wind blew and the leaves fluttered, and that was how I knew time was passing, though I didn't care. Pei-Pei writhed once, digging her bare elbows into the wet detritus and curling up her whole body. If she had been pretending to be an animal, it might have been funny. Instead, it was frightening. She emitted a sound that, if I'd heard it out of context, I never would have guessed was human. Leaves slapped together somewhere behind us.

A great length of time passed, but it didn't matter. A ringing or whistling began. Wind blew across my ears and pressure built in my skull. Then I heard a voice. Just a person. "Natty! Natty!" it called. A man's voice, but not my father's. I listened to it for a while as it drifted farther away and then closer and then farther again. Yes, Natty—my brother—was missing. People were searching for him. I opened my eyes and put my hands in front of my face. They had lost their outlines. I was blind.

I choked out some kind of sound. When there was no response, I screamed, "Here! Here! Here!"

As my eyes adjusted to the moonlight, a thin figure appeared over me. "It's you," he said. "What happened?" He crept to Pei-Pei and crouched low over her, bending forward and resting his hands on either side of her head—he looked like he would kiss her. It was Collin. I had answered his calls for my lost brother. I had wanted someone to come, anyone, and had tricked him into finding me. But he didn't say anything about it. He put the back of his hand to Pei-Pei's cheek, her neck, her arm.

He turned to me. "Can you get up?" he asked. Without waiting, he shoved his forearm beneath my armpit and helped me to stand. He let go and watched as I stood on my creaky legs. I tried to raise one foot off the ground. To my surprise, it worked.

Collin took off his coat, lifted Pei-Pei's torso, and spread the coat beneath her. He slid each of her arms carefully through the long sleeves and reached into the wrist holes to find her hands. He zipped it all the way up. Then he scooped his arms beneath her, as I had tried to do. He staggered a little under her weight but managed to heave her off the ground.

"We have to get her home," he said, and started to walk. He was firm, serious, efficient. Though he carried the weight of another person, it was hard to keep up with his long strides.

In the dark, he walked in a single direction, and I stumbled after him as quickly as I could, my soft legs paddling the soft ground. Below the canopy there were no stars to navigate by, but somehow he seemed to know where we were and where we were going. All of our time in the woods—they had opened to him in a way they had not for me.

"The lights," I said. "Did you see them?"

"What lights?" he asked.

"Just a minute ago . . ." I said, but I trailed off. It might have been hours ago.

Collin had already forgotten my question. He was barreling ahead.

"Where are we going?" I asked.

"Your home," he said.

Was my mother there? Could I face her without Natty? My joints ached, my knees buckled, and I fell behind.

"Wait for me," I said.

Collin stopped. Without the rhythmic crinkling of the coat that Pei-Pei was wrapped in, I could finally hear how hard he was breathing.

"I have to go," he said.

"No, wait," I said.

He began to walk again, then stopped and turned. He lifted a knee, shifted Pei-Pei's weight in his arms, and said, "I need to get her inside." He readjusted her again.

I stepped up to them and put my hand on Pei-Pei's calf. Her pants were soaked through.

"Keep walking this way," he said, and his voice was not unkind. But he had to leave me. I had to be left. "You'll see the path soon enough," he said.

Then I was on my own, careening through the dark, floundering in what I could only hope was the same direction. The cold pressed into my face. I had never wanted to get somewhere so urgently or dreaded it so much. Forces pushed and pulled me and I wondered if I was running in place. My heart was bucking around with fear and exertion. I had to come to a full stop and press both hands to my chest, to keep everything safely inside. But once I was still, I started to rattle in place, as though someone were grabbing my shoulders and trying to shake my bones out. So I ran again.

Finally, there. The path. The path. I almost wept again. Instead, I kept running. The familiar bends of the path gave me a surge. Even in the dark, I knew where I could just run straight, and where I had to slow for the curves.

As I burst out of the woods and onto our lawn, I saw with a shock that every light on the ground floor of our house was on, so that it glowed like a ship in the brine of darkness. But on approach, I saw no one. My footsteps became harder—more real; the ground near our house had frozen over. I slid the glass door open. It made a sound like a long sweep of a broom.

I walked into the den, where Collin was holding Pei-Pei's wet shirt in the air. She was lying on the mattress with two blankets over her.

"Help me," Collin said. "Make the fire. Make it a big one."

I knelt in front of the woodstove and slid the last of the firewood in. I poked at the embers a little, watching out of the sides of my eyes as Collin rearranged Pei-Pei's bare, limp arms next to her body and pulled the blankets up to her throat. All of his movements were slow and deliberate, as though she might be shattered from an accidental flick of his hand. It was a strange sight, his gentleness.

Collin rose on his knees and looked around the den for a place to put Pei-Pei's soggy shirt and pants. With a dull ache in my chest I watched him notice everything. The sloppy bed in the middle of the room, the small piles of clean and dirty clothing along one side. In the wall itself were a series of nails that we were using as a drying rack near the stove. If he spoke to me, I would tell him—it hadn't always looked like this; there had been a sofa and window blinds. But he didn't speak. Instead, he spread Pei-Pei's wet clothes on the carpet, then returned to her. He leaned over her with his ear very close to her mouth. He stayed so long I thought she must be awake and speaking. I leaned toward them to hear better, then realized he was only listening for her breath.

In the tight space behind the stove, I saw my father's boots. The collars were stretched from wear; his ankles couldn't possibly fill them. I reached out a hand. The outer leather was hot to the touch, and the soft collar was nearly dry.

The fire began to catch. Although I was right in front of the stove, it didn't seem any warmer. I tried to stop shivering by holding tightly on to my feet.

"Do you have clean clothes?" Collin said.

"Me? They're upstairs."

"Change out of that wet stuff. It's sucking the heat out of you." He looked at me until, uncomfortable, I backed up to the doorway near the stairs. I preferred all the other versions of him I had ever met, including the one that tormented me. I didn't know how to handle his concern, his seeing eyes.

For the second time that night, I made my way up to my room and left a pile of wet clothes on the carpet. This time around, everything was slower—the climb up the stairs, the peeling of the clothes, the search for dry socks, which I eventually abandoned. I tugged four separate shirts over my head, one after another, most of them dirty. They restricted how far I could swing my arms and I found I liked it, the constraint, as though someone were holding me back.

I stopped to use the bathroom, but the door was locked. I stood outside for a few moments as my heart raced. "Natty?" I said.

The doorknob clicked as it was unlocked from the inside. After a second or two of indecision, I opened the door and saw my father scurrying back toward the tub. He sat down, fully clothed, on the toilet lid. He still held the phone and the cleaver, one in each hand.

"Is Natty back?" he asked. His face was contorted. I glanced up and down his arms and legs and realized I was looking for blood. I wished he would put the cleaver down.

"No," I said. "I don't know where he is."

My father rocked forward and back. "You can leave now," he said.

I backed away and closed the door softly. I headed down the stairs. Collin met me at the bottom.

"Can you get me the car keys?" he asked. "I'm thinking of driving her to the hospital."

I took the few steps to the front door and looked out the narrow window. There was a strong, icy draft coming from the doorknob hole, and I tried to block it with my body so Collin wouldn't notice. I squinted into the night. My father's truck was parked diagonally in the driveway. A hubcap gleamed. His keys were always on him. My father. The man hiding upstairs, with his boots drying behind the stove. The shameful secret of it all. He hadn't gone out to look for Natty.

Finally I said, "My dad has the keys." It was a kind of truth. I asked what I had been holding in my mind like a hot coal. "Isn't she okay?"

"Sure, she's okay. But I think she's hypothermic," Collin said. He looked at me. "But she's okay." He leaned against the wall to gaze into the den where Pei-Pei was sleeping. "I'll call my dad to take us. Where's your phone?"

The phone. "Oh," I said. I thought for a moment, but there seemed to be no way out. Resigned, I said, "It's upstairs. I'll go get it. You stay here."

While Collin went back into the den, I climbed the stairs again. The bathroom door was still unlocked. I entered and found my father in the same huddled position on the toilet.

"I need that phone," I said.

My father slowly extended his arm and held the receiver out to me. The cord dropped and flicked the floor.

I took it from him, and the plastic was very warm where he had been holding it all this time.

"Are you going to call the police?" he asked.

"No," I said.

"It's okay if you do," he said. He shook his head. "It's the right thing to do."

"I'm not going to call them."

"Please call them," he said.

"I said I'm not going to." I pulled a towel from a rack and threw it over his lap so that it covered the cleaver in his hand. I thought about asking him for the keys to the truck, but I didn't know how to explain their appearance to Collin. Pei-Pei was okay, though, he'd said. I shut the door. There was no denying I was my miserable father's son.

Downstairs, Collin watched me plug the cord back into the base. I was grateful he asked no questions. He made a very short call, saying only, "No, it's Paige. You need to come. She has to go to the hospital." This was how they talked, I thought. Adults. Men. People who wanted something to happen and then made that very thing happen.

Collin rolled Pei-Pei up in two blankets. On one end, her mess of hair spilled out, and on the other end, I could see her bare ankles. Those ankles—just skin over nubs of bone. Some time later, Mr. Dolan pushed open the front door without knocking and helped Collin carry her out. I felt a passing itch of jealousy for Pei-Pei, wrapped up and looked after like that. Accompanied. "She'll be just fine," Mr. Dolan mumbled, patting the air in the vicinity of my head, and after that he barely glanced at me. I was glad for his largeness, the space he took up. He focused solely on maneuvering himself and then Pei-Pei through the front door and keeping the blankets from trailing. I closed the door behind them. In the den, I sat down on the bare mattress. The house was quiet again—and colder somehow, though the fire had grown luxurious. I got up and wandered around the kitchen. I lifted the lid on the cabbage soup. It was cold now, and tiny white discs of fat floated on top.

———

THE BACK DOOR slid open and Natty came in. He was nearly silent, and I only noticed him because I was sitting perfectly still at the table and facing the door. His face was very pale at the temples and flushed in the center of his cheeks, and a smear of dirt ran up his neck. His eyes were wide, hyperawake, and as he approached me I saw his lashes were stuck together into spikes.

He put a hand on the table near me. A pink, raised scratch started on his index finger and disappeared under the wrist of his coat sleeve. He smiled.

It unnerved me; I jumped out of my seat. "You're back?" I said. I hadn't meant it as a question. I cleared thickness from my throat. "And where were you? You caused a whole big mess."

Natty grinned at me.

"What?" I said. "What?"

"Did someone show you the lights, too?"

"Oh, the lights!" I said, with more feeling than I'd intended, because I'd forgotten them.

Natty grabbed my wrists. Maybe it was his face, so close to mine and so elated, but his touch was electrifying, and I thought of the charged silence of the colored lights that had skated across the sky. We had both seen something from another world. We had been marked.

"You're home," I whispered. The relief hit me, hard, and I shook myself loose from him to grab the table edge with both hands. It was solid, the table, so solid.

"It was Ruby," Natty said.

"Yes, Ruby," I said. I would have agreed to anything in that moment.

Natty smiled again. Though he was rumpled, wet, and dirty, he looked fine. More than fine.

"Where were you hiding?" I asked.

"I wasn't hiding," he said.

I took him upstairs to change. We stopped outside the bathroom.

"Natty's home," I shouted at the door.

It opened. My father stared at us. He said, "Oh, Natty," and took three careening steps forward. He patted Natty all over. He couldn't seem to stop. Then it was towels—the one I had thrown at my father and two more from the bathroom. My father used them to smother Natty. When Natty shook them off, my father started again, laying one across his shoulder and tucking it here and there, and then adding one across the other shoulder. It made me think of the way we used to wrap rice in lotus leaves, folding the long strips tightly so that the rice was pressed into the shape of a pyramid.

"Enough towels," I said. "He's about to change out of these clothes."

"Yes," my father said, and followed us. He left the cleaver in the bathroom sink.

When the three of us made it downstairs again, my mother was in the den. One by one, our family was returning.

"Look," I said. "Look. Natty's back."

She could barely look at him. And she couldn't seem to speak. Her face got stuck in a grimace for a few long seconds, and she waved her hands in front of herself, trying to unstick it. Suddenly all of her muscles went lax, and she said in a mangy voice, in Natty's direction, "I'll never let you out of the house again." She turned away from him and worked her mouth.

Here we were, then. All standing beside the communal bed in the den. But there was something else still lurking, something I hadn't yet dissipated into the air. "Pei-Pei," I said, and for a moment all I could see was the image of her lying in the forest with her arms spread open to the cold. The next words rushed out. "She's in the hospital. Mr. Dolan took her there."

My mother whirled back around. Her mouth opened and she pursed her lips. She clamped them shut again. She said, "Why would she go to the hospital?"

"I think she got too cold," I said. "Hypothermia."

"Hypothermia!" my father said. He began to rub the back of one hand.

My mother fixed her eyes on a nail in the wall. Her chest was fluttering with shallow breaths.

"I'll drive to the hospital," my father said. "I'll just change out of these clothes and go." He gestured at his work clothes and gave one of his belt loops a nervous tug.

"Yes, go," my mother said. "Change your clothes and go, and

then don't come back." The raggedness of her voice frightened me. She looked straight at my father. "Don't you come back."

My father stood there empty-handed with a silly expression on his face.

I wanted to tell him: She meant don't come back without Pei-Pei.

My father swiped at the carpet with his socked foot. We had tromped in and out of the den all night and tracked mud everywhere, and some of it had dried into clods. My father kept rubbing hard at three of his fingers.

"Hypothermia," I said. "Not frostbite."

"I mean it," my mother said.

My father gave me an uneven smile. I sensed he wanted me to look away, so I pulled up my layered sleeves and examined the waffle print that was embedded on my wrist. My mother barked, "Go. I told you to go." My father's footsteps drifted up the stairs.

"When will this stop?" my mother asked.

I shook my head.

"Everything that's gone wrong—it's been your father."

I clenched and opened my hands and kept my face very still.

"We can't live like this," she said.

I wished she would stop talking. Everything she said in that cracked voice caused strange vibrations in my spine.

"We can't survive."

When my father returned, he was wearing a button-up shirt tucked carefully into clean, belted jeans. Over his arm was his damp coat. He dropped a soft canvas bag on the floor. Unzipped, it gaped open, and I saw too many socks and all of the towels from our bathroom and a great deal of empty space.

I brought him his boots from behind the fire.

"Thank you," he said, as quiet as a leaf landing. He knelt to put the boots on. The collars were dry, but he had been working in the rain, and I knew the insides might still be wet. He laced the top eyelet hooks and yanked them tight, and I imagined the cold water pressing into his socks.

He approached cautiously and placed a heavy palm on the back of my neck and the other hand on Natty's narrow chest. "I'll call soon from the hospital," he said.

I nodded. "Okay," I said, because my mother hadn't answered.

He lingered. "Don't worry," he said.

I nodded again.

"Because I'll call."

He tapped Natty's chest playfully. "And where were you tonight?"

"With Ruby," Natty said.

My father nodded as though this were a reasonable thing to say. "I was very worried," he said. "You can't know how worried I was—I nearly went out of my mind. But now that I see you standing here, I can leave."

But still he didn't leave. He pulled on his coat and zipped it closed more slowly than I had ever seen it done, tooth by tooth. When he finished, he looked at Natty and me once more.

"Go," my mother said.

He picked up the canvas bag. It was light in his hand. "I'll call," he said. Still he lingered, reluctant to turn his feet toward the door.

When he had finally driven away in the truck, my mother said, "At long last." She gazed at the door for a minute and then gave it a kick, though it was already firmly closed. She busied herself in the kitchen, reheating the soup. "Sit," she called back to us. "At the table where I can see you. And if you get up, I'll beat you to death."

When it was ready, my mother brought two bowls of soup to the table and tested the temperature by raising each bowl to her own mouth and dipping in her upper lip. When she handed one to Natty, he tipped up the bowl and chewed sloppily on the sodden cabbage like an animal. Then he tapped the bottom for the rice that clung there. Had he ever eaten like this? It was how Ruby used to eat, striding into oblivion.

He put down the bowl and asked for another.

My mother came to the table. "You, too," she said to me. "Eat your dinner."

I dipped my spoon in and swirled it.

My mother brought the pot to the table and refilled Natty's bowl. Then she ate out of the pot by lifting its long handle.

"I'm done," Natty said. He tilted his bowl to show us. He looked happy. He'd returned to a version of himself we'd forgotten.

"Stay here," my mother said. "When everyone's done, we'll go to bed."

I took my time. The phone rang. I looked at my mother.

"You answer it," my mother said.

I walked into the kitchen and lifted the receiver. "Hello?" I whispered.

"Pei-Pei is all right," my father said. "But she needs to stay a little longer."

"But she's okay," I said.

"Yes. They say she will be fine. Tell your mother she'll come home tomorrow."

"Can I talk to her?" I tried to think of what I would say and drew a blank. I just wanted to hear her voice. She had been unresponsive to me all night. Even when I had cried, she had not comforted or chided me.

"No," my father said. "Not tonight."

But she would be home tomorrow. I hung up and sat down at the table and told my mother the news word for word. Then I finished the soup quickly, clinking my spoon against the porcelain, soup dribbling down my neck. While I ate, Natty fiddled with something in his pocket. When he finally uncurled his hand to show me, the little green Monopoly house sat upright on his palm.

The three of us crawled into bed without brushing our teeth. The mattress was spacious now, and we stretched our limbs, unrestrained. Later, in our sleep, disturbed by overexhaustion and cold, we wormed toward the center again. Or perhaps Natty stayed still while my mother and I crowded him on either side. I found myself sleeping on top of one of his arms, pinning him down.

——

IT WAS MR. DOLAN who brought Pei-Pei home the next night. He spoke to my mother in the kitchen. He lowered his voice from his usual shout, but it remained loud enough to hear every word. He asked about our electricity. That's lucky, he said, but if they haven't yet, they will soon. He asked if we still had water.

Someone would come to shut it off, he said, and drain the pipes for winter.

"Where's Dad?" Pei-Pei asked. She was sitting on the floor and leaning against the wall, and I studied her for signs of bodily damage. A blanket covered her legs and her head lolled to one side.

"Is he on a job?" she asked.

"Wasn't he with you?" I asked.

"He was at the hospital last night, but he left in the morning."

"I guess he might be at a job," I said.

Pei-Pei adjusted the blanket over her legs so it covered her feet. She was wearing socks from the hospital, and they were thick and powder-blue. "He said something strange last night," Pei-Pei said. "He leaned way over me and said, 'I used to be an engineer, you know.'"

"It's true," I said. "He was one, before."

"I know," Pei-Pei said. "But it sounded like he was lying."

"He wasn't lying."

"I know that."

"Well, I don't know what you're trying to say."

"Forget it," Pei-Pei said. She pedaled her legs beneath the blanket and said, "It's pretty chilly in here."

It wasn't until my father had been gone for a full week that I tried to ask Pei-Pei to return to the subject. What had he said again? How had he said it? She only shrugged. "I don't remember," she said.

And that was it. I had nothing else to examine, only my memory of his hand on my neck and the inadequacy of his packing. We had eaten soup and gone to sleep, and when we had woken he was gone for good. Had he tried to come back and been turned away? Or had that been it, that lingering, sweaty hand? This was how people in our family disappeared. In a long haze of night. Without our full awareness. Without our permission.

19

ADA STOOD AT OUR FRONT DOOR. A LITTLE SNOW FELL ON her shoulders, but her crimson coat and hat were mostly dry. Her father must have dropped her off, but his van was nowhere in sight.

She handed me an envelope. "Your ticket, it won," she said. She nodded in response to a question I hadn't yet formulated.

"What?" I said.

"We bought a ticket for you," she said. "For the snow lottery. And your ticket won." She was a little breathless, and her words ran together. She asked, "Isn't that good news?" with a stretched-out smile, and I understood she was reciting this speech.

When I took the envelope, she grabbed my wrist. She patted the back of my hand. "Take it," she said, though it was already in my hand. "It's yours. It really was your ticket that won." My face grew hot, even in the fresh, bracing wind.

Ada tipped her head back to gaze at the sky, and I watched

a flake of snow head for her nose and veer toward her eyebrow at the last possible moment. Her eyelids pulsed in one slow blink. "It's going to keep going for days," she said. "It won't be a hard snow, but it'll be a long one."

That sounded more like her. Ada, my friend. Still, my mind was cluttered with the things we were not saying. Collin had come into our house, into our den. Their father had hoisted Pei-Pei up in blankets. What did Ada know? It made my whole scalp crawl. What did she know of us?

She yanked off her hat and shook a bit of snow from it. Strands of her long, fine hair rose above her ears and tried to float away. "I've got to go now," she said, pulling her hat back on so it sat crooked. I wanted to reach out and adjust it, but she whirled around and ran down the steps.

I closed the door and lifted the flap of the envelope. What I saw—hundred-dollar bills—made me shut it again. I shoved it into my waistband and walked around the house with my secret, letting the corners of the envelope scratch my skin. The feeling of so much money was sharp and stinging. When Pei-Pei asked me to stop pacing, I stood stiffly against the wall.

I lasted nearly a full day before I showed it to my mother. She snatched it from my hands and didn't give it back. "Who?" she said, already counting the money. "Who brought this?"

I told her and rubbed the spot on my hip where it used to sit.

"Finally," my mother said. "Our luck, it's come, it's here." She made a snatching motion in the air. "We take it."

"Luck," I said, bobbing my head up and down. "We won. We won the lottery."

She pressed her palms together and smiled at her long, narrow thumbnails. Her eyelids fluttered with possibilities. I wanted her to say it, that we had won this money, but she didn't.

"It's done," she said. "Over." She spread her arms. They grew wider and wider to include the room, the house, the forest, the state, and, it was clear, our existence in these cursed spaces.

———

WE STOOD in the Anchorage airport with just a few suitcases at our sides. Our messes shut away. It was remarkable: we blended in.

"Why Seattle?" I asked.

"Why anywhere?" my mother said. She had stopped speaking of Taiwan, and I didn't know why.

Natty sat in the window seat and stared out fixedly, even after we had broken through the cloud cover and there was only white fleece to see. I watched him watch the sky. I had read about the lights in the newspaper. On the night Natty hadn't come home, a woman had driven off the road. Others had called the police, who had taken garbled notes on the "visions." What we had seen, the article explained, were pieces of a rocket that had launched a Russian satellite. Space junk falling from low orbit and entering our atmosphere, burning up as it came into our world. I kept this to myself. From my aisle seat I could see only Natty's cheek and jaw, and both were smooth and slack. He touched the small plexiglass window as though it were alive.

When we arrived in Seattle, it was November but felt like the late Septembers of Southcentral Alaska—gray, wet, with darkness touching down at dinnertime. A September that had gotten stuck, lasting months and months. At the fringes of the city we rented a two-bedroom town house, where the only out-door space was a rectangle of weeds the size of a rug. We left it to its own devices but it never sprouted anything of note or grew quite wild; it seemed restrained by some kind of decorum, and even the spring blooms were small and wan.

Pei-Pei took one of the bedrooms for herself. When I sat on her bed, it wasn't like before. She used to prattle on about any-thing that bounced through her brain—the sun was getting brighter, in 1.5 billion years our oceans would boil away, our atmosphere would leave us—but now she let none of it out.

"How was school?" I asked that first day.

"There are a lot of Asians here," she said. Her face and voice were blank, so I couldn't tell if this was a good thing. I had al-ready been confused for not one but two other boys, and I liked it. I felt protected by a shroud of vagueness. Anything I did would be attributed not to me, but to the air that floated over us. No one would ever see me.

Pei-Pei stacked her textbooks along the edge of her desk and began to wrap one with a cut-up grocery bag. She folded two corners neatly and taped the paper down. I watched as she cov-ered each of her books and then titled them with a marker: *Biology, Trig, American History*. Her handwriting was slow and precise. She turned the books and lettered their spines, and I marveled at her meticulousness.

"Will you wrap mine?" I asked.

She shrugged. "Sure. Go get your books."

"Nah. I'll do it later." I had only been curious what she would say. I flopped back on her bed, a full-sized one, huge. I rolled from one side to the other and kicked her pillow. Still she didn't yell. With her back to me, she organized her pens and binders, and her motions had a small range.

My mother flourished. Almost immediately, she found a job at the post office. She also fell in with a trio of mothers, speaking Mandarin with them rather than Taiwanese. After they discovered she was not from Taipei or Kaohsiung at all but from a seaside village, they invited her to the market, where she demonstrated how to choose fresh clams. They called our house for instructions on scaling a fish. Once, they crowded into our tiny kitchen to watch my mother prod at oyster omelets with a spatula. They were loud, and they spent a good thirty minutes entering the house and another thirty leaving it. My mother played up her fascination with their face creams, their sturdy shoes, their endless advice on vitamins. She told them that our father had been a stomach doctor, and that he had died many years ago.

She slept in the second bedroom, against the wall opposite from Natty and me, and at night she told us the secrets of her day across the expanse of shadows. Five of her coworkers smoked cigarettes out back, and one of them always snuck in an extra break. Another squirted Easy Cheese straight into his mouth. A customer once tried to mail a dead cat.

One night my mother climbed into my bed and talked about a boy in her village. They had grown up together. They invented games out of shells, and at night they raced down to the cliffs and jumped off higher and higher rocks into the ocean until one of them balked at the dark water. It was usually the boy, she said. He had a pointed nose, tiny wire glasses, and soft cheeks, and he grabbed her hand when they sprinted down to the beach. They slid all over the rocks, skinny as eels, their clothing paled by the sun and their brown skin showing through. Was it the boy, she wondered, or simply that they were children? It was as happy as she had ever been.

"It's not because you were a child," I said.

"Isn't it?" my mother said. "Because I can't get it back."

"I want to go to Taiwan," I said.

"Me, too," she said. But still she didn't take us there.

We hadn't gotten very far. There we were, in the Pacific Northwest yet, in a city that probably had more Alaskan transplants than any other. By many measures we were doing better, our lives more stable and restrained. But sometimes I felt uneasy. What were we doing there? The feeling persisted through my life, no matter where I went.

———

IN THE SOMBER LITTLE LIVING ROOM of our Seattle town house, we watched the news coverage of the *Exxon Valdez* spill. Natty and I perched on the love seat for nearly all of spring break. Sometimes Natty slid off the cushions and sat on the floor, where he could practically touch the screen. When she came home from the post office, my mother cried at the wasteland contained in our sixteen-inch box. Two hundred thousand birds, dead. All those uncountable fish and mussels and clams. Even the seaweeds were deeply mourned. "That coast," she moaned. She asked us to turn down the volume, then went to sit in the kitchen.

But Natty and I were riveted. By the black beaches and rocks, all the dead, slicked fish, squinting seals, oiled birds trying to fly. The cleanup crews sopped up the shores all day, only to have them tarred again by the next tide. One evening Natty lifted an upturned hand at the television. On the edge of the screen was a figure faced away from us. There was duct tape on his splattered rubber slickers. His way of pressing on his knees as he straightened up was achingly familiar.

My chest convulsed. Could it really be him? A second later the scene changed to show a worker raking up crude oil that had been hemmed in on the water.

On the couch, Natty and I didn't say a word to each other. My father had sent two letters before we'd left Alaska. They were postmarked in Anchorage and Juneau. His simple statements in English—"Dear my children, all is good and working is fine"—seemed heavily coded, but I never was able to decipher them.

It had to be him. He'd only flashed across the screen, but wouldn't we know? It was a gift. Now we could imagine him walking the coastline of one of the southern islands, or stopping for supplies in Valdez, a sudden boomtown, among thousands of temporary workers. We'd watched enough news to put a high-pressure hose in his hand, or a net of black carcasses behind him, or a sick otter in his arms. He was saving lives, saving the water, saving the land.

In a year, half of the rescued otters would be dead. Workers from the cleanup crews would start coming down with respiratory illnesses. If you dug a few inches into the sand on some of those beaches, oil would fill up the depression you'd made.

I asked my mother for my father's address. Natty's head ticked, a fraction of movement, as he waited for her reply. She said she didn't have it.

20

WHERE OUR HOUSE USED TO BE IS A NEIGHBORHOOD—MY
father's old dream. The grasses in the yards are all mowed to
different lengths, but there are no grasses so long you could lie
down and disappear in them. The forest is smaller now and no
longer filled with spruces. A fire came through, and now aspens and birches—fluttering things—dominate. It's a paler,
sunnier, friendlier version of the woods we used to know. The
Dolan house still stands on the other side, duller in color, with
the yard cleaned up. I didn't step any farther than the edge of
the woods. I was afraid, I realized, that someone—Collin or
Ada or their father—still lived there. I stood at the border and
recalled the dark spruces that had parted here, and how the sudden aperture of the Dolans' backyard had been a lovely shock,
a rich apricot pool where the late afternoon light gathered and
stewed.

I was driving away from it all when a radio broadcast came
on and an astronaut mid-mission began to read a letter to his

son. It was a bunch of nothing—plain declarations of love and unoriginal philosophizing—but a shaking fit overtook me, and I had to pull off the road. Who knows what it was? Those same gray mountains through the windshield, or the thinness of the clouds. My father would have liked to be that man, I knew—he'd fancied himself some kind of pioneer—and maybe I would have liked to be the son of someone who had ventured and succeeded. Or maybe it was just the direct address coming through the speakers at me, all the way from space. The expanse made him totally unfettered. The distance stripped his words. There was no self-consciousness, only sentiment: I'm out here, and I'm thinking of you.

———

I WENT TO TAIWAN, trying to find the village that lived in my memory of my mother's memory. Those rocks, those cliffs, those hunched old women scraping limpets and mussels at low tide. I slept on my aunt's floor. We walked the shore often. Ropes of seaweed covered what little sand there was and housed thousands of jumping bugs. They made the seaweed tremble.

We gazed at the cloudy water. "Have you ever seen a whale?" I asked.

"They're out there," my aunt said. "I believe they are."

My aunt didn't look like my mother at all. There was none of my mother's smallness, quickness, or nervousness. My aunt had large, muscular arms and a thick blanket of straight black hair that looked like it belonged to someone half her age.

Her breakfast spreads intimidated me. She brought out ramekins of salted, shredded fish, platters of deep-fried silver

pomfret or yellow croaker, crab legs, and broths made by simmering small oysters and clams in water. Sometimes she served
the broth in big, upturned crab shells. She showed me how to
take a chopstick and detach the yellow and gray organs from
the shell, mixing them into the soup for flavor. When I tilted the
shell like a bowl and drank, she nodded. "That's right," my aunt
said. "Keep at it." She had no children. Her gaze on me was hungry, and she broke it only to suck an oyster or clam shell clean
and add it to the pile on the table. They clicked like poker chips.

Week after week of eating like that, shellfish and fish at every
meal and little else, my lips grew fat and the skin on my face
flamed and thickened. Welts appeared on my arms and legs.

And why are you still here, people asked. How long are you
staying? On the crooked street outside my aunt's house, a little
girl fed a dog with teats hanging to the ground. When she saw
me, she buried her face in the dog's matted neck and laughed.
"Huan-á," she whispered. A phrase reserved for white Western-
ers. Halfway between foreigner and barbarian.

I'd thought I might live there. I had imagined the village as
a home I couldn't visualize but that my body would recall. Some
smells—fish-heavy trash, reused cooking oil, the damp remains
of a typhoon—were like buried memories. I luxuriated in the
humidity, the temperate breeze. But the allergies. The language.
The sidelong glances. It was a kind of violence, what my father
had done. He had brought us to a place we didn't belong, and
taken us from a place we did. Now we yearned for all places
and found peace in none.

THE YEAR SHE DIED, my mother asked me to cut her hair. In her studio in Seattle, she showed me the scissors she used for regular household tasks. She held them by the blades. "Help me. Just a trim in the back," she said.

"There's a salon down the street," I said. "It's a five-minute walk."

"They want thirty dollars from me," she said.

"You need hair-cutting scissors to cut hair."

"What's the difference?"

"There's a difference."

For weeks my mother had been asking me for a haircut. My reluctance had to do with her hair itself; it was getting sparse. Her part had widened, exposing a distinct strip of scalp, and near her forehead there was an especially disturbing bare patch. It shone. When I glimpsed that patch full-on, it felt like I'd seen something I shouldn't have.

I spread out a layer of overlapping newspapers in the kitchen and lowered a chair onto the center. My mother was prim as she settled herself on it and perched her hands on her knees. But when I did nothing, she grunted in exasperation. "Just cut straight across," she said, and made a short chopping motion behind her head.

I pinched a thin section of her hair between my fingers and pulled it flat. It was variegated gray. The white strands were especially wayward. As an experiment, I cut off the smallest length I could, maybe a quarter centimeter, and a sprinkling of hair dust fell from my fingertips.

My mother twisted her head back and examined the newspapered floor. "Don't be a coward."

"Turn around," I said.

"That's not going to do it. I want it off my neck."

"Get someone else to do it," I muttered as I made the next cut. But I knew she didn't have anyone else. Her friends had not lasted, and her children had scattered.

"Your mood is bad," she said. She used the phrase "sim-tsîng," which broken down into its two words meant "situation of the heart."

I stopped cutting. "This is how I am."

"I know it," she said. I couldn't see her face, but her voice had dropped.

Did she mean that she knew—even knew it well—this enduring strain of unrest?

Later, I let myself into her cramped studio with a bag of groceries. The lights were off, though the day was on the wane. A feeble glow entered from the kitchen windows. From the door, I could see my mother's figure in the armchair by her bed. Both of her feet were pressed into the carpet. She was making a rhythmic movement, raising one hand above her head and flicking her wrist.

I stepped closer to turn on the lights but stopped. Her fingers, pinched together, tossed something to the carpet. While I watched, she repeated the gesture six or seven more times, with an air of absentmindedness. She stared right at the old television, which was off. What other permutations of her life would have led her to this point? This plucking of the hair, strand by strand. She was making herself bald, and I wasn't sure she knew it.

Silently, I approached. I didn't touch her, but I should have. Such things were possible at dusk, when the lights were off and our minds were sliding through time. We had been unthinking with our movements once, bed-hopping, kicking, clutching. She had run along the water with me, the sky opening wider and wider to accommodate us. In her way, she'd loved that place.

I gazed upon the ravages of my mother's hair. It used to be thick and willful. I thought of a patch of barren dirt. Then I thought of the lush, long grasses that had lived at the border of our woods, and how we had rustled them as children. We plucked their tips and gathered them into small brushes, and Ruby painted our faces with them, clumsily dusting our foreheads, cheeks, eyelids. "Before, you were ugly," she said. She held our chins with her small, firm hand. "Now you are beautiful."

ACKNOWLEDGMENTS

I'm enormously grateful to Emily Bell and Jackson Howard for taking on this quiet, small thing, and for understanding and bettering it so thoroughly. Thank you also to Lauren Roberts and the team at FSG for their care, and to Richard Abate and Rachel Kim for a potent mix of insight, real talk, and advocacy.

The Martha Heasley Cox Center for Steinbeck Studies, Henfield Foundation, Truman Capote Literary Trust, James Jones Literary Society, and Headlands Center for the Arts kept me going with generous support and recognition, and the Iowa Writers' Workshop opened a world to me. I'm glad for the friendly stewards of these institutions, especially Holly Blake, Nick Taylor, Jan Zenisek, Deb West, and Connie Brothers.

These mentors mattered very much to me: Charlie D'Ambrosio, who gave colossal gifts of time and unsparing attention; Ethan Canin, who delivered instruction and kindness in equal measure; and of course Sam Chang, who's known me and guided me since I was a pup. Others have left marks as well: Marilynne Robinson, Yiyun Li, Sara Houghteling, Kevin Brockmeier, Leah Price, Daniel Bosch, Pam Houston, and Joshua Mohr. Twenty years ago, Patricia Powell set me on this path.

For reading this novel in its garbled state, I'm indebted to D. Wystan

Owen, whose compassion (for characters and author alike) saved this book from the recycling bin, and Alex Madison, who saw the things I couldn't see and constantly held out her hand. Alongside these two, Jamel Brinkley and Sarah Frye supplied therapy, hilarity, and white lies that sustained me through the writing. Garth Greenwell showed me true generosity and is my model of kindness and grace.

Iowa City would have been a lonely place without Willa B. Richards, who accompanied and inspired me. I'm also grateful for the friendship, strangeness, and brilliance of Yaa Gyasi, Lakiesha Carr, Nyuol Lueth Tong, Will Shih, Noel Carver, Jake Andrews, Vanessa Roveto, Sophia Lin, and Ellen Kamoe. The enthusiasm of Magogodi Makhene and Sorrel Westbrook-Wilson pushed me onward.

The inexhaustible faith of old friends came in handy when I ran low; thank you to Charlie Black, John Hsu, Jonathan Fuentes, Beth Hillman Tagawa, June Rhee, Rachael Trapuzzano Pruitt, Roger Huang, Daniel Nazer, Kate Leahy, Wendy Yu, Gloria Huang, and many others. Every single day, Frances Chen and Adrian Lu gave me a swift kick in the pants, while Sarah Cove cheered from afar.

Daniel Mosteller, Greg Schmeller, Christopher Busch, and Chieh-Ting Yeh answered odd questions with patience. Thanks also to those who welcomed me to Anchorage in 2004, particularly Gail Voigtlander, Laura Sarcone, and Ambler Stephenson. The exuberant *Anchorage Daily News* articles of the 1980s supplied a little fodder while greatly brightening my days.

At the heart of it all: thank you to Alan and Bin-Bin, my little family, my whole world, my home.

A Note About the Author

Chia-Chia Lin is a graduate of Harvard College and the Iowa Writers' Workshop. She lives in the San Francisco Bay Area. Her stories have appeared in *The Paris Review* and other journals. *The Unpassing* is her first novel.